PRAISE FOR VICTORIA DALPE

"Dalpe's horror stories are equal parts intriguing, compelling, and appropriately macabre. *Les Femmes Grotesques* tidily secures Dalpe her position as an author to watch."

— MONICA S. KUEBLER, *RUE MORGUE*

"Reading like a mashup between *True Blood* and *Already Dead*, with a soupcon of *Warm Bodies*, Dalpe's latest novel pulls out all the stops. A luminous and raucous reworking of everything you thought you knew about the undead, witches, necromancy, and parallel dimensions. Fun, funny, and sexy —but also thoroughly blood-soaked."

— BRIAN EVENSON, AUTHOR OF *FATHER OF LIES* AND *LAST DAYS*

"Dalpe wields literary black magic yet again. Cool, sardonic, and asking the big, pointed questions about life, unlife, and death. *Selene Shade: Resurrectionist for Hire* kicks off what promises to be a tremendous new series."

— LAIRD BARRON, AUTHOR OF *NOT A SPECK OF LIGHT (STORIES)*

"Victoria Dalpe has woven a magical mythology you want to get lost in, combining elements of the macabre, the cosmic, and the slyly mundane. *Selene Shade: Resurrectionist for Hire* is a wonderfully clever ride through death rituals, contract work, and the possible end of the world."

— NADIA BULKIN AUTHOR OF *SHE SAID DESTROY*

"Victoria Dalpe's *Selene Shade: Resurrectionist for Hire* is at once a gripping suspense tale and a phantasmagoria of magic and mayhem. At varying intervals, I found myself begging for Selene to catch a break and praying for more monsters...and more murder, just to see what Selene would do. Dalpe could easily borrow her heroine's moniker, for only a Zombie Queen of the darkest and most delicious talents could cook up a work so devilish, so twisted, and so gratifyingly written."

— CHRISTA CARMEN, TWO-TIME BRAM STOKER-
NOMINATED AUTHOR OF *THE DAUGHTERS OF
BLOCK ISLAND*

"Dalpe masterfully weaves a world full of darkness and imagination that knows no bounds. Eloquent storytelling that doesn't hold back on the nasty bits."

— ARON BEAUREGARD, AWARD-WINNING AUTHOR
OF *PLAYGROUND*

"With a zesty heroine, a likeable style, and a touch of grue, *Selene Shade: Resurrectionist for Hire* is the first installment in what looks to be a tremendously enjoyable series of dark thrillers. I ate it up like a zombie with a fresh plate of brains and am already hungry for more."

— POPPY Z. BRITE, AUTHOR OF *EXQUISITE CORPSE*

Selene Shade

Resurrectionist for Hire

Book One

Victoria Dalpe

HORROR

Copyright © 2024 by Victoria Dalpe

Cover by Daniella Batsheva

ISBN: 9781960988324

CLASH Books

Troy, NY

To my Friends and Family: I am infinitely blessed to be surrounded by so many amazing, creative, and wonderful people.

PROLOGUE

I want her back.

She lay dead. Washed and draped in a crisp white shroud. Her features sunken, especially the eyes. Her white hair thin and wispy. Fluff clinging to a dandelion.

When did I let her get so old?

I run my hand over hers. The skin paper thin but soft. Room temperature.

The funeral home smells overwhelmingly of lilies: the scent stifling and strangling. I so desperately want to be away from it all, had avoided being in a room like this since my parents' funeral all those years ago. But I can't leave her, not yet.

I ignore the line of shifting anxious mourners standing just outside the door. They're waiting for me to move along; they'd have to keep waiting. I'm not ready.

When I arrived at the funeral, I was shocked at the volume of cars and number of people who had come. How did she know them all? How could they all love her? It almost felt like a betrayal. She had all these people and I only had her.

You could bring her back.

No. No, I can't. She doesn't want to.

So?

My guts twist at the thought of taking away her will. *Hers.* I just can't. My selfishness isn't a good enough reason to bring anyone back. Even her. Especially her. It would be wrong. She didn't want to come back, we'd discussed it. Several times. On this she was adamant.

Any more wrong to bring her back than all the others?

Shut it. Just shut up.

I lean over and kiss her cool forehead, allowing myself the physical affection she would have shaken off in life. I breathe in her smell, what little remains hiding there under the lilies and the chemicals. Her scent was already changing with the blossoming decay. It was over.

I wish her safe journeys and I turn to leave. On the way out, I keep my eyes down, never once looking at the mourners. A voice I recognize calls my name. I ignore it. Someone else reaches for me. I ignore that, too.

As I exit the building, sunlight hits my face. My jaw is clenched tight enough to shatter teeth. My eyes burn. I get into my car and drive away.

Only when the funeral parlor is in my rearview mirror, only when I'm somewhere no one can see, do I let the tears flow. Away from all those eyes, I wail and scream and punch the steering wheel. I give in to the grief that had choked me, slowly, methodically, all these months of watching her get old, get sick, and die.

She was my best friend. My only friend.

And now there is no one. I am alone.

PART ONE: WAXING CRESCENT

I

Can death be sleep, when life is but a dream,
And scenes of bliss pass as a phantom by?
The transient pleasures as a vision seem,
And yet we think the greatest pain's to die.

II

How strange it is that man on earth should roam,
And lead a life of woe, but not forsake
His rugged path; nor dare he view alone
His future doom which is but to awake.

—"On Death" by John Keats

ONE

The Plains of Anchu were never still as the winds from the Si Mountains snaked down from the north, then mingled and collided explosively with the gaseous bubbling unrest of the sulfurous Lan Lakes to the south. The Anchu plains, trapped between, became a battleground of strange weather: psychedelic hurricanes, acidic precipitation that gnawed at the rocky barren surfaces, and scorching fume-filled heatwaves. Though the plains were harsh and hostile, there was also alien beauty there. Rainbows of colors painted the air and water as the gasses mixed. What little growth survived was hearty and unique. Twisted roots clung to veiny clay, while gnarled scrub fought for nutrients with the few stalwart creatures of the plains. Those creatures were hard-backed, low to the ground, burrowing things. Their meat was sour and stringy, the aftertaste thick with ammonia.

In the skies, there were large things that hunted, great creatures, so vast as to be impossible to see all at one time. These creatures lived on or in the storming clouds of the plains. Huge iridescent creatures that swam above the plains often glimpsed through the tumultuous weather, the tornadoes, the storms. Always hungry and hunting.

And so, with the air and water poisoned, the meat hard to catch and harder to eat, and the skies filled with predators, the true residents of the plains, the sentient upright sort, had taken to living underground. As the

Plains of Anchu became more toxic and uninhabitable, they went deeper still into the earth. These survivors, the Pale Ones as they were known, dug and dug, creating elaborate warrens that would impress with their complexity and maze-like mathematics. Whole cities of clay, damp, and darkness. There was little food, less potable water, and even less hope. The one thing the Pale Ones had in abundance was magic, a pure energy that could be absorbed and manipulated; the atmosphere positively throbbed with it. And with little else to sustain them, these hungry magicians turned to cannibalism both of the flesh and of one another's lifeforce. They grew stranger. Craven. They had little choice, but to cull their herds, split the weakest amongst the strongest.

Hungry.

Everything was hungry on the Plains of Anchu. Desperately trying to eke out an existence from the highest points in the heavens to the deepest coolest points in the ground. All the creatures yearned for survival.

Or better yet, a door out.

The resurrectionist didn't look how Peter expected. For starters, she was young, probably late twenties or early thirties. No makeup, her skin clear, and her brown hair swept back and knotted tight and low at the nape of her neck. Prim, like a schoolmarm or a nun. She wore a white blouse tucked into gray dress slacks. No jewelry. Plain.

Then he met her eyes.

They were the lightest blue he'd ever seen. It was the arctic blue of husky sled dogs and glacial ice. They were secret springs at the farthest reaches of the world. His entire body crawled with goosebumps when he looked into her eyes, and his heart froze up mid-beat. Inhuman. Unnatural. Their otherness reminded him why he was there in the first place.

He tried to ignore his sister beside him, agitated and shifting, and no doubt glaring his way.

He cleared his throat, "Thank you for seeing us on such short notice, Ms. Shade. I will just cut to the chase, as I am sure you are very busy. Basically, my father has been moved into hospice and has decided to change his living will. Apparently, he doesn't want to...die anymore." Peter looked away, feeling embarrassed before the resurrectionist. As if talking about death was somehow vulgar. Which was absurd considering it was literally her job. Peter's family had always been pretty conservative when it came to interacting with the more inhuman elements in society. They went to church, they were members of exclusive country clubs, and they, like so many of that generation, just kind of existed like there weren't monsters living openly in the world. Because of that, Peter felt quite uncomfortable and sheltered facing someone inhuman.

"It happens more often than you may think." Selene Shade shifted forward, both hands on the desk, nails cut short, unpolished. "Mr. Partridge, I will tell you the same thing I tell all potential clients. Not everyone is a good candidate for resurrection. The desire to live on in the twilight of life because you are dying and scared and the desire to live *after* death are not the same."

"Meaning?" Iris, Peter's sister, interrupted. She had her arms crossed over her chest and a pinched look directed at Ms. Shade. Iris didn't like any of this and her flirtations with *very* anti-magic born-again Christianity made this meeting all the more of an ethical and moral sticky wicket for her.

"*Meaning* that he may not want to come back after he dies. That he may prefer to be dead, once he is dead. Not everyone wants to be pulled back and put into a dead, reanimated body. It's close, but not the same as being alive. He'd have to live with the restrictions and it's important he knows them. Many reconsider resurrections once they know everything."

"Oh, he has a real zest for life." Iris answered her chin held high, eyes red-rimmed. Ms. Shade's face was blank, no doubt in her line of work, everyone had a zest for life, or unlife as it were.

"If that's the case, then he would put down a non-refundable deposit and sign the resurrection agreement. But I always recommend we allow the living all the information and the deceased the choice. Once dead, he may prefer it."

"I highly doubt that, Ms. Shade, as I said my father has a lot of vigor left in him."

The resurrectionist sighed, not bothering to hide her dislike for Iris Partridge anymore. It made Peter like her more, made her seem more ordinary. It wasn't a buyer's market after all and Iris was a pill. A negative review online was not going to stop the dead from dying. There were only two resurrectionist firms in the Goat Hill area. She could afford to let them walk.

"If he agrees and signs the paperwork, then the next warning is that only parts of him may return, or something that is not him at all. It's rare, that happening, and never at our firm, but it can happen. It's not an exact science as you can probably imagine. So, there are risks to consider. More so, if he is mentally unbalanced, there could be issues."

"Like *zombies*?" Iris whispered the word like it was a swear and Peter grimaced. The resurrectionist leaned forward, her face stern.

"Ms. Partridge, let's call a spade a spade, shall we? He would be a zombie if he was reanimated—though I don't like that word—he would be in a dead body, a body that decomposes, and he would need to be fed a particular diet. Not brains like movie zombies, but living flesh and lifeforce, to stave off decomposition. He would require a care-taker. This isn't a brand new, better than ever, father for you. This is an elderly man in a frail, reanimated body. It's not miracle healing, it's *death magic*. It's a big choice and commitment for your whole family."

She looked between the brother and sister, skewering them with her icy eyes. "He would be your responsibility."

"Fine, yes we understand." Iris shot back, her knuckles white.

"Twenty-five thousand for standard Reanimation. Non-consen-sual, in this case, if his faculties could not guarantee he understands exactly what this entails, is one hundred thousand dollars. Non-refund-able. Contracts have to be signed by the dying and the individual who would be taking the caretaker role." She paused and looked at them both again, "You take the paperwork and give it to your father, and have him really read it, really understand it, with a lawyer. Since once he is back in that body, the only way for him to get out of it is to see me for a Release, which costs another five thousand dollars, plus the addi-tional funerary body disposal costs at that point."

"That's absurd that you can justify charging that much," Iris said.

Ms. Shade quirked a brow and spread her hands wide, "If you wanted to save that money you could let him die."

"What is a Release?" Peter interrupted. "Why is it so much?"

"In the old days, the resurrectionist would be the animus. The problem with that is, if I get hit by a bus tomorrow all my half-lifes would drop dead. Moving the magic to an object protects against that.

"To Release him, I would need to do a ritual that severs the connec-tion between his spirit and body. Without the ritual, you would need to destroy his brain and damage his body beyond repair. It's cheaper, but it's not pretty. Believe me."

Iris gasped, her hand literally clutching her pearls. Peter bit back a smile. It was all very grim business, but under her austere mask it was clear Ms. Shade had a dark sense of humor. The idea of "Iris the Priss," as she was known in high school, bludgeoning their senile zombie dad to second death to save a buck was both horrific and sort of funny.

"Take the paperwork, show your father, and let me know what you decide. If he's in hospice, you may not have a lot of time."

───────

"I did not like her tone at all," Iris said once they were in the car.

"We want her to turn dad into a zombie. It's pretty fucked up, no matter what tone she uses." Peter rested his forehead against the steering wheel. His father, a man who would cross the street to avoid encountering anything he felt unfit or unnatural, wanted to become one of their ranks. It was unbelievable.

"It's what he wants! God, Peter, do you want Dad to die? To be gone?" He could feel her eyes on him, picture the glare without look-ing. He'd been avoiding those glares since the day they were born. He wanted to tell her that he found the idea of half-lifes repulsive. That he did not want his father to be one.

But the selfish part of him also had come up with a good idea in the resurrectionist's office. He wanted to write an amazing article on this process and his family, and who knows, maybe win a Pulitzer. He was already mapping out the long-form personal journey of a religious man, who hated the supernatural, through his change of heart late in life to his death and later resurrection. It would be intimate, it would capture how the world had changed so much in one generation. Sure, there had been plenty of articles and books in the last thirty years as the archaic practice of resurrection gained popularity and went main-stream. But they were often so clearly biased. Others were just plain schmaltzy like the memoir, *Bringing Back Janey*, written by the mother and father who had forced their daughter back to life then sacrificed everything to give her a "normal" life again. Then there was the long-running blog, *The Zombie Life*, the daily ramblings and inane observa-tions of a random half-life.

Peter was planning an article that would cover it all: the history of the practice, the real-life effects, interviews with resurrectionists, the lucrative and bizarre business model and how all of it was remaking the idea of life and death. There was a class angle of who "gets" to come back to life. Told from the perspective of a former bigot who ends up becoming one of the creatures he so detested.

"*Well?* Peter? Are you listening?" He lifted his eyes to meet his twin. So similar to him in appearance and yet so different. Same thick auburn hair, same hazel eyes, same pinched wrinkle from frowning nestled between their rusty eyebrows.

"Mom is gone, Peter. If he dies we'll be orphans!" Iris said.

He couldn't help but laugh, "We're thirty-five years old Iris, we'll be *fine*. It's the natural order of things after all. Old people die."

"It doesn't have to be, I have seen plenty of half-lifes and they are okay. Thriving even. Look at Joanne Danvers."

"She had cancer, sis, and two little kids to take care of, it's different. Though honestly, even in that situation, it just feels...creepy." He started the car, wanting to be away from the whole business, "Besides, Joanne Danvers could walk unassisted and she didn't have the early stages of *dementia*. Honestly, is she really happier? Have you asked her?"

Joanne had been a family friend since they were kids. Iris had to use her as an example because she was literally the only half-life Iris knew. It had been so tragic when she was diagnosed with aggressive pancreatic cancer and, with it, a guaranteed death sentence. She had toddlers at home. When she eventually succumbed to the disease, she was reanimated. Was she the same though? He flashed on the last time he'd seen her: chalky skin, rheumy yellowed eyes, thin-lipped tight smile. Empty, forced. No, she wasn't the same, she was a fucking monster. He hadn't even spoken to her, just raised a hand and kept his distance.

"Of course, I haven't asked her, Peter. God! That would be so rude." Iris put a hand to her chest piously.

He rolled his eyes, his mind already back on his article. Maybe a title like: "My Father the Half-Life: A Journey Investigating Beyond the Veil." He could swallow his fear and interview actual half-lifes. Could start with Joanne. He could talk to lawyers, doctors, ethicists. Half-lifes only recently had gotten the ability to vote and serve in the armed forces. He could talk to movement leaders in their community who demanded equal pay. Peter liked to think he could bring a human-interest element. Even a class issue, since the cost was so high and clearly insurance wouldn't cover it, most half-lifes came from money. He could write it either way, tracking the process, and how hard a choice it was for everyone.

"Peter? Seriously can you focus for like a minute?"

Peter groaned, "Fine. You talk to Dad, show him the papers. I'm going to call up Joanne, get her perspective on all of this. Her husband too." *On the record even*, he left unsaid.

Two

The animus was placed over his heart, the chain draped around his head. The small metal pendant still warm from my hand. I'd been doing raisings for so long that I didn't need to use the necklace as a point of focus, but found that the ritual, and having a physical element for clients to see and associate with the process, helped all around. The necklace helped the magic stay balanced.

I laid my hands on the cool chest, it was concave and covered in tattoos. At my touch, all the sounds and sights in the room faded as if the light and volume button had been turned all the way down. The room darkened until nothing remained but myself and him. Or rather his body, which was nothing, just an empty vessel. But the thing that made me a resurrectionist, called a death witch in other cultures and times, was my natural affinity for the dead. Like poles of magnets, drawn together by some invisible compulsion. To me, a dead body felt like a promise, something holding its breath, waiting. I hungered to touch them, to fulfill that promise, and they welcomed the contact. This mutual hunger, felt both by the dead and the resurrectionists, was not spoken about outside of resurrectionist circles. Easy to understand why; craving the dead, wanting to fill them, to undo nature...it doesn't make for polite conversation.

I cleared my mind and focused. Where my palm pressed over his still heart, a vortex opened, a perfect hole straight through him, through reality entirely and into whatever was past the mortal plane. I cast my consciousness into that hole.

The feeling was akin to how I imagine an astronaut feels, out there in space, barely tethered, surrounded by darkness, mystery and cold. Alone in a place indifferent and achingly silent.

Jason Jacob Devries, come back to me.

Out in the darkness, the twinkling of billions of stars. Each star a soul. Some were hungry and lonely, drawn to me. Others drifting further back, away, fleeing my pull. I, the black hole, searched amongst them.

Jason Jacob Devries, come back to me.

There! A small glow, dim, but drawing nearer. Curious about me. It was him. I could always tell if it was the right one.

By the time I noticed him, he'd drifted too close to turn back and was pulled into my snare. I dragged him back with me. His essence struggled in my grasp. I imagined him a fish, and I the hook. Through the wormhole tunnel *pull pull pull*, he fought, but his will to live or die was weaker and no match for mine. Like being born all over again, his soul, his *anima,* was pulled back through into this reality. Poured into his body through the hole in his heart. I sealed the passage, like piling boulders in front of a cave mouth.

Then he was trapped inside his corpse.

The body was still, though the spirit inside was frantic. The body can't reanimate without my command. The dead flesh tingled beneath my touch, always so patient. It's the clay and I'm the sculptor. Breathing out, I will the soul and body to reconnect. I will life where there was none. The soul melts and fuses back into the flesh, reactivating it. This body would move now, once I commanded it. My mind spoke to the soul inside, luring it out like a scared animal.

Jason?

Where am I?

You are home, back in your body.

Back? I died?

You are dead. You overdosed.

I don't feel anything. I can't move.

You will.
Now.

With a great gasp of air, the body of Jason Jacob Devries sat up. He rubbed his arms with trembling hands, his head darted around. Panicked. His hands fluttered to his animus, the pendant around his neck. It was a physical harness that kept his soul and body in harmony together. Half-lifes didn't need it, but it was a powerful meditative tool that we found helped them to stay connected mind and body. Otherwise, like a transplanted organ, there could be a bad match. It was also an insurance policy, as if a half-life did not have an animus to attach to, their lifeforce depended exclusively on the resurrectionist. If a piano fell on me, all my half-lifes would drop dead. Since half-lifes could potentially live a hundred years, or more, better to remove the resurrectionist as the magical lynchpin.

Jason was frightened, breathing rapidly, and was just about to leap from the table, that was until he caught my eyes, and stilled. Like a trained dog waiting for a command.

"Hello, Jason. My name is Ms. Shade, I am your Resurrectionist."

I waved out the office window as the car pulled away in the spring rain. Jason, once dead now reunited with his parents. Jason the junkie, now Jason the half-life. Watching me from the back window of the car, face lost.

Jason the zombie.

He would not be shambling around begging for brains, like in the movies. Or, at least, the old movies. Before undead rights activists convinced the public that it was deeply problematic to depict them that way. That it enforced stigmas. Which I agreed with, since it was hard enough living as a half-life, passing, fitting in, without people fearing for their brains. No, he would just be a paler, more distant version of himself. Almost alive. Almost. The need for drugs would be gone, and hopefully, in its place, some peace. But he wouldn't be free of hunger; the magics that kept spirit and flesh together, in a body that had suspended rotting, demanded a constant supply of fresh lifeforce.

But like a pet snake, he would grow accustomed to eating a mouse or gerbil every few days. A small price to pay to be alive again. Or half alive.

I sat at my desk and covered my face in my hands, tired. The process of soul-searching and planting was draining. Jason Jacob Devries was my third of the day. Unfortunately, my client list kept growing and growing. As half-lifes had become more normalized in society, more people lined up to become them. Good for my bank account; bad for my mental health.

My tepid coffee was not enough, rarely was. What I needed was help, I was putting out a lot of magic, not to mention the emotional toll of all the grieving clients. I was keenly aware of the empty desk opposite mine.

Dot's desk.

If she were there, she would be busting my balls about something or other. She'd never seemed tired, always saw the work as a calling. Loved her clients and half-life progeny like they were her own family. Such a perfect blend of sarcasm and wise medicine woman charm. The office felt so empty, so wasted, without her yelling at me all the time.

We had worked together for twelve years, she'd apprenticed me, and now she'd left me.

Alone.

I took her for granted, that I knew for sure, I hadn't realized how much I loved and needed that grouchy old lady until she was gone. It had been months. As I stared at her desk again, I could hear her voice in my head: "Quit mooning over me. You're tired, you look like shit. Hire some help, you idiot!"

I shook my head and smiled. It was true. Everyone dies, even Dot. Though unlike some, Dot wasn't coming back. It was time to find someone.

Before I lost my nerve, I started to draft an ad for a new resurrectionist. It would take a while to find one, especially one I would want to work with. We were rare, and good ones tended to get snatched up fast. Most likely I would be forced to take on an apprentice and train them myself. The good part of that is then I had control over their

techniques and client services, the bad part being a standard apprenticeship took at least a year but normally two. Beggars couldn't be
choosers though, I was too backlogged to do all the reanimations alone.

The idea of emptying Dot's desk and clearing out the last remnants
of her (dusty sweater on the back of her ergonomic chair, lipstick-
stained coffee cup) made my eyes fill with tears. No. Not yet. I wasn't
ready for that. I wanted to encase her desk in glass and preserve it like a
snow globe.

I was alone too much and I was getting weird with clients, I knew
it. *Curt and mean* according to my bad online reviews. I'd used Dot as
my social outlet, she'd stood in place of dating and friendships. I hated
to admit that, even to myself, but I was lonely. I'd never had many
friends and I hated the awkward fumbling of dating. But it had been
months of eating takeout alone and only talking to people who
paid me.

The red-haired man, the improbably named Peter Partridge, had
caught my attention at his consultation. In romance novel terms, he
was rakish and surely something of a cad. While the occasion was serious, his eyes had a twinkle to them, and he carried an air of good cheer.
He woke something up that had been collecting dust on a shelf. Not
desire per se, but interest. I was interested in him. But he was a potential client, so best to cast my attentions elsewhere.

So, perhaps a dating profile. Though the idea of typing in my occu-
pation made me uncomfortable. Just because some aspects of the
supernatural were becoming more mainstream didn't mean there
wasn't a ton of hate and fear still. People still got burnt at the stake on
occasion. Since I could anticipate an inbox filled half with bible-
thumping evangelicals calling me the devil and the other half with
fetishistic wannabes, I wasn't too eager to put myself out there again.
So, maybe I wasn't ready to online date yet.

Don't overthink it. *Get laid*, as Dot would say.

How else would I meet anyone these days? I was too fried after
work to go out. Was I going to sit at bars waiting for people to talk to
me? Take a pottery class? It all seemed kind of pathetic.

At least an online job listing and an online dating profile would
involve staying seated at my desk, and not talking to anyone just yet...so
win-win. If I didn't want to respond I could ignore their messages or
delete the app.

I had finished the rough draft of the job description when my door buzzed downstairs. Due to security issues in my line of work, having a secure entrance with video cameras and heavy-duty locks was imperative. People felt pretty passionate about life and death, regardless of what side they landed on it.

The man outside wore a tan car coat and dress trousers and tie. Hair neat and very short. Dark sunglasses. Official looking in posture and manner.

Three minutes later, Detective William Marlow of the Goat Hill City Police was sitting across from me. His brown/black eyes sized me up as if he didn't trust me. He was very fair, with light sandy blonde hair cut military short. He was handsome in a grizzled civil servant way but his aura was weird. It wasn't as colorful or lively as most people's. He had the look of a man who'd seen things, lived things. Which was probably cliché, considering he was a cop. Through the hardened professional exterior, I instantly sensed he was uncomfortable being in my presence. Just little clues: his aversion to shaking my hand, the way his body, although seated, seemed to be inching away and just about to spring up and run. Sadly, it was not abnormal, people were often afraid of me, but it seemed especially unprofessional in a cop, in my personal opinion. Especially a cop who clearly wanted something.

"So, Ms. Shade..."

I smiled, more teeth than necessary, "Please call me Selene."

"Selene, thank you for seeing me. I came here to talk to you about a matter of some delicacy. Have you been reading the papers, keeping up with the news?"

"Not so much as I'd like I'm afraid, but I am guessing this is about those murders."

"Yes, *those* murders," he replied stiffly.

Apparently, our little slice of the world had itself some sort of serial killer. If three bodies in three months was enough to count as such these days.

"The previous two victims were totally mutilated. But this young woman, number three, he wasn't able to finish, he must have been interrupted."

"Meaning..."

"Meaning she is intact. That is where you come in."

I sighed, putting both hands over my eyes. "You want me to bring her back?"

"Yes, exactly, she can ID her own killer, perhaps give her testimony, help us stop this guy." He sounded a little too confident in my abilities and I was tempted to laugh him out the door. But as I glanced his way, something about him stopped me. He was throwing very peculiar vibes. I looked a little closer, allowing the thing that made me a resurrectionist, my third eye, sixth sense, whatever you want to call it, to open. This detective's aura, which I thought of as the soul or spirit, was very strange. I'd have loved to stare longer but he was waiting for my response.

"Maybe you should talk to my competition, Dania Barabas, she's more experienced than I am...and she tends to be more touchy-feely, she may appreciate the publicity."

"Is she more skilled? Would she get better results?" I twitched at that, my ego warring with my desire to send this cop packing. The two resurrectionist firms had always been competing for the same business. Dot had really disliked Dania, and vice versa. I'd never met her. Most clients visited both of us when making a choice, they checked our rates, compared our personalities. Dania was more maternal, definitely more into the crystals and incense, delved more into closure issues and all that. Worst of all, she was a hugger. I liked to think of myself as the more clinical option. The DMV of death magic. I provided a service, but we didn't have to get all into each other's business. Dot had always come in someplace in between. The grouchy aunt type, filled with tough love.

"Certainly not, we—*I* am the better resurrectionist."

"Good. Because Ms. Barabas flat out refused, says she never works with the police."

"Oh, I see. So, you went to her first, huh?" I scowled at him.

His lip twitched, "You have a reputation for being a bit curt, Ms. Shade."

"Ah, see you read my reviews."

"I'm thorough." He had to be desperate, to be in my office asking for help. He did not want to be there and his discomfort was obvious. The murders must be pretty bad if the cops were looking to magic and the occult for help, definitely not the first choice for the very human police department and their limited budget. I squinted thoughtfully at Detective Marlow and he shifted in his chair, eyes anywhere but on me.

This cop's aura had my alarms ringing like a buzzing in my head. I've met plenty of people who were repulsed by me, by what I do, plenty of regular folks who think I'm hellspawn. But the detective was practically squirming in his chair and he had yet to meet my eyes once. Detective Marlow was hiding something. I wondered if he was human at all.

All people have an aura, and for those like me who traffic in death, we see a twin image: the physical flesh, and the spirit that is tethered to it. The spirit tends to bob in and out, like a balloon tied to a belt loop. It inflates and deflates, it changes colors with emotion. Detective Marlow's spirit was suspiciously still, bluish-gray, and faint. This ability to see the spirit inside a person was a unique ability only resurrectionists had. Witches could do a version of it with a charm, but it was a pale imitation.

He leaned forward hands between his knees, "Well, Ms. Shade? Selene? Will you help us? This is time sensitive. Three young girls have already lost their lives."

"It's more art than science, Detective. You may not get the answers you want."

"I appreciate that but, well...I am still asking," he said.

"And frankly, I've never raised someone for the cops." This was the first time I had been asked to assist with an investigation. On the occasions they came knocking, Dot had always handled them. She had better bedside manner and a bigger sense of civic duty than I ever did. I glanced at her empty desk missing her for the hundredth time that day. The familiar pang of grief and loss like a heavy weight across my shoulders. But even in her forty-year career as a resurrectionist, Dot had only helped the police maybe a handful of times and only in a fraction of that handful was she of any real use to them.

"The trail has gone cold, Selene, and we know...well, we know these crimes aren't over. We need information, information only the victim could provide us." Cops had a hard time understanding that not all murdered victims were floating around looking for vengeance. They weren't wandering ghosts locked to their deaths, another myth the movies really convinced people of. Ghosts were real, yes. But ghosts were merely shades recreating a moment, a stain on reality. Weirdly, I couldn't see ghosts all that well. Human psychics saw ghosts and some necromancers. Ghosts were energy, replaying scenes like a movie scene rewound and recreated over and over. But there was no sentience or intelligence to them.

The dead rarely had a sketch of their killer ready to show me if I did drag them back into their bodies. Death and time and reality don't work like that. Normally the dead are gone, off to wherever they go, and they don't want to return, or when they do, they don't even remember dying. Talking to them is similar to talking to someone with Alzheimer's: moments of clarity, surrounded by fog.

"It's not that I don't want to help you, Detective..." My hands fluttered in front of me, I was trying to think of a way to succinctly lay it out for him when he finally met my eyes.

The connection between us was like an electric shock. The feverish intensity of his eyes, his odd gray aura, I suddenly knew why he was so uncomfortable and I knew what he was. No, not regular people at all this one. I tried to hide my surprise and my excitement.

I cleared my throat and sat up straighter, hands clasped in front of me, feeling a little smug for solving the riddle. "I don't like doing involuntary resurrections under normal circumstances. And performing one on someone that died in a state of trauma? It's like rape." I shifted in my seat, looking closer at his face, his hooded eyes, his lips in a taut thin line. Then I decided to knock him off his game. "Like I am violating them all over again. Surely you remember that...from when *you* first died."

His eyebrows rose, eyes meeting mine again. *Gotcha.*

Then, I snorted, killing any mystique I may have created, "You pass, really well actually, it even took me a moment to figure it out."

I could see for a second that he wanted to deny it. But then his shoulders slumped a bit. "You got me," he said. I smiled.

"Were you made undead voluntarily?" This was an inappropriate question, but I wanted to prove my point, and I was generally curious. That and I hated, hated, forcibly reanimating the unwilling.

"Sort of. But I have known others..."

"I am sure they weren't too pleased. This poor girl was murdered, reanimating her as a living corpse to discuss her murder...it feels abusive to me. Cruel. She may just want peace."

"Yes. She may well. But I can promise you this: if we don't talk to her, others will die. Violently. This guy...he's not going to stop. Unless we stop him."

The words hit me harder than I expected. The dead may want peace but he was right, there was also a duty to the living to consider.

I leaned forward. "Fine. But I want a retainer. I am up to my eyeballs over here now that Dot is—well, since my partner passed away. It takes a toll."

"A toll money will fix?" he replied coldly.

"Not fix, but it helps."

He stood and handed me his card. We arranged to meet at the morgue that evening. He was a few feet from the door, hand hovering on the knob when he stopped and turned.

"I have to ask; how did you know?"

"I told you, you are good. Really good actually. Besides being pasty. But from your aura I can feel, sense, however you want to call it, the death on you. That you have been touched by it and changed by it. That you paid the price for the trade. It's kind of exciting. I've never met a vampire before."

"I wondered if you'd be able to tell." His back was to me as he said this.

"That why you were afraid to come here?" His head shot up, appraising me. It's said vampires have a natural fear of resurrectionists and necromancers. There is even a theory that vampires were an accidental creation of necromancers trying to create half-lifes thousands of years ago. Or so I'd heard, this was the first time I had actually talked to one. But since vampires were cousins of half-lifes, and I could control half-lifes, then perhaps I could control them all? Interesting theory that explained their fear of us.

Since I valued my jugular, it wasn't a theory I was going to try out anytime soon.

"Could be that you just have a scary reputation," he responded and I laughed, caught off guard.

"Very curt." I crossed my arms and leaned back on my desk. Trying for a cool effect.

"Selene, my personal situation is not public knowledge. And I would like it to stay that way."

"On the force you mean?"

"Everywhere. I would appreciate discretion."

"Of course, Detective Marlow, your secret is safe with me." I waved him out. I watched him get in his car through the window, thoughtful as he drove away. While half-lifes had rights and citizenship, vampires still occupied an in-between space legally. It made sense that the detective would keep his undead status a secret at work.

Vampires were apex predators and humans were their preferred food group. Half-lifes ate hamsters on occasion, it was a big difference.

THREE

Peter Partridge sat across from Joanne Danvers, the half-life, and her husband, David. Peter sipped his tea, ignored the plate of biscuits, and tried to act totally normal. He did not stare at Joanne, though he desperately wanted to.

The house was tidy, especially so, and there were fresh flowers in vases all over. Even a cluster of petals in a bowl on the coffee table. The effect was overwhelming, like being in a florist. He wondered if the flowers were masking an odor that could not be scrubbed out of the place, like decay? A grandfather clock ticked loudly, and though there were two kids in the house, he did not hear a peep out of them.

"It's so nice to see you, Pete, been a long time," David said genuinely. He shifted his weight on the sofa, leaning back. Joanne stayed still and upright, spine ramrod straight, eyes on Peter with total focus. He fought the urge to fidget.

"Oh yeah, thanks for having me by. We are all so busy these days, you know?" He stared into his teacup, trying to find tact. When none came to him, he plowed on, "But the reason I'm here, god, it feels so rude after not talking to you two in so long, but the reason is my dad... he's in hospice."

"So sorry to hear that," David said, his face tight.

"He wants to get resurrected, doesn't he?" This from Joanne, who had barely spoken or emoted in any way since he arrived. Even now, her voice was monotone.

"Yeah, it's that obvious, huh? Well, he is dying and is thinking about becoming a half—well I mean, he is thinking of being brought back. Just wanted to talk to some people who have experienced it."

David sat back with a forced chuckle, "Heck of a responsibility you've given us, Pete. Right, honey?"

Joanne was staring down at her hands. Finally, after the silence stretched to awkward she looked back up. "It's not the same. I was so young, my babies...were so little. I just couldn't see a world where I didn't get to raise my children. For me, there was no such world. But it's not the same. He's had a long life."

She touched her heart. "It's so quiet, in here. I feel like a machine sometimes. Everything black and white, all around me everyone sees color." She met Peter's eyes and he was chilled by the desperation there, his entire body crawled with goosebumps.

David chuckled good-naturedly and took his wife's hand, "Oh honey, we should be telling him the good stuff too. Like you get to be here with us. And you're working down at the grocery store now and thinking about taking some classes. It's not all bad, Pete, just different. Right, hon?" Her smile was brittle as she nodded.

Peter stayed as long as politeness would allow, before bowing out. He was nearly to the door when two kids quietly ventured out of their rooms, thin and wide-eyed. Was it his imagination or did they avoid their mother? David offered to walk him to the car.

Once outside, door closed, David sighed, "Tell your dad no. He will be so old and frail, and hungry. That's the only thing that gets any rise out of them really. Feeding time." He shuddered, "My garage looks like a pet store."

Peter waited, unsure how to respond.

"I mean we make it work, Jo and I, we have to. We made our choice. At least until the kids are done with school..." He wanted to say more, but something quieted him. Peter followed his gaze to the front window where Joanne stood sentry, arms crossed, watching them.

"Good seeing you, buddy. Keep us posted on your dad, and if you ever want to get a drink or something."

"Yeah, sure man," Peter said as David walked back toward the house. A doomed man.

The body lay on the slab, though her face was relatively unharmed, no one could say she was sleeping. Her pallor and sunken eyes, her bluish lips, even the limpness of her long curly hair said dead. Dead.

I was not afraid of the dead. If anything, I felt a kinship with them often more so than I did with the living. They were just husks after all. Harmless and empty.

But I still felt a pang as the sheet was pulled back, revealing her face. Something about her youth, her beauty, and the violence of her death. The knowledge that she died in fear, I could almost feel it staining her. A wrongness.

"Maybe I am just sexist, but there is something about pretty dead girls," I muttered.

Detective Marlow stepped closer to me, and her, "It's true, Poe said it '*The death of a beautiful woman is unquestionably the most poetical.*'" I turned and raised an eyebrow.

"*He reads*, what else can the mysterious detective do?" I teased, trying to calm my nerves.

His face sobered and I kicked myself for being overly familiar.

At that moment a tall older man in scrubs with a white beard, Max, and a small dark-skinned woman in a burgundy pantsuit, badge on her belt, entered the room. The woman introduced herself as Detective Regine Robinson, Marlow's partner. The doctor was the resident in charge of forensics. Detective Robinson regarded me with a level of loathing that made me think she was both a hater of the supernatural and also probably religious. There was a certain indignant disgust that comes from true believers, a certain flavor of hate that just feels different. I don't blame them per se since I can do something that only Jesus was supposed to do, after all. But I also didn't have to love the witch-burning glares I got.

Made me think back to the Partridge brother and sister. The sister had a bit of it too. The certain judgment of the righteous.

"Thank you for coming, Ms. Shade, we realize you are busy, and we don't want to take too much of your time," Marlow said with a smile, all icy formality with me around his colleague. Now that I knew what he was, I couldn't not see it. The predator eyes, shiny and flat like a shark's; the white sharp teeth, carefully tucked away behind his pale lips. The always-still aura superimposed over his flesh. I caught myself staring and averted my gaze.

"This is Belinda Curwen, and she was murdered last night. Witness interrupted the crime, perp fled, but it was too late to save the victim," Detective Regine Robinson chimed in.

"So, you want me to find out what happened?" I replied sullenly, looking at the dead girl.

"Yes, anything you can find out would be helpful. The other two victims had their heads removed, making it impossible to...ask them." This again from Detective Robinson, her expression sour. She was probably five inches shorter than me, but she was thick, and I got the distinct impression she could beat everyone up in the room.

"No offense, but isn't finding out what happened, *investigating*, your job? As I told your partner, it's not as easy as just waking her up and asking 'hey, who killed you?'"

"We have been doing our jobs, Ms. Shade, we would not have even entertained someone like *you* coming in if it was not urgent that we stop this guy." Robinson glared up at me, "So just do your job to the best of your ability."

"I expect my retainer regardless, I can't guarantee results." I said this to Marlow as he seemed the more reasonable of the two.

"Just try your best, Ms. Shade. Now if you please, she's scheduled for her autopsy tonight after this session," Marlow said.

"Fine! Let's dive in and see what we can find." I clapped my hands and rubbed them together. My bravado masked my discomfort, poorly no doubt. I met Marlow's eyes again, and there was some sympathy there, he knew I didn't want to do this. It made me like him more, not much, but a little. "I need access to her bare chest, above her heart."

The medical examiner, Max, was so still I forgot he was in the room all this time, leaned past me and pulled back the sheet, exposing small pert breasts and a strange bruise over her heart. I produced an animus and holding it, I placed my hands over the bruise, skin to skin, and closed my eyes.

The room slowly darkened, as I pulled myself in, lit now only by the living-lights of the lady detective and medical examiner, and the cooler stranger light of Detective Marlow, they glowed around me, like floating lanterns in the dark. Until even they were gone.

Then I was through the wormhole and into the ether, calling to her. Over and over. The space was infinite, billions and billions of burning stars. And I was lost out there, hollering and hollering. I felt like a pet owner in a forest. Calling out for Mr. Whiskers. It was different looking for souls when you weren't invited.

Belinda, Belinda, Belinda.
Please come back, just for a short while.
You are safe. You are safe with me.

Am I?

There she was. A small voice. Surprisingly close as if waiting for me.

Yes! Yes, of course. Come back with me, just a short while.

Back where?

To your body. Just a short while. Please. You will be safe.

Then she was.

Her eyes opened at the exact moment mine did. I heard Detective Robinson gasp and step back. Marlow was as still as a statue beside me. Belinda sat up, arms limp at her sides, and turned to me. Pale-blue eyes only for me.

"Welcome back, Belinda. My name is Selene, and I need your help."

She hesitated, eyes glassy, before whispering, "Ok."

"Tell me about your day. Tell me all that you remember."

The dead girl went still. Thinking no doubt. The stillness is one of the tells of the undead. Humans move, and pace, and itch, and tap. They snap gum and twiddle their hair. The dead do none of those things, they are more like the spinning wheel on a computer screen.

"I went to class. Then a shift at the coffee shop. Went out for a drink with James. He was walking me home. And then...and then..." Her eyes widened and she looked at me, horror across her face.

"I'm dead, aren't I? This body, my body." She felt her chest and arms. Hands grasping, I noticed her broken nails. They were caked in mud and dried blood. No doubt defensive wounds, from fighting and clawing. I swallowed a lump of nausea.

"Please stay calm. You are safe with us. I just need to know. Who is James? Did James hurt you?"

"James? He goes to school with me. We have a comparative religion class together. He is cute. Shy. Harmless. I said that to my roommate, she didn't like him, said he was 'creepy.' No, he is just shy, just harmless."

"Did James kill you?" Detective Marlow said, voice soft but urgent.

I repeated the question to Belinda. "Do you know his last name?"

"I don't know his last name. I can't remember."

"Try," I said pushing gently.

"Did he kill me? *Did he?*" She reached out to me. I took her dirty bloody hands in mine. Cold.

"What happened on your walk home? Think back, try to remember..."

"He told me that I was perfect. That he had been looking for someone like me. A *perfect vessel*, that's what he said. That he was in love with me. Nice things. He kissed me. I felt a bit drunk, and asked him to take me home, but instead he laid me down. I said no, not there, and I fought. Then another person was there, holding me down. And they...they..."

She drifted, eyes looking away. Her hands pulled away from mine and went to her lap, bunching the sheets in a fist. "They raped me. James held me down. The other he..."

"What did he look like? Did he say a name?"

"Darkness. Living darkness."

"Dark skin?"

"Black."

"A Black man?" Detective Robinson responded. My skin was suddenly covered in gooseflesh, a flash of a figure, naked, made of shadows, its inhuman flesh undulating and rippling like oil. An open mouth, blacker still, and out of it the sounds of wind. I was sharing Belinda's memory of her attacker. Or was I? The image was terrifying but also oddly familiar.

Belinda turned to the lady detective, her eyes haunted, head cocked. "No, not a man at all. Not skin. A man made of shadows." She pulled the sheet away from her body then and I sucked in a breath.

From the waist down, her body was stained with old clotted blood. Her genitals so mutilated they looked more like ground hamburger meat than a human body. Both her legs had been ripped from the sockets and hung like old puppets off the gurney, held on by skin and sinew. The only reason she could sit up at all was her inability to feel pain. I glanced at Detective Marlow mouth open in horror and was not reassured by his wooden expression.

"They chanted over and over. He ripped me apart. I screamed and screamed but no one came. I was bleeding, I knew I was bleeding to death. No one came. I died. I'm dead. Oh god, oh god. NO ONE CAME." If she breathed normally, she would be hyperventilating.

"Do you remember what they chanted? Or if they had any ritual tools?" Marlow asked.

"I don't know. I don't know. I didn't want to die. I was so scared. No one came to help. No one—"

"—I am so sorry for what happened to you, Belinda. Thank you for helping us," I said, I could feel tears burning down my cheeks. I did not want her to get any more agitated, she was pulling at her hair, eyes rolling. "I'm going to let you go now. Back to sleep if the detectives are done."

"Wait! Wait! You can't just put me back in the ground. You can't just let them get away with this. I don't want to die! I don't want to die. Selene, you can't do this! You promised I would be safe. Save me."

My stomach flip-flopped. I looked at Marlow. "Can I talk to you?" He nodded.

"Belinda, be still and calm." I commanded. She instantly stopped screaming and sat like a propped-up doll. "Detective Robinson will be with you until I return." Max the medical examiner and Detective Robinson watched Belinda, lifeless as a statue.

I rushed from the room and pressed my back against the cool cement wall, gasping for air. Marlow closed the door and came to me.

"What happens now, Selene?"

"You get what you want? Please tell me you have. She's suffering and needs to be set free."

"We got something. But we could use more—" he replied, voice remaining composed.

"More? This girl is a victim of a horrible crime, and she didn't want to die. Now she is in it, all the trauma, in her broken body, again. It's cruel and traumatic. She's losing her mind every second she is forced to be in there. I'm surprised she was as lucid as she was. I don't like to raise the unwilling. It's a violation. That's why Dot used to handle this police shit!" A flash to a funeral, twin coffins, a hand on the edge. Everyone screaming. I pushed it away.

Marlow leaned toward me, meeting my eyes, "Okay, okay, Selene. I get it. She gave us what info she could, now let's give her peace, and find the ones that did this." I glared at him then turned and marched away from him.

As I re-entered the room, Belinda turned, eyes eager and loving as they took me in.

"Thank you for coming back to us, Belinda. You've been so brave. Thank you for recounting your horrible ordeal. But it is time now for you to leave this body. It is broken and you are free from it."

"Please don't do this, Selene. I'm not ready."

I smiled sadly, taking her hands in my own. "No one ever is. I'm so sorry for your loss. Safe journeys."

With that, I severed the connection I'd created between her soul and body. With a snap, the tether broke, and the body fell back with a wet thump, limp and lifeless again. Her mouth hung open, slack, eyes cloudy and wide. I breathed out, my whole body exhausted, my spirit battered.

I staggered from the room, running my hand along the wall until I got to a water fountain. I put my face into the cold water burbling out of it, washing the weight of the reanimation away.

Marlow was at my side, silent, and watching.

"Thank you for doing that. I know it was hard for you."

I looked up through wet eyelashes, glad it hid my tears. "What really was the point of that? I'm sure you could have found out she was out with James from her roommate. Christ."

"But that shadow man. That was new, good intel."

"He obviously isn't human if he is able to rip her body apart like that. Not to mention shadow black skin," I muttered wiping my face off. "Good luck getting him for a line-up."

"Can I buy you a drink? You look like you need one." I raised my eyebrows at him. I was tempted to say no, but the image of the Inky Oil Man and Belinda's desperate voice, felt like worse company. I didn't want to be alone just yet.

So, I let the vampire buy me a drink. He owed me.

FOUR

Hank Partridge coughed wetly and dabbed his mouth with a monogrammed handkerchief. Peter, his son, fought the urge to gag and glanced at his sister. Iris was applying makeup with a compact and acting oblivious. There was a lot of phlegm in hospice after all.

"You think it's a bad idea?"

"Yeah, Dad, I do. We talked to the resurrectionist, and I talked to a freaking half-life face-to-face. You would still need your walker and you'd have to eat fucking hamsters. It's not like you'd be magically younger or able to move better."

"But I'd be alive, and I would have no pain and no medication."

"Yeah, no pain but you'd be in a dead body!"

"Peter, this is Dad's decision. It's his money, it's his choice."

Peter glared at his twin, "Will half-life Dad be moving in with you?"

Iris flustered, "I have two little ones so that is not a great idea, Peter. Just because we don't have the space, Daddy, not because we wouldn't want you there."

"Yeah fucking right! Well, you aren't living with me in my tiny apartment, which means you will need to have the budget to be in an assisted living facility that will provide you with your...vermin. On top of the money to get you reanimated."

"Then I guess I'll start looking into those places. Iris honey, will you help?"

"Anything for you, Daddy. If this is what you want."

Peter stood and swore. "What is wrong with dying with dignity? When did that go out of style!" He stormed out, slamming the door behind them.

A nurse was in the hallway, Hazel? Hannah? An H name, he'd seen her before: pretty and petite, clipboard in hand.

"Everything all right, Mr. Partridge?"

"Oh fine, my Dad is hellbent on becoming a fucking zombie. Can you talk some sense into him?" Peter's anger had surprised him, but after talking to Joanne, he found the whole idea to be terrible and wrong.

She smiled sympathetically and came closer, lowering her voice, "More and more of our patients seem to be going that route. But what kind of life is it? Between me and you, I think they are creepy."

"Same. Thank you, Hannah."

"Harley."

"Sorry, thank you, Harley. Hey, what are you doing after your shift?"

I sipped my vodka soda and stared off into space a moment, trying to relax and collect myself. The whole ordeal with Belinda was still too close, I could feel her desire for life, see the desperation in her eyes, taste her fear. I couldn't save her. She was already lost.

I couldn't avoid flashing on the ink man again, looming over her. The horrible way he killed her. The nightmarish familiarity. I knew him from somewhere. There was an ache in me, both physical and spiritual. A helplessness. I wished Dot was with me now more than ever. She would know what to say, she would know what to do.

She wouldn't have let me go there in the first place.

The vampire detective sat across from me, a scotch neat sitting relatively untouched to his right. The bar was dark, the booths tall and leather, creating an intimate feeling, almost like being tucked inside individual clam shells. Benign ambient music floated above us. It was a good place for discreet conversations.

If we'd been having one, that is. We'd been nearly silent since ordering drinks. Two strangers with nothing pleasant to say to one another.

Finally, Marlow spoke, "Is it harder to raise murder victims than those that die naturally?"

I raised my eyebrow at his choice of icebreaker. "Unnatural death is traumatic, it hurts the body and the mind. That's why there's 'police work' and not just defaulting to magics and all that shit. There was an equally likely chance she would have just started screaming and clawing her face off as soon as she woke up. There is a heavy toll meddling with that stuff. If they are expecting it and wanting it, they transition a little better."

"I understand. I do. But we needed a break. And now we know something."

"Yeah the 'shadow man' doubt that'll be easy to track down. But this James fellow, you really didn't know about him before I raised her?"

"James was already a suspect. But there's something weird about him, too. No James on the roster for the class. Classmates, even the roommate, remember seeing him and talking to him, but no one can accurately describe him."

"Obfuscation spell sounds like. Or he is just really fucking forgettable."

"Exactly. We know he's at least dabbling in some dark magic, and he obviously runs with a scary friend."

"More than likely they aren't just really heavy-duty rapists. This screams ritual sacrifice or something akin to that. Especially the perfect vessel stuff. The other girls were missing their heads?"

He met my eyes, thoughtful. "Yeah, does that mean anything to you?"

I rubbed my temples, tiredness pulling at the edges of my vision. "Makes them unable to resurrect or communicate with post-mortem. Even for a necromancer working only with their salts. Without heads you won't get too much more than a gross science experiment. If they don't want their failures leading back to them, and it makes them harder to ID in general."

"Makes sense. And frankly a relief to not call in necromancers. *That* is a worst-case scenario. We already brought you in. Not to mention the monetary cost to the department."

I nodded and looked away. Resurrectionists were disliked, but necromancers were loathed. The conversation dried up and I sipped my drink.

I'd noticed that for a sort of dead guy, he was not very still, he fiddled with things on the table and moved his drink around. It was not a behavior I would think a vampire would have. Did I really put him at this much unease?

I wondered about him, as it was impossible not to. But that was cliché wasn't it? It's what everyone wants in the end. The story: the vampire's really good story.

"Tell me about yourself," Marlow said finally, breaking the long silence. I chuckled at him beating me to the punch, wondering if he was a little telepathic.

"You tell me about yourself," I countered, half smiling.

"I asked you first, and besides you know more about me than most people do already. You have me at a disadvantage."

"There is not much to tell. I am a resurrectionist. I was raised in the Goat Hill foster system, went to college at the local university, apprenticed with Dot. That's it."

"Dot is Dorothea Wraith?"

"Yeah. Yeah, she taught me everything, and she was my partner, and best friend. Though she would probably say I wasn't hers. She had a cruel sense of humor. And other friends and family."

"People at the station speak highly of her, she helped with some hard cases over the years."

I settled further into my booth, slumping like a teenager. Dot did everything better, always had. Marlow noticed.

"Selene, I'm sorry about today, but it does help to give us some leads. We do appreciate what you did."

"I'm sure. Your partner looked like she wanted to burn me at the stake."

"Robinson? Yeah, she was not too keen to bring you in."

"Oh, it was your idea? That's surprising considering I give you the heebie-jeebies." He frowned, annoyed, and something about it made me smile. I think I liked bugging this vampire.

"You don't give me the 'heebie-jeebies.' God, are you twelve? No, I've just never crossed paths with one of you. On purpose. I wasn't sure what would happen."

"And now?"

"It's strange, I would know what you were, or an idea of it, even in a crowd. You feel different than other people, it's like a vibration. But instead of being repelled or scared...I'm drawn in. You're not doing something to me, are you?"

I laughed. "Uh no. I don't think so, and besides, you invited me here, and to the morgue, and came to my office. I have to admit I was curious as well. I haven't had any interaction with you guys either. I think historically there is enough bad blood that we've kept our distance."

"Yeah. So, the 'shadow man' doesn't ring any bells for you?"

The dark figure flashed into my head unbidden, just as it had before, the windy howl coming out of its open mouth. I shuddered and squeezed my eyes shut a moment.

"I saw him. Or rather Belinda saw him and we shared the memory. He is definitely not human, barely humanoid. No, you'd notice this guy. His skin looked like an oil slick. No facial features, just a hole for a mouth. Scary stuff."

But was it only Belinda's memory? Again, something about him made me wonder, just familiar enough to bother me. A déjà vu sensation that perhaps this shadow man had appeared to me before.

"I will pull in the occultist we have for cases like this, see if he's mentioned anywhere," he said.

We finished our drinks and I declined a second one. We'd taken separate cars so it was easy to say goodbye and just leave. I was tired after all.

I was out of practice talking to anyone besides clients and the dead these days.

City traffic was light this late in the evening on a weeknight, and I was grateful for a quick trip home. I lived in a small brick townhouse in an "up and coming" neighborhood on the West Side of Goat Hill. The homes around mine showed their age but still brimmed with enough character to be charming. A lot of hardworking immigrant families and excellent takeout. But definitely not a cool neighborhood for hip young singles. Dot teased me when I renewed my lease that I was signing a spinster contract.

I pulled into my parking spot and hurried up the steps, keys in hand, embarrassed that the day had left me on edge and fearful of shadows. But there *was* something in the shadows, a dark thing, with a mouth made of wind, and the strength to tear my legs off my goddamned torso. I was entitled to a little sleeplessness over that wasn't I?

I didn't feel safe until I was inside, deadbolt secured and chain affixed. I washed the residue of the morgue off my face, stripped and pulled on an old T-shirt, crawled into bed. Fear and exhaustion battled to allow me to rest: as long as my dreams were nightmares.

Miraculously, I fell asleep.

Marlow drove slowly under the overpass, clocking each of the figures standing along either side of the tunnel. Ladies and men, posing provocatively, others pitifully, all trying to entice the right John. A younger woman with a bit of baby fat caught his eye. She had blonde hair in pigtails, an oversized fur coat, underneath she wore a skimpy black dress.

She teetered over in sky-high heels and leaned in the passenger side window, he was relieved to see fine lines on her face in the dash lights, she was young-looking but not that young. She chewed gum, watermelon flavor, and it filled the car with its artificial scent.

"You looking for a date?" she said in a husky voice.

"Hop in."

They drove a few blocks down and pulled into an alleyway between two buildings.

She pulled her jacket off, snapping her gum, and faced him.

"Ok, ground rules: hands are ten, mouth is twenty. Pussy is fifty. Rubber is mandatory. Anything more adventurous is a hundred and a discussion beforehand. Cash."

He appreciated her directness, she was nothing if not professional. "And for blood?" He asked as gently as he could. Her expression changed, surprised, she hadn't taken him for a bloodsucker, so few do. He thought it was a gift, to be so passable, it allowed him to have a relatively normal life. There were others who weren't so lucky.

"I don't normally do that, don't like the marks." She said timidly. She'd lost her businesswoman bravado in the face of something dangerous.

"How about one hundred cash and I will be very, very discreet?" She finally nodded, not meeting his eyes.

"Alright, but not too much."

He spread her legs and nuzzled between, easily locating the femoral artery with practiced ease.

FIVE

Harley lay asleep beside Peter, snoring softly. They'd had dinner at some American fusion gastro-brewpub-type place, then had drinks, then more drinks, then to his place. He hadn't expected company and his poor apartment had the eau de bachelor look and scent about it that caused him some shame.

Thirty-five and he still couldn't manage to get his dirty towels into a hamper without the threat of company, and more often, not even then. Maybe everyone was like that deep down; he hoped at least that the world was full of pigs, and the only reason to civilize was a fear of judgment. He could hope at least.

Harley hadn't seemed to mind, she barely looked around the place before pulling off her scrubs and getting down to business. She'd confessed to having a crush on him for ages, ever since his father had been admitted. Harley was a talker, she was from Maine, a farmer's daughter, went to nursing school because it was one of the few jobs that weren't affected by the economy.

She told him all of this as she rode atop him, breasts bouncing, and he wondered what kind of evening she thought this was. It was like a porno job interview. She was a nice enough girl but the whole thing just felt like a mistake. He wanted a distraction and someone to bitch about his father to. It could have been anyone really, as long as they agreed with him. But now he had her sleeping beside him, oblivious and content, thinking this was a love match. Peter groaned and wondered what it was about him that attracted these intense, needy women that he didn't like much.

He tried to imagine David and half-life Joanne having sex. They must after all. All he could picture was her lying stiff, eyes open and unblinking, not even breathing, while David hammered away. Was she cold inside? Did she even feel anything? Did she secretly hate her husband for bringing her back from the dead? Forced to an afterlife in grays, surrounded by friends and family that were just a little afraid all the time.

The resurrectionist must feel that way too. Everyone just a little uncomfortable around her, she was like a walking *memento mori*, if you see her, it's too late. Those creepy inhuman blue eyes. He wondered if she raised Joanne. It was possible, there were so few reanimators out there.

He couldn't sleep and finally dragged himself out of bed and slowly padded out of the bedroom and sat himself on the couch. The resurrectionist and the half-lifes bothering him just enough to drag his laptop toward him and fire it up. A little research never hurt anyone. The Wikipedia entry caught his eye:

It is believed that the ability to reanimate is inborn, and that resurrecting the dead is basic biological function for those with the talent. Resurrectionists are always female, with blue eyes regardless of ethnicity, and the ability is not always hereditary but can run in family lines. Most individuals with this very rare ability are trained and apprenticed by an experienced resurrectionist. An untrained individual can create dangerous uncontrolled undead. It's why a good apprenticeship is imperative. Without a resurrectionist exerting their will on the undead, the creatures can be volatile, violent, and essentially mindless, save for hunger. All the great zombie incidents have been sourced back to one untrained resurrectionist, often in a state of heightened emotional distress.

Again, Peter thought of the resurrectionist and her otherworldly blue eyes. How disturbing to have such a skill. How isolating, he mused, people must cross the street to avoid her. He felt a little more sympathy for Ms. Shade, it must be a lonely life.

Finally, as dawn crested the rooftops across the street, Peter was able to curl up on the sofa and fall asleep.

Germaine Whately sat in Java's coffee shop on her laptop looking for jobs. As she had been for two weeks. Even with her loans, she was coming up short for the semester and her parents were tapped out. She was only a Freshman, how would she finish school in four years at this rate? Cashiers...supermarket, mall jobs. There was one thing she could do that would pay better, but it was the thing she wanted least in the world. She groaned.

She was about to close up for the day when she saw one that caught her eye:

Resurrectionist Wanted:

Small boutique Resurrectionist on Goat Hill's East Side looking to hire part-time reanimator for basic reanimations, office duties and light filing. Prefer some experience in the field and references. Serious inquiries only. Willing to offer apprenticeship for right candidate. Inborn talent only, no necromancers need apply. Thank you.

She scanned the shop conspiratorially, as if anyone cared what was on her laptop screen and reread the listing. Germaine had moved to the East Coast and away from her family, away from her few friends, away from that life to hide what she was. She wore brown contacts. She planned to be an English teacher. To be normal.

Germaine hadn't understood when her farm-vet father begged her to stop coming along to his client's homes with him. The horror when she learned she was bringing back all the euthanized animals and that they dragged themselves home to be with her. She tried to picture her father, Gene Whately, the gentle man that he was, bludgeoning dead animals with shovels, cutting their heads off, and burying them again, all to hide the truth from his young daughter.

Shame bloomed in her, coloring her cheeks. The familiar shame of being a freak.

But that would certainly pay more than a job as a cashier and if she didn't figure something out, she would have to drop out next semester. Besides, no one at school had to know.

Before she could talk herself out of it, she wrote up a quick cover letter and shot it off, resume attached. Exhaling as she did so.

"This seat taken?" She glanced up to see a young guy, early twenties, in a Meridian University T-shirt under an unzipped hooded sweatshirt. "I wouldn't bother you, but the whole place is full." She glanced around and confirmed that yes, there were no empty tables.

Germaine moved her stuff aside to make room. She found herself nervous, boys in Bixby, Oklahoma rarely talked to her. They all thought she was a freak: a chubby resurrectionist with frizzy red hair. She was basically a pariah back home. It was nice for a guy to want to even just sit near her, be seen near her.

"Thanks for being so nice. Oh, my name is John, by the way." He had brown hair that curled a little at his jaw and tan skin. Handsome. He also had a unique aura. She wasn't particularly skilled at seeing them, and back home in Bixby she didn't encounter much besides the standard human variety. But John's was interesting, like most people, he had the floating spirit that fluctuated in shape and color, but in addition, the spirit itself had little tendrils or tentacles reaching out around him. Like the rays of the sun.

"Hi John, my name is Germaine. Nice to meet you," she stuttered out, realizing she'd been staring.

"Likewise." They held each other's gaze, even when she felt herself blushing.

Everything in my bedroom seemed normal, but something woke me from a dead sleep. I followed the contours of the room, looking for anything amiss. Slowly. The bureau, from a thrift store, an old antique coatrack, weighed down in jackets and scarves. A sagging bookshelf, an old ratty chair, two big windows with blackout drapes, my nightstand. Back around again, bureau, coatrack, bookshelf, chair, *dark figure crouched behind chair*, two windows. I froze, body coated in cold sweat, and slid my eyes back to the chair. There it was, the *off* thing in the room, the shadow man, crouched low and watching me with two twin pools of ink for eyes.

I was paralyzed, staring at the thing, a vulgar approximation of a person. My body awash in electric icy adrenaline. It was like living shadow that was untethered from its owner. I blinked, hoping it was the lingering vestiges of a bad dream. But it remained watchful and waiting. When it was clear that the thing wasn't going anywhere, I swallowed and forced myself to speak to it, heart frantic in my throat, "What do you want?"

—a door

Its mouth stayed firmly shut but I heard its voice. Whispery and scratchy, it sounded like wind in my ears, like the buzzing of insects.

I blinked and he was gone as if he'd never been. For a chilling amnesiac second, I was so disoriented that my bedroom, my body, *my life*, were all totally unfamiliar. I was empty, a total blank. The moment passed and everything flooded back in: the mangled body of Belinda, Detective Marlow, and the shadow man, full of howling wind. The man who wanted a door.

I so badly wanted to talk to Dot about all of this. Tell her about the case: she had a fantastic way of approaching problems, seeing them from a different perspective. The familiar ache of her absence, the empty knowledge that I couldn't call her ever again.

Well, you could...

Oh, shut up, I am not bringing her back from the dead because I was scared.

It was true that I couldn't pick Dot's brain about any of this, but she had been married to a necromancer academic. A very knowledgeable one at that.

I was already reaching for my phone. I hadn't even thought about Karl the night before at the morgue, or how he may be able to help with the murders. They'd been divorced for ages, hell, she only called him *Shithead* for the last few years of her life. He was still a *somewhat* respected necromancer, if such a thing existed. I'd last seen him at her funeral, he was one of those men who became more chiseled and handsome with age. He looked like a cross between a men's hair dye model and a B-movie villain. Close-cropped goatee, smoky lensed glasses and a black turtleneck. He was also a professor of death and death magic with a predilection for adoring TAs and undergrads.

It was 6:30 in the morning, I chanced waking him. A few rings later a sleepy voice answered.

"Karl? It's Selene, Dot's former partner."

"I know who you are, Selene. Is everything alright?" Vague concern in his voice.

"I don't know. I had to assist a murder investigation last night and something the victim said has stuck with me. I wanted to run it by you. She described her killer as a *shadow man*? He's basically a black outline?"

"I am assuming you don't mean an African American man?"

"No, no, black like ink, not human. Like a living shadow. He may be trying to open a door?"

"Hmm, well there is an obscure figure like that referenced periodically: The Nigrum Porta, or Black Door. That sounds pretty close to me."

I stopped listening, feeling nauseated. *A door*, he said he wanted a door. The Black Door. I looked at the empty space beside the chair where he'd been crouching moments before. I told Karl to go on. He explained Nigrum Porta was a gatekeeper, believed to be like a ferryman or key, some translations even referred to him as a dark god.

"So, if he was being invoked..."

"What do you mean *if*? This is an archetype figure mentioned in various ancient texts, not a murder suspect."

"*Three* murders, and it looks like it's a young guy and this Black Door are raping women to death..."

"Raping women? That seems a bit mundane for a celestial gatekeeper. I've never read anything like that about him."

"Could you put together some information and have it sent to me?"

"Sure, sure. I'm out of town on sabbatical and don't have my books, but I can have one of my TAs put something together and get it to you ASAP. Anything to help." A long pause, "How are you doing otherwise?"

"Fine. I'm fine." I heard him breathe out, loudly.

"That's good. I worry about you, all alone. I still can't believe she's gone, y'know? Like the world is lonelier without her in it."

I wasn't going to have this conversation, it hit too close to home. "I have to go now, Karl, but thanks."

"You can talk to me, Selene, about her. Anytime. I know you have a pretty sullied perception of me, but I loved Dot too. She thought of you like a daughter, and I know she was your only family..."

My eyes burned, I wanted to just hang up, but that would have been childish. Instead, I steeled myself, let out a shaky breath, "Thanks for your help and support, Karl. I appreciate it. I do have to run though. Send me anything your TA digs up and...take care." Then I hung up, before he could get another word in edgewise.

I set the phone on the nightstand again and pulled my knees up to my chest, hugging them tight.

My only family.

It was impossible not to think of my actual family. My parents: two vague figures with blurred faces. Time and lack of photos had worn down their memory like stones on the beach. But I could remember a soft touch, a ghost of perfume, a laugh. A date night, while an elderly neighbor watched me, and later I would learn a car accident took them away from me.

Then their funeral. Me sitting in the front pew, crying and crying, wanting everything to go back to the way it was. But it didn't, and the priest droned on, and my heart felt heavy, and I just wanted them back. My pure childlike desire reached out to them, there in their matching wood boxes. Then my parents pulling themselves from coffins, their bodies weeping formaldehyde, stitched mouths tearing, garish doll-like makeup, glued-shut eyes. Everyone screaming.

I slammed the door on memory lane and dragged myself up and through my morning routine, tired of my own looping self-pitying thoughts. Can't stay alone where the ghosts of the past and the horrors of the last twenty-four hours could follow me around. I needed to keep my head on straight and look forward. Girls were getting killed. My past griefs were nothing in the face of that.

I got in the shower. I went to work.

Six

Peter Partridge was sitting in his car in the resurrectionist's parking lot. He admired the old historic mill building and the expansive view of the sea beyond. Lazy windmills circled in the far distance. He was watching a flock of seagulls rummaging in the overflowing dumpster when a silver sedan pulled into the lot. It was her. When she stepped out of her car, he felt the same spooky thrill he had in her office on that first meeting. It was a strange sensation to be so intrigued and yet so repulsed simultaneously by someone. Like a kid peeking through splayed fingers.

She wore oversized sunglasses, her chestnut hair, still damp, was pulled tightly in a bun, this time on the top of her head like a ballerina. She had on a black leather jacket and slacks. She was holding a coffee, and her mouth was downturned in a frown. With her eyes hidden away, he could admit she was attractive.

He had planned to wait till she was settled into her office, but somehow, without thinking, he was already out of the car and calling out to her. She startled and frowned at him, confused. She did not instantly remember him. Great. Especially since she had been crowding his thoughts since last seeing her.

"Hello, hi. Sorry to scare you. It's Peter Partridge, came in with my sister, Iris, just the other day..." She nodded and forced a smile, spooky eyes unreadable behind reflective shades. "I know I don't have an appointment. But I was hoping to talk to you a little more. Without my sister around." She gestured for him to follow her as she unlocked the door and got into the elevator.

Once in the elevator, she took her glasses off and those arctic eyes speared him through. Like a butterfly pinioned under glass. He didn't think he could lie to this woman, which caused a trill of panic since lying was kind of his default. "I just wanted to talk to you, person to person. Iris can be really difficult."

"I am quite busy, Mr. Partridge—"

"—Peter."

"Peter. I am very busy, what exactly is it you wanted to talk to me about?"

"I went and talked to a half-life I know, to help me understand it all, and I just don't think—I don't think it's right, do you? I know it's presumptuous to ask, and I mean no offense, as it is your career and also something you can't control as such. Sorry, I am babbling..."

The elevator swished open and she stepped out, heels clacking on the wooden floor. She fished out her keys, balancing her coffee, still not answering him. He moved foot to foot, unconsciously crowding her.

The door opened and he followed her in, it was the same space as before. Same big windows overlooking the water. Same industrial loft style. Same ominously empty, dusty second desk. She had set her things down and turned on her laptop. When she saw him looking, staring, at the empty desk she cleared her throat.

"I'm glad you're doing outside research and actually talked to a half-life about it. Most people choose to be reanimated because they are afraid. They don't want to die, or they don't want their loved one to die. But all choices have consequences."

"It's a bad choice, right? They aren't happy, can they even be happy? Or are they ghosts of their old life? Is it just like this terrible limbo?" He was pacing, hands in pockets. Manic energy. He was tempted to pull out a notebook, take notes.

"I can't answer that Mr. Par—Peter—some are happy for the time and their family, others find the limitations of a half-life unpleasant, unsatisfactory. Some like it very much. It depends. For your father..."

"He is going senile! It's wrong and disgusting and my sister is just being overly sentimental! He's also a huge bigot who fucking hates monsters." He blanched at his outburst, embarrassed. "God, I am so sorry. You probably hear this type of thing all the time. You're right, I should go, you are busy. It's not..."

"Have a seat, Peter. Do you want some coffee or tea or something?"

"Got anything stronger?" He answered dryly, sitting heavy and putting his hands over his face. She stood and opened a cabinet, a moment later she handed him a glass with two fingers of amber liquid. Breakfast of champions.

"This doesn't get easier, huh? It's all just such an ethical gray area." He met her eyes across the desk. "I just find all this supernatural stuff so freaky. Guess the apple doesn't fall far from the tree."

"I understand your fear and wariness. It feels to you like the world has changed a lot in a few short decades. That the rules have changed. But that's not what happened; you just learned the way it always was. I was born into the club, so I have no choice but to be a member. But wanting to become a half-life while hating them and what they represent is not a good choice. What kind of life is that? I don't think it's for your family, Peter." She was now perched on her desk, arms crossed over her chest, reminding him of lady detectives on TV. "I don't know if they are happy, or if it's the right thing to do. I like to think that for those who want to live so badly, it's worth it. I like to think that I am helping people, giving them closure, or a fresh start, or giving them more time. But I don't know. Frankly, that often scares the hell out of me."

"Because you can't help it right? It's involuntary? You have to raise the dead."

She grimaced, "Guess you have been doing some research, *questionable* research." Peter darted his gaze away in parts insulted that she would question his research skills, and also knowing that he basically just googled it. She continued on, voice gentler, "I don't know if involuntary is the word, but there is...something akin to a body function, or a compulsion, this *need* to reanimate. But I don't have to do it. And I can't believe I was designed to hurt people. I choose to think it's all bigger and more complex than that."

"Thanks for being so honest with me, Ms. Shade." Peter wished he'd asked for her to be on the record, wished to have been taping this. This could be a very thought-provoking piece, not about his father, but about those rare few who are born different with enormous power. She could be the face behind the growing movement of opting out of death. He smiled thinking of a cover story with her face on it.

She smiled back, "Call me Selene."

"Selene. Since I'm being unprofessional all over the place already, can I ask you another question? This one will hopefully be easier to answer."

She nodded, eyes warmer.

"Would you go out with me sometime? For a drink or food or something? Not to talk about my problems or my Dad or what have you. Just to talk and get to know each other, I find you interesting."

"Seems like a conflict of interest, don't you think? You being a potential client and all."

He shrugged, "It's just dinner. I am not much for following rules. Never have been. Between us two, I am going to fight like hell to not be a client of yours."

She laughed, and it was a nice sound, a hearty deep chuckle. He liked her more for it. She nodded and his heart fluttered. Peter wasn't sure where his professional curiosity started and genuine interest ended, but decided to go with it.

Robinson dropped a stack of folders on Marlow's desk with a dramatic thump, and crossed over to her own desk and sat.

"And this is?" He asked, not looking up from his computer screen.

"Rapes and murders from the last ten years."

"I doubt any will fit the profile. You hear back from our occultist?"

She leaned back in her chair, arms folded over her chest. "She's got some stuff, wants us to meet her to talk about it. Sounds excited."

His phone rang, "Detective Marlow."

"It's Selene."

"Oh hello, what can I do for you?"

"It's what I can do for you, check your email, I had a necromancer professor I know put together everything he could find about this shadow man."

"Can you sum up what you found, while I open it up?" he said balancing the phone between chin and shoulder as he opened his email, noting the large document attached.

"Well, he is an obscure heavy hitter, sometimes even seen as a god. He has a name: Nigrum Porta also known as the Black Door."

"Black Door, eh?" He held a finger up at his partner. "We have an appointment with our resident occultist, so we'll see if all this intel lines up. If so, think we have a good lead. Thank you, for taking the time, I know you didn't have to."

"I want these guys caught, and I really don't like the idea of what kind of door this dude is."

"Same. Thanks, Selene."

He flinched at the expression on his partner's face and hung up the phone.

"The resurrectionist? You guys on a first name basis now?"

"She's trying to help, it's the least I can do." He proceeded to show Regine the attachments and references she'd forwarded along, and while it was obvious his partner didn't approve whatsoever of dark gods and ritual sacrifice, she was impressed with the amount of potentially useful information Selene had decided to share.

Though her next question was to ask why Selene would help them.

"Saving people from being raped to death in magical rituals is not enough of a reason?" he asked. "You saw her the other night, she was clearly upset by the whole thing."

"I don't know, I get a weird vibe from her."

"I think that has more to do with what she is and what she can do," Marlow said.

Regine shrugged, "Whatever, come on let's go see Lila."

Lila Goodtree was a former professor of the arcane and the occult, one foot in magic, one foot in academia. She was long retired and had been working with the police department in a consultant role for well over ten years. In the five Marlow had been with this department, he had avoided meeting her. Like resurrectionists, he just preferred to keep his distance.

When he stepped inside the old dilapidated house, all he saw were cats and books. Cats and books stacked all the way to the ceiling. The only ways through were narrow warrens that he suspected even the lithe cats could barely navigate. The paths zigzagged through the swaying pillars of paper and debris. He exchanged looks with his partner as they both put hands to noses to cover the overwhelming miasma of cat piss and dust.

A voice, old and smoky, called out amidst the piles and layers and they followed it, deeper and deeper into the stacks, emerging in a small central parlor, filled with overladen once-ornate and now destroyed furniture. One wall was covered with hundreds of overlapping mirrors, such that the wall resembled the scales of a huge dragon. The opposite wall was covered with cuckoo clocks, cat clocks, and large institutional clocks; grandfather clocks ran along the floor, grandmother clocks were stacked on top of them. They all ticked, a maddening collection of hundreds of metronomes keeping near but not exactly in synch time. The reflection of hundreds of clocks in hundreds of mirrors was off-putting, to say the least. The whole space made Marlow feel anxious and claustrophobic.

In the center of the strange room was something desk-shaped. Its surface was so weighed down with books and papers and curios he could barely see over it. A threadbare leather office chair shifted to the side, overflowing springs and stuffing, and settled within, like a tiny mouse in a nest, was Lila Goodtree. She was quite small, with nut brown skin and a shock of white cotton fluff hair on top. She was draped in a colorful moth-eaten shawl, and wore thick black-rimmed glasses that comically magnified her cloudy brown eyes.

"Have a seat, I have so much to share!" she said excitedly as she pushed a fat old tabby off a stack of papers on the desk. The cat moved a foot and settled onto the keyboard of an open laptop.

The two officers glanced at the piles of debris, and like a unicorn in a magic eye poster, eventually two chairs presented themselves from the mess. After clearing them off, the two sat, both careful and dubious of the chair's strength. The old woman stood and hobbled around the desk, walking with a gnarled wooden cane that looked like some sort of wizard's staff.

"First, introductions! I am Lila Goodtree, PhD, occultist, worked for the university, specialized in ritual, specifically *human sacrifice* in ritual. As such, I have worked with the police and provided expertise for...a long time now. Christ, since before mundane folks even believed in all the magic and monsters! I don't think I've met either of you two before!"

Robinson made the introductions, her dislike for it all plain on her face. She was very allergic to cats and already her eyes were red and irritated. Goodtree seemed indifferent to it, she was far too excited by what she had discovered. She barely glanced at Marlow before moving on to her findings, to his relief.

"Ok!" The old woman clapped her hands together, speeding along. "This is most definitely a ritual, folks. All three deaths have been. Not just some random sex crime. Took me a while looking at the crime scene photos and reading over the autopsy reports to see what ritual though. There are no sigils, no protective circles, no salts or herbs. Just the body. Whatever the process, it leaves the body destroyed from the inside out. But there was something about them that said ritual to me. Especially considering their similar ages, the similar locations, and the timelines. Nothing about these murders was random. I started to look into sex rituals...covering all sorts of cultures. Started thinking, maybe something quite old, that may predate writing."

"Does Nigrum Porta ring a bell?" Marlow said interrupting, impatient.

The old woman stopped her pacing and squinted at him. A sly smile. "You beat me to it. Spoiled my surprise."

Robinson caught Marlow's eye with a frown. The occultist had not been told about the shadow man, just given the photos.

"The Nigrum Porta, or Black Door, is a strange figure who shows up all over various cultures and cults. The practice of invoking him has often, but not always, been sexual."

"What does the sex do? I mean for the ritual," Robinson asked stuffily. She fished in her pocket for a tissue.

"The ritual is a mockery of how human life starts. Life is created and then passes through the womb into being. In that way, the woman's body is like a door. I found evidence there was a ritual that uses sex as a passage for Nigrum Porta."

"So, is he the door, or is he passing through the door?" Robinson asked.

"He is both, my dear, I know it is rather vague. The summoning is to use him as a door, or I guess he is the key and the womb is the door? It's like the trinity in Catholicism. And equally confusing. It's all and one, besides, this is all theory after all since no one has done it and succeeded obviously."

"Why would anyone want to summon him?" Robinson shook her head.

Marlow stepped in. "Yes, what is on the other side of the door?"

"Nothing that we would want in this world, I'd imagine. Something bigger and badder that couldn't get here any other way."

"Safe to assume then that the ritual hasn't been working," Robinson said.

Lila nodded. "The women, known as the vessels, were not right—would be my guess."

"James called Belinda a vessel in her testimony," Marlow said.

"Would the right *vessel* survive to birth the door?" Robinson asked as she pulled out her notebook and pen for notes.

"No, I doubt even a proper vessel would survive. If you actually believe that Nigrum Porta is real or this type of ritual is real. But, for the sake of argument, let's say for the ritual to succeed her womb is the door." Marlow could see the wheels turning as Lila hobbled back to her desk, as she opened the case files she said, "The autopsies report that it's like the wombs were destroyed from the inside out. Like something tried to get out...but couldn't."

"If we can figure that out, it may help us to better understand the killer's motivations." Marlow said.

Robinson continued on, "Exactly. How is he selecting his victims? What is the perfect vessel? What's the profile? What would our killer be looking for?"

The old woman settled back in her chair and pursed her lips, thoughtful. "My first guess? Virgins. Cliché, yes, but I have two references to this ritual: both quite old and from different parts of the world. One hints at purity, another hints at power. Of course, remember these are both translations of translations. But, look at the three victims, find the common thread. They look to be young college-age girls. What caused our guys to pick them in the first place? And what are they trying to summon? You've got a little time, since we know the ritual is tied to the new moon. A couple weeks at least."

"Thanks, Lila." The detectives stood, Robinson shaking the old woman's hand. Marlow hesitated before reaching out, but Lila shook it unfazed. She was far more academic than occultist after all. He was relieved walking out.

SEVEN

I laughed out loud, nearly spitting the olive I was chewing all over my date.

Date? Maybe, it sure felt like a date. Crazy. Crazier still that I was having a good time.

Peter had taken me to a tapas place, and our table was so covered with small plates there was no top left. We had ordered nearly everything on the menu.

"I really like the melon with prosciutto," Peter said, stuffing a large hunk into his mouth. He chewed loudly, face ruddy with drink. In the time we had been there I'd learned a few things, mainly that he worked as a journalist, mostly online. He and his twin did not get along, nor he and his dad. He was a bachelor who was engaged once in his early twenties. He loved to travel and he hated sports.

I liked listening to him talk about ordinary things. Regular mortal issues—his crazy family, his stressful job. It was all so human. My life was only life and death. Literally.

"What about you? I feel like I have been talking about myself all night." He grinned, showing somewhat crooked teeth. His hair a messy mop as if he'd just raked his hands through it. His hazel eyes were warm with laugh lines crinkling at the sides.

"No, I like it," I said, thinking of my face, so unlined by life. "It's nice to learn about you."

He smiled graciously, "Well thank you, but seriously, tell me all about you, who is Selene Shade? I'm so intrigued..."

"Oh, well. Not much to tell. My parents died when I was quite young, and I grew up in foster care. Then I went to college on scholarships, I met Dot and apprenticed with her to be a resurrectionist. She passed away recently, and now the firm is mine. That's it really."

"What about day-to-day, like: Who do you hang out with? What do you do for fun? Or to unwind?"

"It's pretty dull I'm afraid, umm...Dot and I used to hang out a lot. Eat, watch TV, go to day spas for mani-pedis, stuff like that. Dot and I were really close. Without her, my caseload literally doubled. Doesn't leave me much time or energy to do much beside sleep when I get home. I like to read. I want to like yoga more. Mental clarity is super important in my line of work. Wow, I guess I am pretty boring." God, I was so dull. I was a dreadful date. A depressing date who could only talk about death and wishing they liked yoga more. Ugh. *This must be how the grim reaper feels making small talk*, I mused bitterly.

Peter shook his head, "You can raise the dead! Talk about burying the lede, Selene, give yourself more credit."

I flinched reaching for my wine. "Most people learn those things about me and it's all they can see. Like I am some kind of sideshow freak you know? It's part of what makes it hard to make friends, or date. People tend to be both overly curious and then, openly disgusted."

"Well, help me understand it. What's it like?" I bit my lip, eyes sliding away to the other tables around us, the happy faces of people on dates, enjoying each other's company. I bet none of them were talking about the undead.

"It's complicated, Peter, and not necessarily what I would call *dinner date* conversation."

"But you can *raise the dead*. Defy natural law. That's so weird and cool. Don't you think? What gives you your abilities? Did anyone in your family have the power?"

I shrugged, stuffing a piece of meat in my mouth. "I don't know. They've tried to isolate what makes us able to do what we can, but similar to earth witches, and necromancers, whatever gives us our abilities isn't something they've been able to find in a test tube. Guess it has to stay 'magic' still." The date had shifted in tone to me as the focus, like it always did. I hated having to explain what I was. Hated feeling like an oddity and outsider. I couldn't blame Peter, he seemed naturally inquisitive and had been so put off by resurrection and the supernatural. I reminded myself he was trying to understand. But I didn't have to like it either.

But if you don't open up, how will anyone know you? Dot's voice ghosted into my head.

"I am making you uncomfortable, aren't I?" He leaned in conspiratorially, "I don't mean to really, it's just I am so curious. I am a reporter so nosey by nature. We can talk about something else." Peter had soft eyes and a kind smile, he knew how to put me at ease. A people person one would say. *Manipulative,* a darker voice whispered.

"Peter, what I am naturally sets me apart from other people." My hands hovered, trying to aid in my explanation, "I have always had a hard time connecting to regular people for this reason. I don't like having to talk so openly about something that is so personal. I understand that you are curious, and I actually appreciate you wanting to learn. I was just hoping to spend some time, for once, not being a curiosity. With ordinary people, I often have to play teacher."

"I think I understand. Do you have others like you to hang out with?"

"Not really. Resurrectionists are just very, very rare, so we lack much of a community or traditions or anything that other supernatural groups have. I think our outsider status, in part, is because resurrectionists, unlike witches, or necromancers, or vampires, or most *other* things are born into this life alone, we can't choose it, it chooses us."

"Are these supernatural groups like private clubs or organizations?" He smiled, eating. Trying to hide that curiosity.

"They kind of are. Remember the regular world just learned about all of this in the last thirty years and has been forced to adjust, but we've been around since the beginning of time. These small groups have depended on each other to survive. It's how we remained safe and not burned up at the stake. Tight-knit communities with long memories who aren't inclined to let in outsiders. Necromancers and their lot tend to belong to cabals. Magic users are often in covens..."

"What about vampires? Definitely never seen one, outside of that TV show host. What's her name?"

"Sandrine Scarlet." Her show, *Midnight Chat,* was a late-night talk show hosted by an "out" vampire. I'd seen her show here and there, but it was definitely on the trashy side. A lot of couples with infidelities, people with fetishes, and manufactured reality TV scripted fights. She also had dyed black hair, skintight black dresses, and blood-red lips, very much playing the vamp part. I doubted most vampires would want her speaking for their group.

"They are loners, for the most part from what I've heard. Apex predators. Like big cats. Don't really hang out together. But I really don't know much about them." Marlow's face popped into my head, so unlike my idea of a vampire. He did not seem like a predator at all. A rumpled, underpaid civil servant trying to fight crime and make the world a better place. I'd always heard vampires were sexy, selfish, dangerous, obsessive and possessive, vain, and paranoid. Did I, the dullest resurrectionist, meet the most boring vampire? Not that I was a good judge of anyone, but that would be kind of funny.

"What about half-lifes? You could hang out with them," he said. I wanted to ask why he was trying to find me friends, but I held my tongue.

"I could, sure, and I do sometimes. They have communities and gather together and there are support groups for the newly returned, to help acclimate. I do have clients I keep up with as well. But they are clients, not friends, and on top of that, there is a power dynamic that can be problematic. I made them and that complicates a relationship." I left out because I can literally control them, like a puppet master if I wanted to. That my control was so absolute I could force them to kill for me if I commanded it. They'd kill their own children. That was the stuff that scared people about my kind, hell, that scared me.

For that reason, half-lifes earned the right to keep a little distance from their creators. I could give life, but I could also take it, and I could make them my slaves. This of course, was the reason for the fear, from everyone in the end, even other monsters. The reason that resurrection-ists were shunned, the myth of the *Zombie Queen* who could control an army of the undead. That kind of power breeds fear and enemies, it's why we were killed as heretics so often throughout history. At least that was a hate crime now, the stake burning, though it still did happen on occasion. I didn't share any of this info with Peter, already feeling I'd said too much and revealed too much.

"You just got really quiet. Penny for your thoughts?" Peter pressed.

"I met a vampire recently." I regretted saying it out loud instantly, it felt like a betrayal to Marlow. But it was too late now, I lowered my voice and leaned in, "He wasn't what I expected. Much more normal.

Think he felt the same about me. He'd never met a resurrectionist. Think we were both a little disappointed, being the big bad guys in our community."

"So, he was totally normal? No fangs?"

"Not that I could see, no. But if you can pass as normal you probably aren't hanging out with huge bloody fangs. I almost didn't even recognize what he was. He was that convincing."

"See that's creepy to me. That he looked so normal. Like you— with your eyes? I'd know what you were. I can't believe these pretender races who pass for human are trying to become legal now. People just keep doing what they do, grocery shopping, or whatever, while they hunt us. It's kind of scary." He rubbed his hands on his napkin and glanced around our table before leaning in, "If I am honest, it makes me a little more sympathetic to my sister and her churchy ilk, looking for answers, looking for God. Something good and safe, a promise of something better and less terrifying. It doesn't feel good to learn you aren't the top of the food chain."

"I suppose," I murmured over my glass. I was tempted to remind him I *was* one of the monsters, but held it back. *Pretender* was also a bigoted term, but I did not remind him of that either. Hell, the religious had more problems with my kind than with vampires honestly. Vampires would always have good PR in their 'stay young forever' campaign. We were actively keeping people from heaven or reincarnation. I'd seen *Suffer not a witch to live* on so many bumper stickers I'd lost count.

This was the price of dates with regular guys, they just didn't get it. Across the restaurant I saw a couple enter, two men, on what looked to be a date. I could tell even from across the room, even with his back to me, that one of them was a half-life, his energy a beacon. A familiar beacon. He was one of mine.

"Then again, there are plenty of human monsters out there as well. *Pretending* to be normal upstanding citizens," I said tartly.

"Apologies if I offended you," Peter said. But my attention was across the room, on the half-life, trying to remember him. He must have sensed my stare, because he turned to look back at me. Our eyes met and the whole room hushed around us. Creator and created, attached by a long magical string. His eyes were large, brown, and velvet-soft. His skin, though a dark bronze, had the ashen cast of the undead. Thick black hair. He smiled politely and I did the same. *Amar*

Patel. The name came to me in a flash. He looked happy and it made me feel good.

I did not want to draw attention, especially with Peter so fixated on what I was. But before I could steer him away, Amar walked over to our table.

"Ms. Shade? It's me, Amar Patel." His voice was soft, with a subtle accent.

"Amar, yes, of course. How are you?" I forced my voice to be light and conversational, wanting to see if Peter could tell Amar was a half-life.

"I've been very good, thank you. I received a promotion at my job recently and I am seeing someone." He gestured back to the attractive blond man at his table fiddling with his phone.

"That is fantastic, so happy to hear it."

"Well, I know it's presumptuous but I'd love to take you to coffee sometime if you have the time."

Peter raised his eyebrows, but I ignored him. "Yeah, sure Amar that'd be great. Just email me through my office and we can set something up. Take care now."

Amar went back to his table, and the fact that Peter was still unaware of what Amar truly was pleased me. After all, it proved I did good work. The quality of the undead, both in lividity and appearance, often varied based on the resurrectionist. That Amar could pass so effectively, even under the nose of a reporter suspicious of them and looking for them, gave me a sense of relief. I worried for the half-lifes I sent back out into the world, most people were terrified of them after all. There were plenty of cases of half-lifes being lynched, burned, or mutilated by the classic angry villagers. For that reason, it warmed my heart to see them out in the world, *pretending* so effectively at being human, to steal Peter's word.

I never pursued close friendships with any of those I'd raised, because it was true, that power dynamic was strong and absolute. Half-lifes often hungered to be with their makers and felt compelled to do my bidding. To counteract that, I tried to stay as clinical and professional as possible in raising and dealing with them. Dot had taught me that early on. "Otherwise they get a little stalker-boyfriend," she'd explained. But a cup of coffee wouldn't hurt as long as it came with clear boundaries.

"Did that guy just ask you out while you're here with me?" Peter said, trying and failing to sound like he was joking.

"He's an old client of mine, not that it's any of your business, and clearly, he is here with that man. Not that, again, it's any of your business." The ice in my voice had Peter apologizing. I felt tired of the whole thing.

"A client? You mean he's a half-life?" His eyes narrowed studying Amar.

"I'll just leave you wondering," I said smugly.

The date ended after dessert. Peter offered to take me home, or vice versa. But I declined. I wasn't sure if the conversation had put me off, or just the fact that it was a first date and I was quite rusty in the romance department, but I had zero interest in sleeping with him that night.

I still liked him some, he was cute and engaging, but his morbid fascination and repulsion for death, magic and monsters, made me a little wary of taking it further. The evening had felt like an interview. I couldn't think of one relationship I'd been in where what I was wasn't always front and center. This big thing in between us, always in the forefront.

It was why Dot had married a necromancer. She couldn't be bothered dealing with oversensitive human men. Resurrectionists were fantastically rare, rarer than lightning strikes and lottery winnings, and always female, so dating within that pool was quite limited.

"Selene, did I say something to upset you?" Peter asked at my car, which he'd gallantly offered to walk me to after I declined going home with him.

"No, no sorry. Just a lot on my mind with work," I said as I opened the door. He caught my arm gently and stopped me from getting in the car.

"I like you, Selene. I'd love to see you again."

"I like you too, Peter, thanks for dinner." He wanted to kiss me, I could sense it in his body language. A part of me wanted him to, the lonely part that constantly reminded me it had been well over a year since anyone had been so close, and even that had been a one-night stand, right after Dot died when I was drunk and grieving. But another part hollered no, that he was a reporter, that he saw me as a story and a curiosity. He'd been scared of me at that first meeting.

I wondered if Detective Marlow felt this way, trying to connect but no one seeing past what he was.

The woman was screaming, her body bucking wildly, she was clamped at the wrists and ankles, her splayed limbs forced into an *X*.

A hooded man leaned over her, painting symbols in blood upon her abdomen. She was sobbing and hiccupping, black mascara trailing down her cheeks.

Once the sigils were complete, the man rose and stood over her; a second man, naked, erect, wearing a black mask stepped into the frame.

The video paused.

"Well, then they get down to it. Obviously, this is not the true ritual, with the real Nigrum Porta, but you get the gist." Lila Goodtree sat back in her ancient old chair, wide grin on her face.

"This—this is a...porno? A porno that you think is depicting the same ritual our killer is using?" Robinson's eyebrows were attached to her hairline.

"Yes, my dear, the internet is a magical place."

"But how did you find this, who are these people? Is that woman all right? You think they may be involved?" Robinson asked in a rush. Lila waved her hand in a pshaw gesture and turned to Marlow, trying to find someone who understood.

He said, "Perhaps you could elaborate on what we were just watching Ms. Goodtree..."

The old woman sighed, "I highly doubt these are your suspects, Detectives. This is more a fertility rite role-play, using a specific ritual for a different purpose. Regardless of your opinions on it, I could not draw you a better diagram for what I think they are doing to the victims. Mark my word."

"Okay so give us all the particulars of this ritual," Robinson said to Lila.

She smiled, revealing more gum than teeth and started ticking off on gnarled, arthritic fingers,

"First, they need the new moon, when some believe a woman's most fertile. Second, they need to be outdoors in the woods close to nature. Third, they need the priest figure, this 'James' fellow our victim mentioned is probably playing that role and he summons the other, Nigrum Porta, or some approximation of him."

"We knew all of that," Marlow replied, pinching his nose, frustrated. "I was hoping there was something more specific to be learned. Like a special ingredient that can only be bought in one place. A certain type of victim. A religious sect we could interrogate. Something concrete or admissible in court."

Lila shrugged.

"Ok. Well, we keep looking into the victims then. What is it that would make them good candidates?" Robinson said.

Lila smiled, resembling a sphinx cat. "Right, why did the killers think they were the ideal vessels?"

Marlow rose, too fast to be normal, but he was excited. "All right, if that's all you have, Lila, then all our focus needs to be on the girls."

She nodded and waved them off, eyes enlarged by her Coke bottle glasses.

The glass urn exploded into a thousand pieces just above his head as he ducked, hands over his face.

"You keep failing, and it is deeply embarrassing for me. I vouched for you, I arranged everything, and you keep failing."

James fought the urge to mouth off at Patron. He'd already had something potentially deadly thrown at him best not provoke further.

Instead he rose, cautiously, and dusted off his knees. He faced the Patron, chin up with as much pride as he could muster. Staring into the darkness where he imagined eyes would be since the Patron's face was entirely hidden by a dark medieval-looking cloak. Subtle.

"Begging your forgiveness, Patron, but it is a complicated rite to perform, and considering it has *never* been accomplished with success in human history, I think you need to cut me a little slack. Once I find the perfect vessel..." he trailed off, hands open. The Patron paused a moment, no doubt watching James with whatever counted for eyes under there.

"Very well. Another moon. If you fail this time though, that's it. You will be dead and replaced by one that is worthy."

"Understood, crystal clear, Patron. Now, if you'll excuse me, I have to get ready for a date."

"A date?" Patron scoffed and shook his head. "There is no time for dalliances, we are losing time before the moon."

"The date is me auditioning a potential vessel, sir. I can eat food and interview at the same time, I'm very skilled at multitasking."

With what sounded like a derisive snort, the Patron turned and left. Only when the door was closed, and he was alone, did James breathe out again. False bravado aside, he knew that they would kill him without thinking twice if he failed. The Order of the White Crow was not known for being understanding, or hell even remotely human. They had been trying to summon Nigrum Porta for a millennium and were getting impatient.

James was still unsure why all these hell-on-earth, doomsday, "remake reality in our unnamed God's image" types wanted to unmake the world. But for the reward of immortality, and a position of power in the new world order, he also didn't care that much. Besides, if he didn't do it for them they would kill him.

He was an opportunist after all. He'd been dealt a bad hand in this life, and he wasn't above doing what was necessary to take care of himself.

So, he combed back his hair, inspected his breath and wardrobe, and climbed up and out of the basement apartment in search of prey.

EIGHT

Marlow walked the forested area just off campus where Belinda Curwen was found. He'd been there before when the body was found, but this time, he expanded his search past the immediate cordoned-off crime scene. He was looking for *something* but wasn't sure what. The scents were long buried by the human traffic and night of rain, but the blood smell lingered, as she'd lost so much in the earth below. The crime scene was a clearing in the woods, about twenty or thirty paces from the path and not far from a parking lot. Not particularly secluded, but, on a new moon when the night was its darkest, he doubted many coeds would be by.

Of course, the location could be meaningless. Perhaps it was just convenience. The other two bodies weren't that far from campus either. Victim one was about three miles away on an Audubon preserve. Victim two was just a little into the woods off a commercial area. He made a circular course starting at the body and moving out, maybe the killer left a piece of clothing, a phone, a cigarette butt, who knows, just far enough to be missed. A footprint, even, though that was wishful thinking as so many people had been working the area for the last day. Marlow was a few feet out past the yellow tape when the stink of death came to him.

There on the ground a small brown thing, a mole perhaps, deeply decayed. Strange such a small creature would smell so strongly, he knelt to look closer. There was another little furry pile a few feet away, this one a squirrel, well on its way to being a skeleton. A bit further was a badger, its side rippling with maggots. This was not a normal amount of dead wildlife. He continued moving, pulling out his phone and photographing each animal. All dead, a bird, a bat, a skunk, even a half-run-over cat. As he backtracked, he realized they were almost evenly spaced around the crime scene. But far enough away and apart from one another to go unnoticed.

"Hey, yeah it's Marlow, I am going to need to get a drone to come out to the Curwen murder crime scene. I think we may be missing something. Thanks."

A few hours later, Marlow was looking at aerial photos of all three crime scenes; if his anatomy allowed him to shiver, he would have, because in concentric circles around the crime scene were dead animals, *at all three.*

"Holy shit," Robinson said at his shoulder. "Are they animal sacrifices?"

"No, no they are all in various states of natural decay from what our forensics people say—it's why they didn't make much note of them. It's only when looking from above that a pattern comes out."

"Do you think the killers placed these random dead animals like this then?"

"No, no, you can follow the trails on some of the fresher ones, it's more like...like they were dragging *themselves* toward the victims."

I was at home, watching TV, nursing a fishbowl-sized glass of wine after my date with Peter. I was trying and failing not to feel bad for myself when there was a knock on my door. Which was odd and unsettling since I wasn't expecting anyone and very few people even knew where I lived. Could be a neighbor needing sugar, but then again it was equally likely to be a neighbor with a burning cross. I tied my robe tight, as I was in frumpy pajamas, and looked through the peephole cautiously. To my surprise, it was Detective Marlow alone on my stoop.

"Hello." I said guardedly, through a crack in the door, feeling a little exposed in my cheetah pajamas, threadbare robe and bare feet. Especially since I never gave him my home address. Do you want vampires to know where you live? Do you want to let them into your house?

"Tell me all about resurrectionists," Marlow said in a rush pushing past me, his voice excited as he came inside unbidden. Guess he didn't need an invitation.

"Come on in, no, I insist, it's not rude or creepy to barge in unexpectedly," I muttered closing the door behind him.

He paused, noticed what I was wearing, and then had the grace to look chagrined. "Sorry, Selene, I should have called. I was just excited about a possible lead. I felt this may be a little more sensitive and preferred to do it in person. I have been working on something. Do you mind helping me, enlightening me?" His eyes flashed yellow in the lamplight, like an animal caught in headlights. He could be the best actor in the world, but not much could disguise that. "Please?"

"Fine, fine." I walked toward the kitchen tossing my hands up in defeat, "Geez, resurrectionists seem to be the topic of the evening. It's all my date tonight wanted to talk about..."

"You were on a date? Must've ended early, it's only ten."

"*Anyway*...what do you want to know exactly, Detective?" I pulled another wine glass from the cupboard, filled it, and handed it to him. At least he provided a distraction from thoughts of dying alone or Nigrum Porta hiding up in my bedroom.

Marlow took a sip and plowed on, "Tell me about resurrectionists, when their powers develop, appearance, genetics, all of it, and thank you for the wine." We were back in the living room now, I resumed my seat on the sofa, he took the chair opposite.

I breathed out, "Fine. Let's see, we are always female. Normally the ability to reanimate starts to show around puberty—specifically first menses. But not always, I was a super early bloomer."

"For your menses or your reanimating?"

I pulled a face, "For reanimating, I was only six the first time." I flashed on my parents' funeral and all the screaming as a hand crested the edge of the coffin. Pushed it away. "But anyway, enough about me, let's see, folklore says pale-blue eyes. Dot had very pale, almost lilac eyes, and the few others I've known all did have light eyes. There's a theory that we are the reason blue eyes are seen as evil in some cultures. As far as science tests, not much differentiates us, we do have an enlarged hypothalamus if I recall from preternatural bio in school. But most humans with psionic or supernatural ability tend to."

"And all resurrectionists apprentice and go into your field?"

"No, I wouldn't say that. Hell, for centuries, they were just trying not to get burned as heretics and devil spawn! We are super rare, but even still, there are some who keep it a secret, or may even be unaware of what they are. Others may try necromancy or witchcraft to use their abilities as well as gain others, though our magics don't mix well. Like anything there is a variety of skill levels. Weak ones may only bring back insects and small things, others only animals, still others only humans. Some have a hard time controlling their abilities and avoid places where they may encounter the dead." I took a sip of my wine, Marlow listened closely. "Like I keep saying about all this stuff, there is no exact science to it. We are a rare enough breed to not have a lot of data on us. Honestly, I can count on one hand how many others I have met. The one common trait over the last few decades is our push to legitimize the business of half-lifes, giving us a career and a place in society besides freaks."

"But your kind aren't entirely innocent either," he interrupted, "in my cursory research I have seen a lot about involuntary summonings, mysterious deaths, massive zombie outbreaks, Zombie Queens—"

"Sensationalism mostly. A few major newsworthy events in history. You should know better than anyone that a few bad apples can really change the party line. For most of history, resurrectionists had to conceal their abilities. If you ask me 'Zombie Queens' are just patriarchal nonsense. The idea of a woman gone power-mad leading an army of zombie slaves to do her bidding feels a little preposterous, no? But sure, great emotion and an untrained resurrectionist can and have caused some crazy stuff to happen."

"Crazy stuff. Like zombie murder rampages..." he pushed.

"Sure. The main fear is always involuntary resurrections. But most don't have that kind of raw power. It's also why we use an animus as a physical aid to help lock spirit and body together outside the control of a resurrectionist."

"But someone could do it? Raise bodies by accident?"

I paused again, trying not to think of my parent's funeral. Yes, some could do it. I could and knew firsthand the horror that could unfold. "What does this have to do with our case?"

"*Our* case huh? Maybe." He smiled and sipped his wine, seemingly enjoying my frustration. "But I'm still working on a theory."

"You think all the women were chosen because they were resurrectionists?" His face fell, annoyed. I could feel myself grinning. It was nice to be able to tease someone. I'd been dealing almost exclusively with clients. That involved a certain level of somber professionalism pretty much all the time.

"Tell me about your bad date," he deflected, picking a fuzz off the afghan on the chair.

I laughed out loud. "You must be kidding! You can't barge in here, unannounced, leave me hanging, and then ask about my private life!"

He sighed, "Okay, fine. I've been working on finding commonalities between the victims. So, victim one we found headless a few days after the murder and were only able to ID her based on an ankle tattoo."

He rubbed his hands together and leaned forward, "It was of a cross. She was a waitress, eighteen, not a college student but worked near the college. Religious family, home-schooled, no boyfriend, very sheltered, parents reported her missing. Head never found but according to records, blue eyes. Second victim was a college student, junior, twenty-one, specializing in death ritual and arcane magic. Driver's license says blue eyes. Reported missing by roommate off campus, she was from a conservative family as well, but rebellious. She was found a week after ritual. Then we have number three, Belinda—whom you've met—was studying comparative religion. Blue eyes. Murder interrupted and our killers fled the scene leaving body mostly intact. She was last seen going on date with 'James' and according to her dormmate, Belinda was shy and rarely went on dates."

He raised a hand and began counting his fingers, "We know the ritual needs a new moon, a quiet secluded area outdoors, potentially a virgin, but the third was the mystery, what was it about these specific girls?" I settled both feet on the floor and leaned forward. "They were all young, pretty, blue eyes. But it was only when I was walking around Belinda's crime scene that it came to me." He paused and I could see something dangerous in the glint of his eyes, the predator peeking out.

"Yes, sitting on the edge of my seat here." I replied, anxious.

"Dead animals."

"Continue."

"Each crime scene had an abnormal number of dead animals scattered around the vicinity. Upon closer look, some appeared to have dug themselves *out of the ground* or dragged themselves. Odder still, they were found in almost a circular pattern around the kill site. At all three.

Look at these pictures—" he pulled out folded rumpled copies of photographs from his breast pocket. Each one was a grainy aerial shot of some woods. In the center, yellow markers of a crime scene, in each he'd circled small dark spots and then drew concentric circles connecting them. Like a solar system with the crime scene as the sun.

"Could the victims have done this to the animals?"

"You don't think they were placed or sacrificed. You think that the victims, in distress, were sending out some sort of panic signal and it was unconsciously raising anything dead nearby to come to their aid."

"I do."

I tapped a fingernail against my wine glass, "Very clever, Detective. I think that is a very strong theory."

"Has it ever happened to you? Something like that with animals?" He leaned in curious and I felt my face fall before I could control it. The hands of my dead parents reaching out of their coffins. I shook my head no and cleared my throat.

"I have the coroner looking into Belinda more closely, we did also get some DNA evidence from under her nails of our killer; it's a match with the other two. Sadly, this person isn't in the system. Detective Robinson is working on additional backgrounds of the victims. But I think this could be a strong lead. At least we know what kind of victims our killer wants."

"I agree. Now, here is my question for you, Detective, if the ritual calls for a female resurrectionist, why not just abduct a known one? I'm on Yelp for Pete's sake. It's not that hard to find one if you look."

His face sobered at that, the light dimming. "I have thought about that, our occultist, Lila Goodtree, thinks there may also be a virgin sacrifice angle." He said and I leaned back thoughtful, so if the killer needed a virgin resurrectionist, how was he finding them?

Marlow continued, "They were all young, and from conservative homes or were known to be shy and not date. I think our killer took his time getting to know them." He paused and I sipped my wine and waited. "I think you will be safe. Unless you're a virgin?" he teased, I nearly spat out my drink.

"Hoo boy, this day is just getting weirder the longer it goes on. No, Marlow, I'm not a virgin..." Granted, I'd only slept with a few people, but that wasn't his business.

He leaned back in his chair, grin wide, "With dates ending before nine it's hard to know."

I offered him a withering glare, before continuing on. "Okay, so hopefully your theory is correct. Otherwise you are back to square one."

"Also, I know we were joking before, but there are multiple translations, not all of the rituals emphasize a virgin. Our killer may be getting desperate for results and come for you after all."

Danger.

Nigrum Porta filled my head, his wailing windy mouth, his arms outreached. He knew where I was already.

I forced myself to breathe, "I can take care of myself. It's a dangerous job, Detective. We are up with abortionists and tax collectors on list of favorite careers to shoot at." I had taken a few self-defense lessons, and the occasional kickboxing class. Dot always carried pepper spray. I had security cameras.

I refilled our glasses and brought out a bowl of popcorn. He didn't eat any, instead using my computer to look at all the resurrectionists in the area. Not hard, as there were only two firms now, myself, and Dania Barabas. Barabas was on the fancier North Side— but she was in her late fifties and a mother, so no virgin there either. But she did have employees and kids. He assumed the killers would need victims to be of childbearing age. We then moved on to how our killer would even find untapped reanimators. Outside of the blue eyes, there wasn't much to out a resurrectionist. It must be some kind of spell, but neither of us knew enough about magic, leaving us at a loss yet again.

"We need to talk to a magic practitioner, the precinct occultist is too academic, we need someone—"

"A witch would be good, or a psychic that could use a charmed object to see auras. They must be using some kind of tracking spell to find these girls after all."

"You know any witches?"

I groaned inwardly, I did know one, but we weren't friends. I actually kind of loathed her.

"Persimmon Shaw. She's the real deal, very powerful and a coven leader. She could probably find the spell, or at least bring it back to her coven to think on."

Marlow wrote down the info in his police notebook. "That will help, if we can figure out how James is finding these girls, we could potentially replicate the spell and find them ourselves. Before."

"Potentially, but I am guessing the department doesn't have a resident spell-slinger?"

"No, but they should, they still prefer to look the other way. Hopefully, Ms. Shaw would be able to help with that too. I think the world is still trying to ignore the unnatural and hope it goes back where it came from. They don't want to change laws, or change practices, or think too much about us all hiding in plain sight."

"Yeah, my date wanted to talk about that at length. Pretenders."

Marlow set his glass down, "Ah yes, the date, you've mentioned it a few times. You want to talk about him?"

I laughed, unsure what this vampire wanted. Marlow seemed eager to hang around and to bring me onto the case. He could be as lonely as I was. Having to always be around normal people, trying and always failing to pass, was exhausting. I'd been playing and failing the game my whole life. The detective may have just liked being able to talk to someone without having to hide.

"My date, he's a reporter, he and his sister came into my office about their dad."

"A client?" He put a hand on his chest, feigning offense.

I laughed, rolling my eyes. "Oh please. A potential client. He was nice enough, it's been a while, but I just felt so under a microscope. A freak for him to figure out. You know, I thought about you at dinner."

He grinned, toothless, "Really? On your date?"

Was he flirting with me? I wasn't sure. "Not like *that*, I wondered if you felt like an outsider too, like people can't ever see past what you are. Or if it was easier for you because you can pass for human."

His playful expression dried up, and he sat back. "It's complicated. I have had every kind of relationship. The lies weigh heavy when they don't know. Those who know often do treat me as a novelty, or a time bomb. Or the worst, they're scared of me. Or they want me to turn them. There's always resentment at the end in one way or another."

"Could you date other vampires?"

"No, I've never liked the company of my own kind for relationships."

"Why?"

"We are a desperate lot. We provide each other with little besides competition and everything turns into a pissing match. Even with my wife it was like that, after a while. Any vampire relationship has to be non-monogamous, or polyamorous, so that always adds complication regardless of who you are dating. On top of that, humans are fragile, they age, and they tend to die, faster if in a relationship with a vampire." He sighed and looked away, "As I said, it's complicated."

"You were married?" I asked. I was also curious about the polyamorous comments but didn't want to sound too interested. I kept trying to picture what his wife would be like.

"Yes, I was married. A long time ago. She made me a vampire. It didn't end well."

"That was succinct." He gave little indication he planned to elaborate. I took a sip of my wine, "Guess there isn't a lot of love out there for monsters."

He raised his eyes to mine and his glass, "To the lonely road of monsters."

"Here, here," I replied and clinked his glass.

NINE

Germaine Whately stared up at the old brick mill building, it had taken her two bus transfers to get there. It was remote, facing the water, and lazy seagulls made circles above and bobbed in the choppy water below. On one side a massive mountain of sand, or salt, covered in a white tarp. The other side a mammoth two-story pile of scrap metal towered.

Large boats and barges coasted through the gray waters.

She was nervous. This job was a big deal, it would pay so much more than slinging coffee, or canvassing, or working in the school bookstore. It was a potential career, and one that her parents would be mortified about. They'd worked so hard to hide her, to not let anyone know. They were ashamed of her. If she got this job, then everyone would know what she could do. What she was. No more hiding behind contacts, no more trying to be normal.

Get over it, Germaine, Own it. That was her assertive voice, the one that got her to apply to schools out of state in the bigger cities. The one who craved a fresh start away from the small-town hicks of Bixby who always looked down at her, to that stupid Jesus camp she was sent to every time she brought back another dog or horse. Forced to pray for mercy and to avoid the fires of hell for being an unnatural creature. It was the voice that commanded her to accept being a freak and making some money. To have it work for her instead of against her.

To some she was an abomination, but to others, she was special. She had power. She could save someone from literal death. She had godlike powers.

Germaine had been a little surprised when she received such a quick response from the resurrectionist firm. Must be desperate for help, she'd thought. Then again, it's not a job just anyone could just apply for. Her resume highlighted her office work helping her dad's veterinary office and the one disastrous summer she worked at a burger and shake stand, sweltering in the dust bowl heat.

The curt email back:

**Please meet me for a brief interview on April 30th at 2pm. Be prepared to resurrect. Professional attire and manner expected.
— Selene**

Germaine felt both excited and nauseated by the prospect of resurrecting. She knew she could resurrect (had done it) but with intent? For a paying customer? In front of people? She did some cursory research on the basic rituals online so she wouldn't look totally out of her depth. She then researched the resident Goat Hill reanimation biz, which didn't take long, as there were only two offices. Dania Barabas' firm "Resurrection Artists" in the North, and Selene Shade's "Goat Hill Resurrections" on the East Side. Both businesses had decent reviews and a high BBB ranking. Though Selene was called out by name as being serious to the point of rude and overly clinical a decent amount.

She glanced at her phone, 1:55, time to go in.

Five minutes later, Germaine sat sweaty-palmed across from a stern dark-haired woman with the bluest eyes she'd ever seen. Germaine herself had very pale, cornflower-blue eyes, which she often hid behind brown contacts. She did not wear contacts to the interview so her very blue eyes were visible, but nowhere near the woman before hers in intensity. They positively glowed. No one would look at those eyes and think she was normal. Even Germaine, another resurrectionist, had a hard time meeting them.

The woman's aura was peculiar as well, she had a halo around her head that most resembled a black sun, or some sort of vacuum or suction surrounding her with reaching rays, trying to pull things toward her. Germaine, unable to see her own aura, had only read about the phenomena. A resurrectionist's aura, described as a *net for spirits.* Germaine wondered if hers looked the same and hoped it didn't. It was so different from a regular person's, which was so colorful and alive.

"So, you are a freshman at the University. What are you studying?" she said, her voice deep and clipped. Germaine squirmed under her harsh scrutiny. She willed her cheeks not to flush, but the hotness she felt creeping up her neck told her otherwise. The curse of a fair ginger complexion.

"I'm still undecided, ma'am. My family are farm and animal people out west on the Plains. I have no interest in any of that. I'd also hoped, and, no offense is intended, ma'am, to do something non-supernatural with my studies. Maybe English. But I also need a job as I've maxed out my loans."

"Did you apprentice?"

Germaine blushed fully now, hiding her eyes beneath her pale eyelashes. She shook her head no. "Not exactly, Ms. Shade. After it was revealed that I was taking a lot of my father's dead animal patients back home with me, revived, he sent me to a religious organization that focused more on containment and abstaining from using my...abilities. Through prayer and breathing."

Selene smirked, "Ah yes, the 'pray the devil out' disciplines. And how did that camp experience work out?"

"Not very well. It was kind of a mess, between the magic handlers, the psionics, and the gay kids, I think we were all just trying to make it through under the radar of the counselors. But I have worked on it myself where I could. Mainly through animals, raising them and putting them back down. Once on a person, it was my friend's uncle, he was very sick and passed away unexpected. The family wanted to say their peace, and so I offered to try. I used a locket I had in my jewelry box as an animus. It went well, they all had their time together, and then I released him."

"Well, that is impressive control considering you lacked proper tutelage. I myself apprenticed for years with my former business partner. With more old people alive than ever before and half-lifes becoming more socially tolerated, we are getting a lot of business. Good for my bank account, bad for my sanity. There aren't enough of us around wanting to get into the business. I need help. I need someone to divide the workload, you understand? Sooner rather than later. Someone serious about the job."

"Y-Yes. I do." Germaine gathered her purse and coat, eyes downcast.

"Hey, I am not saying it's a no, I am just saying I want someone with a little more experience, but sadly there aren't many of us around." Selene met Germaine's eyes and held them for a moment, before continuing, "This is a heavy job, not only the raisings, but the grief, the families, the paperwork and bookkeeping, and all the little things that go into it, you understand? We act as therapists, grief counselors, and everything in between. I sense reluctance from you, considering your upbringing and all, does that sound like something you can handle in and around your studies? You can say no."

Germaine shifted in her chair. Her instinct was to say no. Her instinct was to get a job on campus, focus on school, try and get a real boyfriend—her mind flickered to Coffeeshop John's face, his bright kind smile, his overgrown mop of hair. Handsome face with kind eyes. But she also needed to be realistic, this was who she was, and it would be better to learn to control herself, maybe even make the world better for someone.

"I'm willing to give it a try. If you are. I'm tired of hiding what I am and I need money for school."

"Good. Good. I am a sink or swim kind of person, and I have to be at the morgue pretty much now, would you like to come along and attempt the raising?" Germaine's hands sweat, but she nodded. It had said in the ad, prepare to resurrect, but it still left her feeling squeamish.

The two women got in Selene's silver car. News radio played quietly, it talked about the local cult murders. Authorities warned women around the university to travel in pairs and avoid the parks after dark.

"I've been helping with this investigation," Selene said after a long moment.

Germaine cleared her throat, "It's so scary. There are vigils set up at school, and escorts to walk you around campus at night. We never had this sort of thing in Oklahoma, where I am from."

"The one bit of info I will tell you is that it looks like all the victims may have been young resurrectionists. Be cautious until this guy is caught."

Germaine's throat went dry and all her nervous sweat chilled. "How do you know?" she said.

"This guy pretends to be a college student, goes by the name

'James,' and lures the girls away after a date or whatever. He is not grab-bing them from the bushes, he is targeting them, and he knows what they are."

"Wow. I'll be careful, not that I have much of a social life to worry about or anything," she replied lamely, regretting it as soon as she said it. Selene shot her a pitying look.

"Just watch your back, and if you know any other girls like you, let them know. It's not public knowledge yet, but we need to protect ourselves from these guys."

They arrived at the hospital and Selene passed through the rabbit warren hallways of the lower levels with practiced ease. Once at the elevator to the morgue she flashed a plastic badge. "She's with me." She nodded back at Germaine to the security guard. He looked them up and down, nodded, and resumed his crossword.

They rode the elevator down to the morgue, basement level, which opened on long hallways of gleaming white tile and bright overhead light. The floors squeaked under her uncomfortable dress shoes.

Finally, they entered a small room with a single metal table. A body lay under a white sheet in the center. Germaine sensed the corpse and felt the desire to put her hands on it, to fill it back up. The desire shamed her and caused her chest to flutter with panic, especially when she saw the two people standing in the corner. An old mother, and the wife she guessed. "I can't do this," she whispered to herself, *You can! You can!*

"Mrs. Ingersoll, Leticia, so nice to see you both again," Selene said, her voice low and respectful, professional. "I see Jeremiah decided to pass along."

"Yes, Ms. Shade, but it was quick and not too painful." Mrs. Inger-soll said, her voice heavy with grief. "Mothers aren't supposed to bury their babies." She followed up, her voice cracking. The younger woman put an arm over the older one and both began to cry quietly.

Germaine felt like she was intruding. Selene stepped closer to the grieving women, "This is my associate, Germaine Whately, she will be assisting with the resurrection today and I assure you she is most competent." Germaine did not miss the sharp look, the one that said do not fuck this up and get it together.

Germaine nodded, and smiled, reaching out a shaky hand to both women. The younger one, Leticia, looked shell-shocked. Her face a mask, her eyes red-rimmed.

"And Jeremiah, he will be like he was? He won't be a mindless thing, right? He won't be a monster?" she finally said, voice no louder than a whisper, her eyes glued to the body on the slab.

"He will be the man you knew, but also changed by this experience. This was his choice, as well as yours, his disease deprived you two of the life you wanted. This was his way of coming back. Transcending death for life, for love. Hold on to that thought." Selene said gently, but firmly, "This is an act of love." They nodded and Germaine was impressed. She doubted she could ever be that convincing.

Selene gently took the arm of the widow, "Now, if you ladies wouldn't mind stepping out into the hall, there are chairs just outside the door. We'll call you in when it's done."

The two women went, slowly, eyes on the sheet the whole way. Germaine's heart went with them, what a choice they had to make! To let someone they loved die, or bring him back and break all the laws of nature. What if it was her father? Could she let him stay dead, let his body rot away when she knew she could bring him back? She didn't know the answer.

Once the door was closed, Selene came to Germaine, hand outstretched. "Here is the animus, call him back to himself, I will be here to guide you if you need any help."

An hour later, Jeremiah Ingersoll sat with his mother and wife. His face may have been stiffer, his eyes more distant, but his tears were real. His relief at no longer being in chronic pain, his joy at being able to take his wife to Paris as he'd promised and they'd planned. For him, in that moment, it was all worth it. Germaine felt something blossoming inside her seeing that family reunited, perhaps a calling. She'd never felt so powerful.

Selene took a call as they were leaving the hospital, another client had died, and so she was off to the hospital downtown in Goat Hill's city center and the opposite direction of the college. "Ah mortality, never stops." Selene said after she hung up, "I'm booked solid these days. You did good work today. Impressive even. I need to go in the opposite direction from the college, you alright taking the bus or can I give you cab fare?"

Germaine told her she would catch the bus back to the college. Selene was a few paces away, heading to the garage, when she stopped and turned to Germaine, "Think about today, what you had to do, how it felt, and if you want to do it as a job, and get back to me in the next day or two. You did good work today and you are a natural, so you decide on if it's the job for you and I will think on if I want to take you on. Deal?"

Germaine nodded and Selene left in a rush to meet her next client. As Germaine was waiting at the bus stop, her phone beeped. A text, from John.

Want to meet up for coffee tonight?

She thought of the dead girls and of Selene's warning, but what were the odds that nice normal John was some crazed killer? She couldn't always be afraid of her own damn shadow, MU had ten thousand students. And besides, she wanted to celebrate and share with someone about her amazing day. How fulfilling raising Jeremiah had felt, how natural. She'd spent her whole life fighting what she was, denying her nature, it had been liberating to just give in. Take a chance. Life's for living after all, right?

Would love to! Meet at Java's at 8?
It's a date.

Germaine smiled the whole bus ride home. *A date.* Feeling more alive and comfortable in her body than she'd ever felt before.

I shut my office door and locked it behind me. Everyone else on my floor had closed up earlier and the building felt eerily quiet. In the elevator I thought about Germaine, and felt conflicted. Did I want to have an apprentice? Really? No. But, I had to admit that for being so green, she had resurrected Jeremiah Ingersoll beautifully. She'd been artful and gentle. Overall, it was quality work. So, it wasn't skill that would be the issue, it would be the fact that she was so young, eighteen, fresh off a cornfield church bus. I didn't want to be her friend.

She wasn't Dot.

"A shy, chubby girl with bad shoes and a pension for blushing redder than a beet. But she's got raw power and can make the firm money." That was how Dot would've described her. I could almost picture Dot in the elevator with me, readers perched on the edge of her nose, her gray hair swept up into a messy bun, wearing her signature red lipstick. "Germaine lacks any sort of guile, which would actually be good for clients and business. You could offload a lot of work on her, open your schedule up. Besides, you weren't that much to look at when I found you, like a feral junkyard cat."

Locking the external door, I smiled, finding comfort in even imagining Dot's voice, her hard-ass manner, her honesty. I would never be the mentor that Dot was, I didn't even want to be. But I saw the gleam in Germaine's eye, the pleasure in bringing that man back to his family. I could work with that.

I was overworked, and people die every day, so the extra help once she was trained would be a godsend. The benefit of being in a rare sought-after field is that the pay was good and the competition was low. I lived modestly, owned my car, paid my bills on time. Without much of a life, I just kept socking it away. Dot always berated me for not living it up, traveling, or being part of the community more. But money didn't really matter, it was important to be insulated and as an orphan with no family, good to be able to take care of myself. I donated a lot to foster programs and various child outreach organizations.

But past that, what did I really need money for? I rarely traveled, finding little pleasure in wandering around alone and couldn't remember the last time I had a vacation, or a real boyfriend to go on nice dates.

"Sad sack." Dot's voice said in my subconscious, as she slid her glasses farther down her nose to look at me. "Get over yourself will you, you aren't unlovable, you just need to put yourself out there and take a chance. A little lipstick *and* attitude adjustment and you just may be a catch."

If all goes right, I could be saying the same things to doe-eyed Germaine soon enough. Oh joy. Resurrections and self-esteem building. What a team we could make.

I crossed the near-empty parking lot and had my hand on my keys as I always did. It was quiet, save the rush of cars on the overpass. The water was choppy and gray-green and the air smelled of brine. A rusty old barge piled high with garbage slid silently by. Hundreds of seagulls circled it.

I should call Marlow about Germaine, let him know there is another new resurrectionist in town. A university student no less. Did I feel a little thrill at the thought of having a reason to call him I wonder? Or am I just really excited to have a friend? I knew the answer, I liked his company, he made me feel less alone, less like a freak.

But did I *like him*, like him? I supposed in the end, I wasn't that far removed from Germaine. I too was awkward in my own skin and had such a hard time connecting with anyone, either friends or lovers. Resurrectionists lived outside the world, seeing the natural laws as mere suggestions, and our rare and innate ability scared normal people. That is, until they needed something.

I had the key in the car door when movement in the window's reflection caught my eye, I spun just as something hit me in the head. An explosion of fireworks and I was down on my knees, dazed. My purse had fallen to the ground, things rolled under the car. I tried to get my bearings, but I was pushed to the damp pavement with someone crawling on top of me. As I tried to buck them off, my hands were roughly grabbed up and yanked behind me. I was being tied up, I realized in horror. I fought back, struggling and kicking, panic and the angle of my arms making it hard to get a full breath in. I had a moment of victory when the back of my head connected with the head behind me and a grunt came out. My head throbbed.

But the headbutt victory was short-lived as I was lifted onto my knees and slammed into the side of the car, my breath forced out and head knocking against the driver's door. Vision spinning, I tried to wriggle away and a knee pressed against my spine, riding me all the way back to the ground. My chin struck the pavement. I screamed out, only to have my mouth clamped over by a leather-gloved hand, and the other hand held a vial half full with what looked like cigarette ash in front of my face. I had no idea what it was, but I put everything into getting my attacker off of me then. Never let them take you to a second location.

But he had me at a disadvantage, I was hurt, he was sitting squarely on my back and my hands were tied. I'd never even seen his face. If only I had my damn arms, but I was trussed up too tight to get any slack. A hot tear streaked my face as one leather hand twisted my face and neck as far to the side as possible and the vial came closer to my face, uncorked now. A pale smoke drifted out, it smelled of herbs. I tried to jerk away but could barely move an inch. I tried to hold my breath, but with the first searing snorts of the vial's smoking contents, I was gone.

PART TWO:
WAXING GIBBOUS

TEN

A lightning bolt exploded out of the gaseous clouds and speared the scraggy terrain of Anchu. The force of it cleaved a great trench, exposing the underground gathering place, for the first time, to the skies. What followed was screams and sobbing as acidic rain poured in. Terror abounded when the clay roof further collapsed. In the chaos many were left dead, some mercifully killed instantly by force of the earthen roof caving in, others dying slow, suffocating and drowning in the mud, or crushed by the weight. Still others burnt by the harsh water, sloughing off skin with disturbing ease, for the world had truly turned against its inhabitants. Those who clamored to the top were snatched up like worms into the maws of birds. The sky creatures, starving and agitated by the storm, were eager to swoop in and gobble up anything moving in the dirt.

After the horror of the storms subsided, what remained of the Council of Elders gathered, even deeper below, as everyone had moved further into the ground, for safety. Already workers were toiling to block the passageways and stop the torrent of toxic waters from drowning out the underground city. The elders knew that time was slipping away, that the urgency of their plight was drawing ever nearer. If they were to survive, they would need to find a true door, one that would take them away from this dying world.

They prayed to Nigrum Porta that he would return for them as he *promised, all those years ago. When he passed through a door and never returned.*

Persimmon Shaw was not what Marlow expected. He imagined someone like Lila Goodtree, a wizened old crone with a pile of cats and tomes. Instead, he stood before a tall, comely woman with a golden tan and a shock of curly white-blonde hair piled high on her head, wearing a slinky silk sarong and hundreds of jangly bracelets up her arms.

"Detectives," she said, but her eyes were only on him. They were a vibrant green, lit as if from within, and he had little doubt they missed much. Persimmon was, in a word, dangerous. Marlow could feel the power crackling off of her.

She swayed through the small North Side bungalow, richly furnished from all over the world, and over the vibrant colored carpets. The air smelled of incense and fresh-cut flowers, which overflowed from large vases on nearly every surface. The space felt sacred and temple-like and he found the calmness it caused suspicious. As if a spell was being worked on him. Vampires were not as susceptible to magic as humans, but they were also not entirely immune.

He was also not immune to her physical charms. He tried, and failed, to ignore her round backside, nearly nude beneath the thin slip of colorful silk. He glanced at Regine, who smirked and rolled her eyes. He could almost read his partner's mind: a witch and a floozy.

They arrived at a small office in the back of the house with French doors that opened out to a lush, impossibly verdant garden. It was so dense with greenery that the sky was nearly hidden under the canopy. Many birds and bees flitted through a rainbow of exotic flowers. On the ground a spongy moss, like a green velvet carpet, had grown over the pavers in most places. A fat green snake worked its way past. Marlow reassessed the woman before them, since that garden was decidedly unnatural and out of season for April. He had a feeling the garden wasn't much different in deep December.

"Please have a seat." She gestured to the large cushions on the ground. Regine turned to him and raised an eyebrow, he had to fight the urge to smile.

"We'll stand, thanks."

"Suit yourself, could I offer you a drink? Some tea perhaps?" Her voice was sultry and husky.

"We're good," he said. One shouldn't drink or eat anything in a witch's house.

"You're certain you don't want something *warm* to drink, Detective?" She met Marlow's eyes with a knowing wink and he stiffened despite himself. There was mirth in her eyes, but a warning there as well, she knew what he was.

"We're fine ma'am. I realize you're probably a busy woman, so we don't want to take up too much of your time," Regine plowed in, cutting through their unspoken back and forth.

"Of course, Detectives." She lowered herself onto a small garden chair covered in a sheep's skin and put an elbow on the narrow matching bistro table. "So, this is about the murders on the news."

"You were recommended by Selene Shade, a local resurrectionist," Regine said.

"Selene? Really? That's surprising."

"And why is that, Ms. Shaw?" Marlow interjected, genuinely curious, recalling Selene's reluctance when offering the witch for assistance with the case.

"Oh, we went to college together, we had a falling out. I stole a boyfriend of hers. It was kid stuff really. But she is one to hold a grudge, she was always a bit jealous of me. We were roommates in college, you know how they like to put all the freaks together, cloistered away. Witches tend to be a bit more popular, less icky death stuff than the others." Her eyes again snared Marlow's, but her beauty had already lost its luster in just the few sentences she'd spoken. Persimmon was pompous, and it made her unattractive in his eyes.

"I'll just cut to it, is it possible to create a tracking spell to find resurrectionists? In particular young ones, new to their abilities?" Regine continued, unamused by Persimmon.

The witch's eyes lit up, "That is *interesting*. You think the killer is targeting resurrectionists?"

"We aren't at liberty to say, but would love to know if there is such a spell, or if you could create one, to help locate any and all resurrectionists in the area." Marlow crossed his arms, "It would be aiding in a police investigation and any help would be enormously helpful to the department."

"I don't know any spells like that offhand, but will look into it, do some experimenting. Tracking spells of any kind for living beings are notoriously finicky. I should be able to come up with something. It will be a fun challenge!"

"Thank you, Ms. Shaw, here is my card, do let us know how you get on." Marlow said sternly, and started walking after his partner.

Regine took a few steps out of the room and froze, Marlow nearly ran into her.

"Detective," Persimmon said, her voice harder than before. Marlow turned back to her. All the flirtation was gone and a serious woman stared back. This must be the real Persimmon Shaw.

"They are trying to summon something, aren't they? Doing a fucked-up fertility rite?" He glanced at his partner, but Regine was still as a statue. "She can't hear me, I figured better you and I just talk about this. She's mortal after all, an outsider. If they are using resurrectionist girls as vessels, that must mean the thing that passes through is probably incorporeal, or once alive and now dead and spirit." Persimmon walked closer to him, "It's not common knowledge, but reanimating involves pulling the spirit into this reality *through* the resurrectionist. They are a passageway. Or a filter. Like a door. If this ritual is what I think it is and they need that sort of vessel, I don't like to think what kind of thing would be birthed on this side."

"You have any ideas what it would be?" he said.

"It can only be something quite bad for our world. Something very unnatural. Resurrectionists aren't mortal, the way I am, or even you are. Theirs is a magic from somewhere else."

"How do you mean?"

"I am a witch, my roots are deeply tied to the five elements and to nature, you are a vampire, basically a big parasite—no offense—who feeds off other living things in the ecosystem. But you were created by human magic. We both need this world to survive, and it needs us. Part of the circle of life. Resurrectionists are something else...a void, an anomaly, a door to other worlds, a way to ferry the dead back into this world. They break the natural law. They aren't people as much as they are tools."

"That seems a little harsh don't you think?"

She shrugged. "What do you think a resurrectionist's ultimate purpose in this world is? Is it to fill it with zombies, ending death as we know it? Or is it to bring forth something else from somewhere else? Either possibility spells an end to the world we know." She met his eyes and an intensity burned there, "Either way, there is something apoca-lyptic at its end. They imbalance nature, I've always thought so."

"I've never heard anything like this. This your unique theory or is this a common belief about them?" Marlow said, feeling a blossom of protectiveness for Selene. This was her enemy after all and may be attempting to manipulate him.

Persimmon smiled sweetly. "It's not common theory, no. But not something I came up with either. Witches, who strive for balance in the world, see them as a disruptive and foreign element. Alien."

"Necromancers aren't all that natural," Marlow responded coolly.

"Necromancers play with death magic, often with horrible results, but theirs is a mix of human alchemy and perverted witch magic. You lot are basically predators made by necromancer magic. But resurrec-tionists...and the half-lifes they create, have never made sense. It's as if they came from somewhere else."

Marlow responded, "Like another planet?"

She lifted an eyebrow but didn't respond.

"Ms. Shaw, any help you can give on a tracking spell, or way to pinpoint young resurrectionists would be much appreciated. We are running against the clock."

Persimmon reached out and touched his arm, all flirtation gone, in its place a seriousness, "Protect Selene, I can tell you care about her and I sense she's in great danger. I can feel it. You may not know this, but she is enormously powerful, more so than she realizes. If I was working a ritual like this, she is exactly who I'd use."

"Why haven't they tried that then? Why go after these young girls instead? She said it to me herself, she's in the damned phonebook. She and the occultist on our payroll think they need virgins." Persimmon dropped his arm and stepped away, Regine remained still, face a blank, breathing, but eyes glazed over. He found it unsettling.

"You may be right. Plenty of rituals want virgins. I need to tinker with some spells, maybe there is something I am missing. Send me all the case details you can and I will get the coven working on it. But keep your eyes on Selene. If she's not a target yet, I think she will be."

"I will. Thanks."

"I'll be in touch," Persimmon said, and with that, the world resumed and Regine continued walking from the room totally unphased, Marlow at her heels. He quietly kicked himself for avoiding magic and other flavors of supernatural over his long life. He felt he was at quite the disadvantage and didn't really understand what they could or couldn't do.

I woke to hear voices, my head throbbing something fierce and glanced around. I was tied to a chair, arms going numb. Ankles each bound to a leg.

"I told you to bring her to me, not to beat the shit out of her. Jesus." I was in a musty room, alone, in a basement, with a wall of cement and shelves across from me. Plastic tubs filled with holiday crap stacked till the shelves bowed in the middle. Cobwebs in the rafters. Smelled of mold and laundry soap.

"She struggled, I came up behind her but she fucking head-butted me, look at my lip!" The two men were just out of my line of vision outside the thin door.

"You came up from behind? Seriously, this just got so out of control. The salts to knock her out were supposed to be a last resort! You were supposed to ask her to come along." Well that was good at least, as I wasn't supposed to be brained, drugged, and abducted. At least in their initial plan.

I strained my senses to try and deduce where the hell I was and who my kidnappers were. Their voices were totally unfamiliar. As I tested my bindings, the chair I was trussed to creaked, giving me away.

"Shh, she's awake. Hello?! Hello, Ms. Shade? Selene?" The door opened behind me, the voice was male, middle-aged, and approaching me swiftly. The other man, my abductor from his split lip, hit the lights and the room was suddenly awash in stark fluorescent lighting. I cringed.

"How are you feeling, Ms. Shade? First off, I just wanted to apologize, my colleague here misunderstood instruction."

"And what was that instruction?" I said through gritted teeth, trying to ignore the deep throb in my skull, made worse by the bare bulb which felt like a spotlight in my face.

"To bring you here—"

"—which is where?" I interjected.

"Oh, well, this is not where he was supposed to bring you. This is actually my basement."

"Why the fuck was I abducted at all?" I said back. Fear and disorientation were making me much braver, that and the feeling these guys were not the killers, or even very bright.

The big man, balding with a round belly straining his T-shirt, and thick glasses, grimaced. He looked like a high school wrestling coach, someone who'd been strong and fit in his youth. The smaller man, my kidnapper, was weaselly with a sickly complexion and dark hair slicked back like a movie gangster. He had a fat lip. I sized him up, we were close to the same size. Probably would have been easily matched if I hadn't been struck from behind first.

The big man rubbed a thick hand over his mouth before stepping closer, "You see, Ms. Shade, we know you've been working with the police. We too have been investigating these murders. I also know you contacted Karl Wraith."

My blood chilled at this knowledge, Karl was Dot's ex-husband. A necromancer sure, but also a professor and a regular citizen. I thought I could trust him. Who were these guys? As if reading my mind, the big man said, "Karl is an associate of ours, he brought it back to the cabal and we..."

"We? Are you guys necromancers? Does Karl know you've taken me?" I said. I squinted through the headache and looked at their auras, human but with a taint to them, as if they'd been burnt at the edges. Necromancers.

"We are members of the Order of Yama, ma'am. Karl did instruct us to keep an eye on you, for your protection, after we learned that the ritual—"

"Is sacrificing resurrectionists. Did everyone figure this out today or what? I miss a newsletter or something? So, now you guys think I may be in danger of being abducted, so you proactively...abducted me first?"

"Essentially, yes." The big man opened his hands and closed them, taking a moment to shoot a glare back at his weaselly colleague. "It was not supposed to go down this way, ma'am, I assure you. We planned to approach you, tell you our theories and offer help. The evidence points to them needing a powerful vessel to summon Nigrum Porta, and with three failures they are no doubt getting frustrated."

I was chilled to the bone suddenly, the cold basement, the loss of circulation and the idea that I was suddenly on so many group's radars. I squeezed my eyes shut and breathed out. "I thought they wanted a virgin."

"We thought that too, but there is a conflict in translation. The word could be read as pure power or purity, depending."

"I would like to be untied please. I do not think being tied up in your basement is the best thing for my safety. Especially as we don't know for a fact that I am a potential victim."

Big man paced, his face sweaty, nervous. "The thing they are trying to bring back, it's bad. Real bad. Like end-times bad," he said.

I rolled my eyes, "Great. I would be happy to talk more, even get the police to compare notes with you and we can all help save the world together. But, I will not continue as a hostage or a prisoner or whatever you are doing here."

"You are neither! I'm just waiting to hear from the cabal leaders, it won't be much longer. We restrained you as much for your safety as anything. Jimmy and I will go get you something to eat and drink now." He opened the door, face apologetic.

I hollered, jumped around in my chair, but to no avail. The two walked out, leaving the light on, and headed up the stairs. Did I hear a television blaring up there? If I kept screaming would someone hear me and call for help, or would they gag me?

My mind raced, had it really been only a few days ago that my life was normal? I went to work, I went home, wash, rinse, repeat. It had been crushingly lonely and I missed Dot like a lost limb, but it was predictable. And now? Death rituals, cabals of necromancers, vampire cops, and shadowy oil men with wind mouths watching me sleep. And maybe, maybe, if I got lucky could end up the chosen one in a sacrificial gang bang to bring on the end times.

The bindings around my wrists were tight, giving me very little give. My ankles were not as tight, but with no slack to get free either. These clowns were really serious about my safety, Christ. I tested the knots, moving hands back and forth, ankles wriggling, trying to loosen something. I'd never been tied up before and knew what little I did from movies, so my first insane thought was standing and trying to fall back and smash the chair. My next was I should really carry a blade up my sleeve or in my boot. I struggled harder, letting my hips lift off the chair as much they could.

Clatter.

My phone slipped out of my back pocket. Morons. I laughed excited that they did not pat me down very well when they dragged me here. My purse was probably still on the ground near my car, hell, my keys were probably in the dang car door still. That would look suspicious when someone came near it, surely someone would notice I was gone. Hopefully sooner rather than later. I wished it wasn't a Friday though, as there was little activity in the office on weekends. Maybe a night janitor would call the cops?

Hell, maybe Marlow would notice when I didn't check in, he'd been worried about me. Right? Marlow would notice.

Maybe. I squeezed my eyes shut, head throbbing, wrists and shoulder aching, butt falling asleep. I couldn't wait for someone to save me from these guys. Surely there was something I could do. It clicked before I'd even consciously thought it. The murder victims summoned dead animals to help them. I stretched my senses out, unfurling like a net underwater, feeling the lives upstairs, skipping those, looking for the dead, the empty.

There. Many small bodies, close. I pulled little lights from the ether, so delicate, like plucking wildflowers in a vast field. I willed those small things to come to my rescue.

ELEVEN

Marlow pulled into the parking lot, replaying the conversation with Persimmon. He didn't want Selene to think he was a stalker, but at the same time, better that than something happening to her. He was relieved to see her car in the lot as she hadn't answered when he called the office or her cell.

Before he'd even killed the ignition, he could see something was wrong. He was out of the car in a flash, there was her purse, half under the car, a Chapstick a few feet away. The world tunneled in, the pressure roaring in his ears. He was too late.

"Trace that fucking phone! Now!" Marlow yelled, the mask of humanity sliding as he glared at the young desk sergeant.

I could kill this man, I could kill all of them, everyone in here right now. Worse than that, I want to. He knew it would do nothing to make him feel better or bring Selene back.

If something happened to Selene he would not be able to forgive himself. He had seen her just the night before. He should've put a detail on her, he should have been there.

When he tried calling her work and she didn't answer he'd thought little of it, just left a message. Then he tried her cell. Nothing. He decided to swing by to be safe, figured they could touch base, talk about Persimmon. Maybe get a drink and discuss the case some more.

He'd nearly lost it as he dropped to his knees, gathered her things from under the car. He smelled blood then, got down lower, a few drops, human. Ran his tongue over the gravel, it was not hers.

And he'd smiled then, she fought back, she'd made him bleed. Good for her.

But they had her now. They took her, leaving her things on the ground uncaring. That worried him, that was the move of someone who didn't care if anyone knew she'd been taken. But the new moon was over two weeks away.

He'd stood in the parking lot, pulse throbbing, fangs fully extended. He had the urge to punch something, bite something, smash something, *kill* something. Someone. Selene was his friend, and that meant Selene was *his* and no one took what was *his* and lived to tell about it. Vampires were apex predators and he felt like one in that moment. He was hard-pressed trying to remember the last time he'd been this angry, or worried, or hungry for violence.

Marlow forced himself to relax, forced his body to breathe, his muscles to unclench. His fight response was unhelpful, as there was nothing to attack. He needed his wits and his police officer training. Running around like an angry lion would do very little to get her back. Slowly, breathing in and out, forcing calm, his rage ebbed and he was able to walk through the steps to find her, as a police officer.

First, he walked the scene of the crime, looking for any evidence it could offer. Once he searched her bag, finding wallet, cash, credit card inside, he felt confident that this was not an ordinary human abduction. But he had nothing to go on past that, save that there was no phone. The office building was locked up behind her, hers was the only car in the lot, obviously she'd been grabbed when preparing to leave. The camera facing the lot may help, but that would take time, need to find the security management company, get access to it. If she closed up around five and it was six now, that gave them an hour lead. One hour could have them well out of town, close to crossing another state's line. But he doubted they'd left Goat Hill's city limits. He called the station and reported her missing, got that paperwork going, also an inquiry into the security footage. He called Regine and let her know.

As he drove to the station on the highway, his lights flashing, pushing ninety along the breakdown lane, he debated calling

Persimmon and getting her coven involved. But he was a cop first, and the idea of involving more civilians, even magically inclined ones, went against his nature. Her phone wasn't in her purse. Her phone may still be on her person, or they took it and have it on them. A phone could be traced.

"Track her now, this is life or death, do you understand?" he said as calmly as he could. The pockmarked desk officer nodded, fingers flying along the keyboard. Marlow could feel the needle poke of sharp teeth into his lower lip and willed them to retract, hoped the feral gleam would dull in his eyes, in his body language. *Be calm. Be a person, be a policeman, be normal,* he repeated over and over.

"We got the okay from her cell carrier, now I am just triangulating the location, sir. The movies make this look a lot easier and faster, and besides, this is pushing it, she went missing like an hour ago..." He shot a side eye to Marlow.

"With respect um...Thompkins, she is an active member of an investigation on the current ritual serial killer and may in fact be with them now. As the next victim. *So, speed it the fuck up.*" Marlow wanted to rip this kid's head off and throw it across the room. Something of that thought must have been conveyed in his expression because the remaining blood in Thompkins' face drained away. A few more keystrokes and he pointed to a map on the screen.

"It's approximate, by a few blocks and it's residential. Southwest side of town," he said with a shrug. "That's the best we can do."

Marlow was up, grabbing his coat. "Print it out."

———

The tiny dead mice were hard at work chewing my bonds, their bodies mostly dusty little husks, their teeth and limbs brittle and crumbling. There were a few "fresher" ones and I put them on the heavier work, their bodies a little more intact, but much drippier and smellier. I had them push my cell phone to one of my feet, but that was the best I could do. It was on silent from my last client so at least I could hide it under my shoe until my hands were free. My control of the little mice was not sophisticated enough to get them to unlock my phone, unfortunately.

That said, I was both impressed and mildly nauseated by my command of the pitiful dead creatures. They were making pretty fast work of chewing the bindings, what with the challenge of having to climb up my body then down my arms to settle on my sleeves to reach the rope. It was a tickly and strange experience.

My ankles were nearly free when I heard the basement door open.

"Shit," I whispered, testing the arms, the rope squeaked and a few strands snapped, but it was still too tight to get my hands out. I didn't want these cabal goons to see my helpers, and so willed them to scurry into the shadows and hide. Leaving only one to keep chewing discreetly hidden in the palm of my hand. It wasn't the quietest thing though, so as the big man entered I stopped the mouse gnawing.

"Sorry for the delay, ma'am, as I said we're just waiting to hear back from some other members. But I have a sandwich here for you and a bottle of water. I hope you don't mind turkey." He smiled sheepishly and all I could do was glare at him.

"I'll need my hands to eat. Also, I need to go to the bathroom." His face dropped a little at that, and I could see this was not a man who wanted to have a hostage in his basement. Especially not if it involved him holding me over a mop bucket. I wanted out of these restraints, I wanted out of this house. But I also did not want to have to physically fight my way out. This man was a mountain, and under all that bulk was muscle. And I knew from the bruise on my face that the weaselly one had no problem knocking me around.

Necromancers, like reanimators, did not have a lot of defensive magic besides using the dead as weapons. These guys? They didn't seem very adept at all in death magic or life. Especially compared to Karl Wraith, who was a master of the dark arts and had some pretty scary power. These guys looked like teamsters.

"Of course, I will untie you to eat..." It was just then a phone trilled, and the weaselly one came into my line of vision holding it out.

"It's Lucinda."

The big one took it eagerly and walked out, little one on his heels. I immediately resumed the mouse's gnawing and clawing at the rope. All the while stretching my ears out:

"You need to take her to the meetinghouse and before the cabal. No, I think I've done enough, what with the possibility of jail for abduction and forced imprisonment. My kids are upstairs for Christ's sake. Someone's bound to notice she's missing. Dumb shit here dragged her off, leaving her purse on the ground! Of course, I under-stand...okay see you soon."

He trailed off farther into the basement, mumbling lower than I could hear. Okay, so the plan was to bring me to the meetinghouse, what was their group's name? Order of Yama. I'd heard of them, a large organization, probably over a hundred members, from masters to dabblers. I always thought of cabals as quite similar to the Masons, they all loved their clandestine meetings, cloaks, and secret handshakes. Yup, a bunch of schlubby Masons that raised the dead for long-lost secrets and magic.

And these guys wanted to protect me, or rather just keep me from Nigrum Porta. I wondered if there were any other resurrectionists tied up at the meetinghouse, would I be tossed in a room with a bunch of women who could be potential sacrifices? Run into Dania, my business rival?

Big man went up the stairs, little guy behind him. Guess I wasn't getting my sandwich or toilet break anytime soon. My mice continued working and I was grateful that this house had a vermin problem.

With an exciting snap, one leg was free. I stretched it up, rotated the ankle and was rewarded with blood returning. The other ankle followed right after. I was nearly free of my wrist binding when the door upstairs opened again, and footsteps and voices followed my captors down. Quickly, I ordered a little dead mouse, who was barely a skeleton wearing what looked like a little mini mink stole, to push the rope back up and around my feet as best they could, close enough for a passing glance. I felt like a macabre Cinderella watching my tiny army do my bidding, eyes hollow, bones visible, herky-jerky movements all to help me. The poor things, what horror it must be to be back in their dead and desiccated bodies. *Soon I will release you*, I promised them.

A woman walked in, confident in the way the two other men were not. Her hair was dyed jet black in severe pageboy cut with one bold streak of white in the front. Artfully styled, she wore a smart business suit, three-inch stiletto heels, and tasteful jewelry. Gold-rimmed glasses perched on her nose, the eyes behind them hard. Now this was a necromancer. Her aura was nearly all black, she did a lot of death magic. There was a corruption to it, an unnaturalness. I realized that was hypocritical coming from one such as I, but there it was. I have always found necromancers to be vile and their abuses of the dead for their own ends to be barbaric. Behind her entered another pasty flunky dressed like an undertaker and my two idiot captors.

"I apologize for this mix-up, Ms. Shade, and also my delay in responding, I was in court."

"Does this look like a mix-up to you?" I said with as much authority as one can muster tied to a chair.

A necromancer and a lawyer, hoo-boy, I could almost hear Dot's voice in my head saying that sounds like the punchline to a joke. Something like, what's worse than leprosy? A necromancer-lawyer har-har.

"To be frank, Ms. Shade, my associates fucked up, bad. But I don't think this needs to be brought to the human authorities. And besides, in a way, being kept here actually keeps you safer than out there. They mustn't be able to complete their ritual, you understand that, right?"

"I understand and I do not want to be ritually raped and murdered. But I also think your approach, knocking me out, brutalizing me, and locking me down here...what?"

Lucinda was making a strange face, as if she smelled something bad. "You're doing something in here, some sort of magic. Right now. Aren't you?" Her tone of voice sounded both curious and wary.

I was tempted to lie, but she was walking around me, "I can sense it, it has a wild feel to it. No spells, no sigils, just you summoning," she paused, and breathed out. "The dead."

She knelt, looked at my bindings, all the while, tut-tutting. I tried to hide my mouse, but she pried my hand open and there was little I could do.

"Well, hello there," she said, voice honeyed, and proud of herself. "Who is your little friend?"

My mouse, sensing my danger and fear, reacted to protect me and in a flash, darted up her jacket arm and bit and scratched at the skin above her shirt collar before she could do much more than flail her arms. Lucinda screamed, scrambling away while frantically trying to grab her vicious attacker. The mouse was tiny, barely bigger than my pinky. But its teeth were sharp and it had tangled itself in her hair and necklace.

The three men fluttered around her, useless and unsure what to do. Not wanting to miss my chance at escape, I willed the other mice out from the shadows and immediately they set upon all my kidnappers, climbing up their pant legs on tickly bony feet.

Everyone was screaming and yelling now and I knew this was my one opportunity to get out, they wouldn't give me another. I struggled out of my restraints, and shook myself wildly in the chair.

"It's her you idiots!" Lucinda screamed, her face a mess of blood and scratches. "Stop her and they'll stop!"

The big one had pulled his shirt up revealing his big hairy belly to pluck a mouse and throw it against the wall. He was now heading my way, fist tightened into a ball. I cringed in advance, knowing I couldn't even block it with my hands still bound. If he'd only give me a little more time, I could feel the bindings around my middle giving way.

As he closed the distance, another mouse body went flying across the room and Lucinda came forward, murder in her eyes. "If not for the fucking apocalypse, I would kill you myself." Her teeth were white and perfectly spaced. "Hit her Glen, *hard.*" She looked back to the big one.

As he reared back to punch me, the basement door exploded in and in a blur of movement, the undertaker-looking lackey was suddenly on the ground, his throat torn open. He'd cupped his hands over his wound, but it spurted, something vital obviously nicked. His mouth opening and closing like a fish.

Everyone paused and stared at the man on the floor. And then all looked at the new man in the room.

Marlow. His eyes black as a shark, teeth long and mouth blood-smeared. He stood hunched, hands curled into claws, blocking the exit. Lucinda looked at him and back to me. "Did you command him here? Are you that powerful?" Her voice contained a new note, real fear.

"Untie her now, or everyone in here is dead," Marlow said before I could answer, his voice low and lethal. The contained rage was terrifying, my body was instantly coated in gooseflesh and I was the one he was *saving*.

Undertaker writhed on the floor still, the pool of blood around him expanding. Was this man going to die in front of us? I wondered about Marlow's control and if he killed on his off time as a police officer. I also wondered if I actually cared in this moment, since he was also there to help me.

The big guy quickly came to me, opening a pocketknife and bringing it to the last pieces of rope at my wrists. "If you do anything stupid back there, I will know," Marlow warned, watching the man, "one drop of her blood hits the floor and I will gut you."

The big guy nodded, hands trembling. I took this time to call back my mice, and they surrounded me in a protective circle, all pitifully damaged from the battle. Marlow looked down at them and marveled.

I could see the realization as his eyes followed the mice to the spattering of scratches and wounds on my attackers. He quirked an eyebrow and I shrugged, pleased to see the man was still in there, terrifying exterior or no.

Once the rope was cut and I could get my hands in front, I rubbed them, trying to get the feeling back. I stood unsteadily and Marlow quickly wrapped his arms around me. The hug was tight, bone-crushing, and the affection in it startled me. I don't think anyone had ever hugged me that hard since I was a child. Something squeezed tight in my low belly at the knowledge.

"Are you alright?" he whispered, pulling back to look me over and run a hand across the bruise on my face. His expression darkening. I nodded, just wanting to be free of that terrible basement.

"We are trying to save the world you fools!" Lucinda said straightening herself up, trying to regain some control. "They have failed *three times*, they will not abide by a fourth. They thought the vessel needed to be new, virginal, and unschooled in raw magic. But they weren't strong enough, they need a Master of the Dead." Her eyes bore into me when she said that, a combination of disdain and perhaps jealousy there.

"And you think Selene is a Master of the Dead?" Marlow said, fangs retracted, eyes human-ish, only the mouth smeared with blood giving away his regular-Joe look.

"You don't? You're her minion, you came when she called." My eyes slid their way to Marlow. If I could do what she said, I would have done that first. Maybe. "If I'd known what she truly was," Lucinda continued, "we never would have taken her as we did. Karl never said she was this powerful. I'm just lucky she did not bring a zombie horde to take this house down brick by brick. Let alone summoning an actual vampire."

"Karl told you to kidnap me?" My mouth went dry, Dot would be rolling in her grave if he betrayed me like that. If Marlow hadn't had an arm around me, I probably would have fallen back into my chair. I couldn't believe he would betray me like that. We'd never been close, but we'd always been civil.

"No. Not in so many words. He alerted us to the murders and that he thought you may be a target. After our research, we concurred. Especially now." Lucinda raised an eyebrow and gestured at Marlow. I opened my mouth to protest, but Marlow gripped my arm stopping me.

"Now you know what my master can do. Pass it along that she is not to be meddled with by any of your ilk. She *will* be protected from this threat. But not by you."

I could only imagine my facial expression, it definitely did not scream Master of the Dead or Zombie Queen. Marlow pushed me gently through the door, his hand on the small of my back. Once we reached the steps, I turned back and released the little dead mice following me out. Each of their bodies falling dead and quiet like a row of grotesque dominoes. Lucinda and the big man watched, Weasel knelt on the floor applying pressure to Undertaker's neck.

TWELVE

Amar Patel sloshed his tea as he raised it to his lips. Something had caused his hand to shake, in fact his whole body to shudder with a momentary lack of control. He looked around his small apartment for the source of the strangeness.

His home was neat as a pin, tasteful mid-century furniture, white walls and many lamps and mirrors to brighten up the dank little space. The only sounds the quiet squeaks and whirs of the exercise wheels in his rodent cages. He unfolded a paper IKEA screen when guests came by to hide them from sight. Everything seemed ordinary and normal.

As normal as it ever was as a half-life. In the few months of this new state, Amar had been forced to make peace with the dullness of it: food lacked flavor, temperature extremes went unnoticed. Even sex felt almost as if he was watching it from above himself. He was in the world yet felt a million miles away. As if the volume was turned all the way down.

But that moment, that shudder, that he *felt* with every cell of his being. It was a call. It was panic, it was a need for help. He felt a shock of pure sensation, a tingling, an excitement. There was adrenaline flowing and he felt compelled to act. Without thinking he opened the door to his small mother-in-law buildout in a suburban split level, and walked out the driveway. It was Friday night, dark, misty and cool. The street was quiet, most families tucked in for the night in front of dinner tables and TVs. A dog barked, he heard the highway a few streets away.

What was this feeling? The trill in his head, the flutter in his chest, he had no doubt now it was a call. To him.

He walked without direction, following the summoning like a safety line.

Two-blocks down he stopped in front of a house that was nondescript and a little run down, he'd probably passed it a hundred times without noticing. The signal was beaming from this house. Something wanted him to go in there. *To fight, to protect, to liberate.* Where were these thoughts coming from? Certainly not from him. He'd never been a violent person, but a small part of him lit up with eagerness at the prospect. To rend and tear, to bite, to defend...*my master.*

Amar was halfway up the drive when the call vanished as if it had never existed. He stood stark still, listening, stretching his senses. But the call was gone.

"I am losing my mind," he said to himself, worried the residents would peer out a window and see him in their driveway loitering. He could imagine the police response to male POC half-life trespasser and shuddered. No, definitely unsafe for him. He was back on the street, half hidden by the neighbor's shrubs watching the house. After a few quiet minutes of nothing happening, Amar began to feel silly. He'd taken one step toward home when the front door opened. He spun back to see a woman fleeing the house, bruised and disheveled. It was his resurrectionist. Behind her came a pale man with black eyes and a bloody mouth. She wasn't afraid of the bloody man and Amar had the sense the danger had ended.

He almost raised his arm and called out to help but thought the better of it, he didn't want to get involved in whatever had just happened. So instead, he stepped back into the high shrubs and shadows as they headed to a car out front. He was left conflicted as he watched the car drive away, wondering if he should have tried to help. The call to action had ended and the volume of his world was turned back down again. But for a moment, he'd had such a purity of purpose.

Marlow and I passed quickly through the cluttered suburban house and found two children watching TV oblivious to the craziness in their basement. Unbelievable. They barely even glanced up as we passed through. Marlow was stiff as he marched me out, hand tight on my arm, out the door, down the walk, across the patchy early spring lawn, and into his car.

Only once we were in the car, away from prying eyes did he relax, and even then, it was just a notch. A subtle drop in his shoulders. He took a deep breath in through his nose, expelled it, and turned on the car. As we drove away, I turned back in my seat and watched the small brown split level in the working-class neighborhood get smaller and smaller, no one chased us out or tried to follow. But there was a man, dark hair and skin, I sensed him more than saw him, too far away to see clearly, standing on the sidewalk watching us go. A half-life. Odd.

"You came to my rescue," I finally said, as I sat back, hands in my lap, my wrists red and raw from the rope. I thought about how he'd hugged me when he first found me. I so rarely got hugged by anyone. Growing up a known resurrectionist in foster care, I didn't receive a lot of affection. Dot wasn't much of a hugger either. I'm practically a stranger and he hugged me. I knew I should've been using this time to tell him about the necromancers, but my brain kept going back to that hug. I could still feel it.

Marlow cleared his throat, "Looks like you had it under control, your mouse army was impressive." I chuckled, feeling myself blush.

"That was *crazy*. I never would've thought to do something like that—manipulate dead animals, if it hadn't been for the crime scenes. It always seemed kind of gross, to mess with dead animals. But they really came through in a pinch. I was nearly out of my rope when you got there."

"Yeah. So, what happened?"

"I was their hostage. They drugged me and tied me up. Even still, I had to consciously raise the mice. The victims must have been so terrified to unconsciously call animals to their aid without intention." I rubbed at my raw wrists, my fingers still tingling as the circulation returned.

He reached out and squeezed my knee, "It was clever to use them."

"How did you find me?" I finally asked as he pulled his hand away.

"Your Zombie Queen Radar. You summoned me."

"Ha ha, seriously though?" There was a beat when I wondered, before noting his smirk.

"Your cellphone. I was able track it. But it was only a rough two block area so I was running house to house looking for you. Cost me a little time. Oh here, speaking of, I picked it up off the floor for you."

He reached in his breast pocket and handed me my phone. "Your purse and car keys are in the backseat as well. Can you tell me what the hell that was about, who were those guys? I kind of just broke protocol and left a guy bleeding out."

"Necromancers. The Order of Yama, wanted to keep me 'safe' and un-sacrificed. Apparently, Karl, Dot's ex, shared what was going down with his people and they decided...well to snatch me. For safety."

"I can't believe they abducted you like that, and beat you, and tortured you. They still have to abide by human law. It's just so stupid. You could sue them. We can arrest them."

"Yeah. I don't know if it's worth it. They were very disorganized and seemed kind of dumb. They thought they were saving the world or whatever. The worst part? They promised me a turkey sandwich and a bathroom break, and I never got either of them. Evil." I surprised myself, making a joke, no matter how lame. My nerves must well and truly have been fried.

"You hungry?"

"I wasn't before, but now that I'm thinking about it, yes, I'm starving. And I have to pee. And my head is killing me, one of those assholes smashed my head against the ground and I'm definitely going to have a bruise. They also knocked me out with some weird necro salt so no doubt I am getting the after-effects of that too. Wait—if you traced my phone...doesn't that mean people are still looking for me? Shouldn't you, like, call it in to the station or whatever?"

Marlow frowned, "I will, just trying to figure out how best to play it. Especially if that man I bit died. Since all of this isn't exactly standard or mundane human police work. Trying to decide how much they need to know. Your immediate safety is my top priority now. I feel like a fool not putting a detail on you earlier."

"You think you killed that guy?" I said, voice small.

He shrugged, "Maybe, I was a little out of it, I saw you tied up and smelled the blood in there and just kind of reacted. He was bleeding a lot. Odds are good they won't go to cops even if they end up at the hospital, since they were kidnapping someone at the time. Let me worry about that." Marlow was driving fast, his eyes glued to the road, body rigid. Deep in thought, he scratched at his mouth, noting the crusty red blood there. "I am taking you to my place, if that's all right. Just to make a plan."

"Oh. Sure, yeah, guess it wouldn't be smart to go home just this moment."

"No. If they can find you at work, they can find you at home." Ten minutes later we were pulling up to a converted mill building on the rougher South Side. I'd spent very little time in the area, but knew it was filled with underground clubs, artist lofts, poverty, and some fringy magic users. Edgy, but starting to become chic as gentrification creeped in.

Goat Hill was a smallish city of over half a million. The city consisted of the central downtown, where the hospital and police precinct were and the East Side, which was waterfront, where my office was. I lived on the West Side, which was a more residential, diverse area, and also where my abductors lived. Dot had lived in the tony North Side, where the university and the murders had occurred. Marlow lived in the industrial poorer South Side. This case had been taking me all over the city it seemed.

Marlow pushed a button and a garage rattled open on the side of a large brick mill building that matched all the others around it, we spiraled in and down an additional level and parked in silence. When he got out, I followed him, clutching my purse to my chest like it was a cat. I hated to admit it, but I was jumpy, being out in any kind of open. Between Nigrum Porta invading my house and dreams, and the stupid necromancers knocking me around and kidnapping me, I was feeling a bit unsafe and exposed. I liked the idea of being somewhere with walls and a lock.

We got in an elevator, the harsh light highlighting Marlow's unnaturally pale skin and nearly black eyes. There were still a few drops of blood on his collar. For some reason, probably stress release, exhaustion, madness, I found it funny that he made me feel safe and laughter bubbled out of me. He regarded me strangely, a worried expression on his face.

I waved him off, "I'm fine, really. Something about this day, and all its craziness, is just making me laugh." He watched me seriously, probably worried I had a concussion, which only made me laugh more. By the time the doors slid open, I was a little more composed, but only a little. I wanted a bathroom, some food, a gallon of wine and to take a long shower. Then sleep. Maybe cry? If I could do those things at some point I would be fine.

The hallway was long and industrial with visible pipes and hanging lights. The walls were white, but scuffed. There were four doors, two on either side. We went to the furthest on the right. I wasn't sure what to expect and when he opened the door and turned on the light I was pleasantly surprised.

The room was massive, with soaring ceilings, easily fifteen feet or higher. The floors were weathered wood planks from the building's past life as a factory. One wall was made up of huge windows that looked out at the city skyline. While the room was huge, it was well organized to designate an eating area with an enormous rough dining table where I could picture an army of twenty marauders eating mutton and drinking mead at. It was offset by delicate chairs. A living room area with worn leather sectional and red Persian rug and giant television. A library area blocked off with free-standing bookshelves, I could see through the stacks to a desk and a comfy chaise nestled there.

In the corner I spied the bathroom, everything in its glossy black tile. The bedroom was in another corner, hidden partially by an Oriental screen. King bed, simple metal frame, with white bedding.

"It looks like a magazine showroom in here, Marlow. Makes me embarrassed of my place."

He chuckled, "Well, thank you. When not working I am often home, alone. Reading interior design magazines. Now come with me, please."

I couldn't tell if he was teasing me. So, I said nothing and followed him toward the bathroom. "Now, you tell me what you want to eat, I will order it while you shower. I'll give you some sweats to wear okay?"

I nodded dumbly, requested Chinese which always provided comfort to me for some reason. No wait, I knew the reason, Dot loved Chinese and we ate it all the time. I'd even taken to ordering her favorites just to feel close to her. Pork lo mein, eggrolls, and chicken and broccoli. He pushed me into the bathroom with a towel and a change of clothes and closed the door behind me.

In the bathroom I recoiled when I caught my reflection. No wonder he looked so worried. One whole cheek was bruised an ugly purple-green. I prodded at it, hissing. I also had an egg on the back of my head from headbutting him. God, what an asshole that guy was. My hair was a mess, the bun having dissolved into a knot with a wild halo of escaped snarls. I was filthy from being on the ground outside, my blouse torn, my blazer grimy. My blue eyes looked spookier than usual, practically glowing.

I got in the shower and ran it as hot as my sore body and raw wrists would allow.

After a good soak and scrub I felt a little better. Getting out, I toweled off and put on the sweats and the T-shirt Marlow was kind enough to lend me. They smelled of fabric softener and were both well-worn and soft. I could weep for the kindness.

Out on the table the food had already arrived and he had filled a glass of wine for me. "You are really my hero today, Marlow." He laughed and sat with me, sipping his wine.

"I called Regine and the station, let them know you had been located. Do you want to press charges against those morons for abduction and battery?"

I groaned and put my hand over my eyes. "I don't know, a part of me says yes because 'hello' look at my face, but on the other side I would prefer to not get on anyone else's radar. I also don't want you to get in trouble. They did have good, if fucked up, intentions, and were trying to stop the apocalypse or whatever. Ugh, just let me eat and think about it."

He nodded and gestured to the paper takeout containers.

I began wolfing down my food, only when I came up for air did I notice him watching me with a weird look on his face. "Yes?"

"When I found your things and realized you'd been taken, I just about lost my mind. This just feels like it's my fault. You were attacked, imprisoned, and you had to see me, well, not at my best...I'm just happy that you're okay. I'm so sorry."

"It's fine. You can't beat yourself up, really. It's all fine."

"I saw Persimmon, she says hi by the way."

My face gave me away and he smirked, "In all the madness I forgot you even went to see her, how'd it go?"

"She's a real piece of work. Thinks very highly of herself, but she has agreed to help where she can. The coven is trying to come up with some way to find others like you. Resurrectionists. But she seems to think, like those moron necromancers, that *you* are the missing puzzle piece. A Master of the Dead. *A Zombie Queen.*" The food I was chewing turned to gravel in my mouth. I swallowed with a grimace and took a deep drink of wine.

"Are you?" he asked.

"I am not any of those things," I said.

"Why does everyone seem to think you are then?" His voice was soft, eyes kind, but he was also a cop. He was working on a case that kept circling back to me. Hell, he just had to rescue me from kidnappers and could have exposed his nature. He could have lost his job. Did it matter if I was anything they thought I was? Wouldn't stop them from grabbing me and killing me like the other victims they thought were the "one." I desperately wanted to talk about anything else.

He wasn't pushing. I think that was why I could even talk further, outside of Dot and Persimmon in college, there wasn't anyone I felt comfortable talking about this stuff with. "When my parents died, I was so devastated. Nearly catatonic. I just couldn't fathom that they could leave me all alone. I loved them so completely and their death just destroyed me." I blew out a breath, shaking my head to keep the tears at bay. This was a wound that never healed.

"At their funeral, I just kept thinking: this is not real, this is a joke, anytime now they will just sit up in their coffins and smile and I will go to them. I wanted them back so bad. Over and over in my head, *come back, come back*. And then...they did. Crawled out of their coffins. They were all stitched up and covered in makeup. They reached for me, and I went to them, and they held me. And everyone was screaming, and telling me to put them back, that I was evil, that it was heretical to raise the dead in the church. And all the while I clung to my dad, cold, but still him in there."

I stopped, the emotion too much after such a day. I hated the combination of grief and shame this memory brought to the fore. The loss felt as fresh then as it did all those years ago. I swiped at my tears and forced myself on.

"They tried to make me release them, but I was a child. I didn't know how I did it. And besides, I didn't want to, they didn't want to go, they wanted to stay with me. So...they fought to protect me. They were trying to keep me safe, trying to keep our family together. People got hurt. In the end, a police officer put bullets in both my parent's heads, right in front of me. Said it was for everyone's best interests. They thought I'd lost control of them, that they were violent because I raised them without an animus or anything. But that wasn't the case, they were trying to protect me, to stay with me." I paused, slicking my wet hair back. "It was unheard of for one so young to do anything like that before, apparently. It made the papers. They called me a *Little Zombie Queen*. In one fell swoop I lost my parents twice and was branded a freak."

"So, you could be the one." He said gently. I sipped my wine, not sure where to go from there. I avoided his eyes, sure I would cry more if I looked his way. No one knew that whole story, save Dot, even Persimmon had only known a severely abridged version. I felt his hand on mine, and I met Marlow's eyes. "A child's love knows no boundaries, Selene, and yours transcended death. There is no shame in that, you were an innocent."

"Anyways," I pulled my hand back, a little flustered by his tenderness and my honesty. "I have been alone ever since. I thought I had found a friend in Persimmon in college. She made me feel like maybe someone finally had my back, someone loved me and wasn't afraid of me. Then I met Greg through her, human, and totally normal, but sweet and open-minded and he liked me. With Persimmon as my best friend, a boyfriend, and school going well, I started to feel like I had a place in the world. Like maybe I could have a normal life and not always be alone."

"Then she slept with Greg." My eyes shot up, surprised.

"How do you know that?"

He leaned back in his chair, "She told me. She was very forthcoming in regards to her transgressions." I huffed, embarrassed that Marlow knew so much about me.

"It was a long time ago, I can't believe she told you. She never does anything without an ulterior motive."

"Maybe. But she also expressed concern for your safety. She wanted me to protect you," he said.

"Why you?" I felt pathetic sitting in a borrowed T-shirt mooning over noodles. A jilted orphan who gets cheated on and needs protection.

"I would guess because I'm not human and am involved with the case. But more because I...well I consider you a friend and although I don't know you very well, I suppose I *care* about you. I don't want anything bad to happen to you," he said, opening his long fingers wide.

"You sure my Zombie Queen powers aren't compelling you?" I asked dryly.

"No, Selene, I don't think you are influencing me at all. I see a kindred spirit in you. If we are being honest, and you have been very honest with me, I'd say I am a lonely person too. Because of what I am, it's hard to make real connections. I can see that you are more than just a resurrectionist. If you let more people in they'd know that."

"I've tried that before. They tend to leave me for Persimmon. She's the fun one, I'm the spooky, depressing one," I replied lamely, trying to sort through my feelings.

"That was a long time ago, Selene. You were both kids." He continued as I frowned, "She is also vain and egotistical. But beneath all that bravado, she is very insecure. Honestly, I think she was threatened by the connection you and Greg had. She's probably been as jealous of you for being genuine as you were of her for being popular."

"Maybe, and you're right, we were quite young. I...I care about you too, like as a new friend. I catch myself thinking about you when you aren't around, wonder about what you wonder about. Been awhile since I've thought about anybody." I felt myself blush at the admission. Tiredness and wine were making me too forthcoming.

Finally, I risked meeting his eyes, they watched me intensely, they were so dark as to be almost black. And the look felt...more than friendly. That reminded me of all the aspects of vampires I didn't know. How inhuman were they? Did he like me as more than a friend? Could he even have normal sex? Did I want to have sex with him? Did he kill people? Could we just date? Did I want to date him? I just said I liked him as a friend. Ugh, it all seemed a bit heavy for this specific day.

"Well," he said sensing my discomfort, "we now know we like each other, as for what that means, could mean, all of that, we can save that for another day that hasn't been as harrowing. Let's go watch mindless television and relax."

Under a wool blanket, snuggled in pillows, I felt safe and content. "I love this couch, I love this apartment. It's so homey here. My house is basically a place my clothes live and where I sleep."

He flipped around, settling on an old black-and-white movie on TCM. "Oh hey, this takes me back. You know I saw this in the theater?"

I squinted at him over the pillows, "How old are you?"

"Ninety. I will be ninety-one in June."

"Wow. Ninety years old, and how old were you when you..." I gestured with my hand, crooking my fingers like fangs, unsure the PC term for becoming undead.

He sighed and put his bare feet up on the coffee table, he had nice looking feet. "I was thirty-two. So, it's been...fifty-eight years. That's a lot of moves and new identities. As I get older, I understand why the really old ones just stop bothering and live in a hole someplace."

"Why not just be out as a vampire? Out in the world? Then you could just be your age and be you and not have to keep remaking yourself."

He gave me a pitying look, "Not everyone is like you, Selene. Most people are very uncomfortable if they know what I am. Think of how much space people give you and you are human. I wouldn't be able to work, who'd hire me? I don't know that I am ready to be openly shunned."

"How do you get blood then?" His jaw clenched, eyes on the screen, I could see the tightness under the skin, "I'm sorry. If it's not too rude of a question. I have no idea the etiquette. And with us digging through all my skeletons..." My cheeks felt hot.

He kept his eyes on the TV, "I drink plasma from blood bags, they're in the fridge, but that's like subsisting on crackers. I also have live donors. Usually casual lovers or sex workers, whom I pay." He turned and speared me with his eyes, emotion locked away, "Does that disgust you?"

I fought to keep my face neutral, sensing this was a test. "No, no. It makes sense, you have to eat, right?" My mind reeled picturing Marlow hanging out with prostitutes in back alleys. Was I disgusted? The idea of drinking blood made my stomach churn sure, but if the alternative was dying, who was I to judge? "I'd imagine it would be a pain having to hang out at bars and pick up people every time you were hungry. It's hard enough to meet anyone normally. I can't throw any stones anyway since I spent the day with mummy mice of my own creation. I'm pretty disgusting to regular people too."

He patted my foot on the couch. "Let's just watch the movie, it's a nice love story."

I watched for about five minutes before succumbing to the soft pillows and warm blankets. Then I was dead asleep.

THIRTEEN

Germaine sat across from John at Java's. The small boutique coffee shop was a block off of campus, and it was exactly the cool hang-out Germaine always fantasized about meeting friends at back in Bixby. It was in an old bank with a gleaming bronze vault in the back, brick walls, and towering ceilings. The music was obscure, the baristas covered in tattoos and the clientele cool and young. She'd been going there as often as she could since she'd started school, but this was the first time going with a boy. John arrived early and got them the same table they'd sat at before when they first met. There were plenty of empty ones so she knew he'd chosen it deliberately. The thoughtfulness excited her more than she'd be comfortable admitting.

No boys in Bixby had ever really pursued her. Even her prom date Todd was secretly gay, they'd met at the Christian "Make My Kid Normal" camp and he needed her as a beard. She obliged because he was handsome and popular, and no one was going to ask her otherwise. So, she supposed, he was as much her beard as well, for one night she could be a regular girl. But the memory wasn't a fond one and the shame grated. She had to look at the damn prom photo every time she went back home, as her mother had hung it in a prominent spot on the wall in the main hallway. In it, Germaine and Todd were stiffly posed with forced smiles. Her mother was so proud of the proof that her daughter had accomplished something normal, for once.

"Sorry I'm late, I was working on a paper," she said sheepishly, the real reason she was late was trying everything she had on in some combination with every other thing. Her roommate Jasmine came in during this frantic closet exploration and kindly helped her pick out something appropriate: a blazer, a shiny camisole, and a pair of jeans. Jasmine even suggested she wear dressy heels with the jeans. She'd also helped French braid her hair and apply some makeup. It was more than Germaine had ever worn outside of Halloween, but not half as much as Jasmine wore on a daily basis.

"You look amazing, now I feel underdressed," John said, and she blushed. She'd never thought to combine the blazer she wore to the job interview with jeans. The pumps she'd last worn to her high school graduation pinched and she was definitely wobbly in them. But the outfit made her look more mature and almost presentable. Which, considering she couldn't remember the last time she thought anything so positive about her appearance, was definitely a plus.

"What would you like? I love their cappuccino and their cupcakes are really good." She'd have what he was having, she said eventually, too nervous to consider the menu further.

He went to the counter, and she fussed with her hands, deciding to pillow one on top of the other, like a lady. While she waited, she glanced around the room. There were a few students with headphones on, their rapt focus on laptop screens. In the corner, an older man in a corduroy jacket was reading a paperback and sipping coffee from a paper cup. Germaine was a little disappointed that it was empty enough that no one acknowledged them. This time, unlike prom, she was with someone cute because he liked her, for real. It was disappointing not to show that off more, rub someone's face in it.

John returned with the drinks and two cupcakes, "I got the red velvet and the vanilla lavender, hope that's all right."

"It's perfect, thank you so much."

They sat in silence for a moment, the awkwardness of the date settling in between them. She started to ask a question just as he did, and they both chuckled nervously. He gestured for her to proceed, "Sorry, I was going to ask what you study?"

"Oh, I took this semester off, but I am a junior, double major in arcane ritual and finance. It's a funny combination, but I am still not sure what I want to do. Dad is an accountant, and my mom runs her own business. And you?" He sipped his drink, leaving a white mustache of milk foam on his upper lip, it charmed her and she wished she were bold enough to wipe it away with her finger and then lick it.

"I still don't know what I want to major in. I am thinking English."

He frowned, leaning in and dropping his voice, "English? That's surprising, why not do something in magic? MU is known for its magic majors, one of the first colleges to offer them, in fact."

Germaine cleared her throat, "Why would I?"

He glanced around and leaned further, "Well, it's not something I tell everyone but, I can sort of see auras. I can see yours. It's not human...err normal human, that is." He smiled, trying to soften it.

Germaine felt her cheeks redden, she couldn't meet his eyes. She couldn't even have one coffee with a cute boy.

"Hey, I think it's cool looking. I didn't mean to make you uncomfortable."

"I'm not used to talking about it, openly. Where I'm from, it made me kind of an outcast. It's why I wear contacts."

He looked around and lowered his voice conspiratorially, "What can you do?"

Germaine debated lying, or leaving, and in that instant, she recalled Selene's warning about the killer. He was hunting for young resurrectionists. She knew she should be wary of John's interest in her and because of what she was, and wasn't.

But when she looked at him, really looked, she saw he also had a strange aura, subtle, she probably wouldn't have noticed if she hadn't been looking. The edges were dark and fuzzy, reaching out as if underwater.

It relieved her, as he wasn't as human as he appeared either apparently. She felt angry that Selene and the murders intruded on her first real date at all. So instead, she told him about Bixby, and a very edited version of being such an outsider there.

Germaine told him how Bixby was not as progressive as the big cities, only green magic related to crops or weather, or healing abilities, were celebrated and even then, with a bit of side-eye and quiet judgment. Church pews were still more full than empty on Sundays where she was from. She wasn't used to magic being normal. She'd been shocked that MU offered so many magic and ritual classes. She told him that her home state made assisted resurrection illegal. Half-life's were not granted any rights, instead immediately put down if found. It was like there were two Americas, to her, one side that had welcomed the addition to magic and monsters, and the other which still viewed them to be the work of the devil.

"It's a different world there," she finally said, feeling a weight had been lifted in telling him. John was a good listener.

"You know what I think? I think that it's not that different. There have always, always been creatures and magic in the world. Sure, it only went mainstream recently. But there have always been special people, with abilities, either witches with their earth magic, or necromancers and the like who could make things happen using science and ritual. There were people who could see the future, change their bodies, or move things with their minds. They've always been. We just talk about it more." He spread his arms wide, "Welcome to Goat Hill, Germaine, where you can be yourself, whatever that may be. You are far from flyover Bixby and the shame that went with it. Hi, my name is John, and I am a college dropout with an interest in magic but no real power." He extended his hand.

"Germaine Whately and I am a...resurrectionist." They shook hands, Germaine grinning all the way.

"I am so happy to meet you." He replied. And he really was.

After all, it was two and a half weeks until the new moon.

I woke to a dry throat and total disorientation. I stared at unfamiliar brick walls and closed shades. Panic instantly sent my heart revving as I tried to get my bearings. It all came back, the abduction, the squeaks of dead mice, the bindings around my wrists, Marlow's face covered in blood. A tick of a clock, slow whoosh of oscillating fans on the ceiling. *Where the...?*

Marlow's. I reminded myself I was at Marlow's and safe.

With the curtains drawn I could only guess at what time it was, and Marlow was no longer beside me on the sofa. I sat up and looked around, trying to remember where the bedroom was when I noticed him standing, utterly still, in the center of the room facing me. There was an unnaturalness to the pose and my entire body was instantly alert and afraid.

No.

No, that was not Marlow.

Nigrum Porta, The Black Door, was watching me, his strange liquid body undulating beneath the skin and his horrible mouth opened, this time a word I understood came out, *door.door.door.door. door.door.door.door.door.door.door.door.door.door.door.door.*

Deafening as a tornado.

I screamed, the sound of my voice drowned out by that terrible all-consuming word.

"Selene! *Selene!*" a voice said. I swung my arms frantically, only coming back to myself when I felt my wrists being held down. Marlow's face was above me, his eyes entirely black like two polished pieces of jet in the dim room.

"You were dreaming. You're safe, I'm here and you're safe, can you hear me?" he said, his voice trying to be calm. I nodded, swallowing large gulps of air, I let my eyes go to the space where The Black Door was. But it was empty. It did little to relieve me.

"He was right there. I saw him there watching me. It's not the first time. Before you say it, I don't think it's a dream, Nigrum Porta is real," I said in a rush, embarrassed by how terrified I was. "How can I be safe anywhere if he can find me when I sleep?" A few tears leaked out and I swiped at them, my hands trembling.

"Why didn't you tell me you'd seen him?" he asked gently.

"I don't know, I should have. At first, I thought it was Belinda's memory of him, not mine, which happens sometimes. Though even then, he seemed familiar somehow. After that, with all the talk of Zombie Queens, I guess I didn't want to look like...like it was true. I'm scared."

Marlow sat beside me, close, his face serious. "I won't let anything happen to you." I nodded and before thinking too much about it, I leaned into him and he put an arm around me.

"Did he say or do anything?"

"He said door. Over and over. He wants a door." Fear thrummed in me, I wasn't safe awake or asleep. Awake, I could be snatched up to be kidnapped or ritually sacrificed. In dreams, Nigrum Porta could come and go as he pleased, apparently. I breathed in the smell of laundry soap from his T-shirt and pressed my face to his shoulder, desperately needing to be held and reassured.

"So, nothing new then. We knew he wanted a door. Would you be able to ask him more?"

"I doubt it, he's not really a person. More a shape, his mouth isn't even a mouth. The sound he makes is like being in a screaming tornado. I doubt he wants to have a conversation."

Marlow tightened his arms around me and rested his chin on my head. "But he's reaching out to you. He's trying to tell you something, right?"

I sighed, exhaustion pulled from all sides, "I guess. If watching me sleep and saying *door* a lot is telling me something." It was only cocooned in his embrace, feeling secure and protected, that it dawned on me how isolated I was. Who could I stay with? Would anyone, besides Dot, even notice if I was gone? It made my heart ache. There was no one to turn to with my fears, besides this cop I'd known a week. I was alone without Marlow.

As if my body had a mind of its own I lifted my head, rubbing my cheek against his stubbled one. Our lips were millimeters apart now. A tiny movement and they would be touching, my arms still tight around him, his tight around me. I heard his breath hitch, could feel the uncertainty in the rigidity of his body.

"You've gone through a lot these last few days," he said neutrally. I was sure he was questioning if I was just stressed out and trying to distract myself. I knew that I probably was, but the brain can only take so much. I wanted to shut off the fear and the million other things that troubled me. I wanted to be wanted. I wanted to feel safe. Before I lost my nerve, I pursed my lips and kissed the laugh line at the corner of his mouth. And that was all it took. He turned the last scant distance between us and his mouth was on mine. Hungry.

The kiss was electric. My body pressed to his, his arms encircling me, squeezing me almost too tight, and I loved it. Finally, I broke for air, gasping, and our eyes met in the early morning gloom.

"Wow," I said, feeling silly immediately after. His eyes intense on me.

"Yeah," he finally whispered. I could see him starting to say something, but I was tired of talking and kissed him again to silence him. He groaned and pushed me down, his weight reassuring me. His tongue darted inside my mouth. I felt the press of him hard against my thigh, felt his kisses leave my lips, follow my jawline, settle in the crook of my neck. His hands were on my breasts, over my shirt, then under. I wanted more skin contact, I pushed him back and pulled off my shirt, and then his. He kissed along my bra line, pulling it back to take the nipple into his mouth. It was then I felt two sharp points pressing into the meat of my breast and gasped, my heart trilling and my body suddenly still, he went rigid, his face averted. I could feel his breathing, slow and measured, against my stomach. He finally lifted his head up and met my eyes, his were entirely black and inhuman.

"Are you—are you alright?" I said as the reality that I could be in danger rushed in. He was a *vampire*. Hours ago, I saw him tear out someone's throat.

No one knew where I was. I was so stupid.

"I'm sorry, please don't be frightened. I just got a little carried away. It's been a while. I may need to stop..." He glanced away, chagrined. I wanted to trust him. No, I trusted him. He saved me. It whispered through my mind, gentle as a feather and I knew it was true. Hadn't known him long, but I trusted him. I put my hand on his face tilting it back to mine. I lifted his upper lip with my thumb and his teeth were long enough now they pressed his lower lip. They were needle-sharp at the tips and curved in a little, like a cobra.

"Am I in danger from you?" I whispered. He frowned and started to disentangle from me, but I held his arm. "Am I?"

"Of course not, Selene. How could you—it's just that sex and blood can get a little mixed up if I'm not well-fed. We should stop."

"Does it hurt? Your bite?"

"No, no my saliva numbs the skin."

"How much would you take?"

"Selene, I wouldn't want you to feel weird, or forced, or anything."

I nodded, shushing him with my fingers on his lips. "You saved me. If you can handle it, I would like to continue kissing you. If you can handle it, and it won't hurt too bad, then you can bite me."

"Only if you are sure and feel safe." I nodded and his gaze softened. He leaned forward, lips meeting mine, carefully around the teeth, kissing me tenderly. He traced the lines of my face with his fingertips, then worked his way down my stomach with delicate butterfly kisses, freeing me of my pants.

I had the moment's panic of realizing this was Marlow, that cults were after me, that we still would have to work together, that this would change everything...and then his mouth was on me and all I could do was cry out.

When I was climaxing, gasping, and gripping the couch cushions white-knuckled, I felt the twin sting of a bite on my inner thigh. There was the momentary prick of pain, similar to a dentist's needle, and then a swift warming and numbing of the area. I could see his head rise and fall, feel the hot wetness of his mouth on my skin, but there was no pain. After a few moments he lifted his head, lips wet with blood, and wiped his face on one of our shirts.

His eyes met mine, warily, self-consciously, but my goofy smile erased any doubts and he crawled back up to me. "Kiss me," I pressed lips to his, tasting the tang of my sex, and the metal of my blood.

"I would like to fuck you, if I may," he whispered in my ear.

"Do you have a condom?" I whispered, out of habit.

"I can't get you pregnant, I'm undead if you recall. I'm also immune to any human disease." I wrapped my legs around him. Squeezing his midsection. He was lean, but ropey and hard with muscle. I vaguely remembered some fact that vampires have next to no body fat, that the body turns it into super dense muscle when they are changed. It's why they were so inhumanely strong and fast.

I looked at him in the early morning light. Square jaw, shaved short sandy hair, black button eyes. I welcomed him inside, surprised by the tears in my eyes. I wrapped my legs and arms around him, shocked by how starved I was for another body.

Sometime later, we lay together on the sofa. Me on top, our naked bodies pressed deliciously together. Sated. I sighed into the embrace, enjoying the feel of his chest against my face. He stirred and kissed the top of my head and the tenderness and intimacy nearly caused me to weep. I never wanted to break apart, or to think about what would happen next. Just a little longer in the moment, just the two of us, two bodies, two spirits, and the rest of the world distant as the moon.

Dot was right, even from beyond the grave, I really had needed to get laid. I smiled to myself and dozed, Nigrum Porta far from my thoughts for the time being.

FOURTEEN

I officially woke a few hours later, feeling rested and contented for the first time in a long time. I could smell coffee and followed it to the kitchen where Marlow was standing over a pot.

"Would you like some toast?" he said.

A few minutes later, I was finishing my fourth piece of toast with butter, watching Marlow nurse his coffee, shirtless in pajama pants. I was struck again by how pale and thin he was, his chest nearly hairless, his body taut corded muscle.

"So..." I said, leaving my words hanging, the reality that we'd slept together hovered between us. After my college boyfriend, I'd barely dated and only slept with a few other guys. Never anything serious. An awkward date or two, going to someone's place, then the "I'll call you sometime" as I left in the morning.

The night before had been nice. I hoped Marlow felt the same and wasn't choking on regret. He'd been quiet as I ate, besides the basic pleasantries of asking how I slept and all that. For a nearly century-old man, who presumably had his share of overnight paramours, he was as awkward as I was the morning after. A part of me wished I could read his mind, see if he regretted it.

Please don't, I don't.

"So, you get enough to eat?" he finally said, his eyes were brown now, the color of wet wood.

"—Do you ever eat? I'm sorry if that's rude, I just realized I have never seen you eat anything. But you have bread here and coffee."

"I don't have much appetite for food. It doesn't taste like anything to me and it's hard to digest. Only blood really has...flavor. But I always keep a few basic food items in the house, out of habit."

"I see." For his guests, no doubt. I bit into my toast, "And...how was my blood? Good flavor?" I asked, as I wiped crumbs from my face. I could feel my cheeks redden, already regretting trying to be playful. I was far out of my depth.

Marlow also looked embarrassed. He cleared his throat. "Well, since you asked, it was excellent, very restorative. Thank you for that gift."

"It was surprisingly unpainful. It's only a little achy now." I probed at my inner thigh, noting the soreness.

"Back in the old days we liked to drink from sleeping victims."

"Ah like big, terrifying mosquitos or bedbugs." He nodded and sipped his coffee.

I leaned back in the chair, looking around the apartment in the daytime. I'd meant what I said the night before, his home felt homier than my own. I liked being there with him. I liked him. As if he picked the thoughts from my head he said, "How are you feeling about everything last night?"

How did I feel? I felt good, happy even. But I was also scared, there was a killer out there and various factions who thought either I was the key to the ritual or the next victim. As soon as the post-coital bubble popped, I would be back out there, hunted. But the way he watched me made me think that was not the everything he meant.

"Good. I don't think I realized how much I needed...well never mind. It was great. No regrets. How do you feel about it?" I speared him with my eyes.

"No regrets on my side either. I have been attracted to you longer than I'd like to admit and be professional. Probably your Zombie Queen powers at work."

Grinning like a kid, I reached out and took his hand, "Really? I had a feeling you liked me. But as far as everything else? I feel scared. Nigrum Porta is in my mind, people want to kidnap me, so I am unsafe at my work and home. I can't hide here forever. I have to work, I have so many clients. People are dying all the time."

"You could though, stay here, at least until the next moon. Hide.

You could watch TV all day, naked if you want, and I will provide you with iron-rich takeout."

"Tempting. But no, if the Nigrum Porta can find me here, then he can find me anywhere. And if our killers are using a spell to track resurrectionists, then they can track me down anywhere as well. What we need to do now is follow up with Persimmon and I want to call Karl and freak out on him about those fucking clown kidnappers." My phone was buzzing, as if on cue, I walked over and pulled it from my purse. "Weird, it's Karl."

"Your powers astound," Marlow said with quirked lips.

I answered, "You have a lot of nerve, and a lot of explaining to do, very quickly, or I will involve the police. I was kidnapped, knocked out and put in a trunk, tied to chair. Fucking kidnapped."

Karl, to his credit, did not try to deny anything, "Selene," he sounded relieved, "I don't know what to say. You are so right to be angry, what happened to you was barbaric and totally unacceptable. I told my cabal about the murders because I wanted their help and of course to protect you, and those like you. I had no idea Lucinda had ordered you captured. It's unbelievable. She is normally so practical."

"Well, I was tied up in some suburban basement, and I am rocking a black eye from your *protection*. Did you call for any reason besides an apology, perhaps with some useful information since apparently everyone thinks I'm *the perfect sacrifice*."

"Ever since we spoke I've been researching. The obscure texts I've found describe the ritual needing an untainted source, a pure resurrectionist, a virgin. I think they were going off of this translation which is why they haven't sought you out."

"Yes, everyone knows that already! Besides repeatedly failing, why would they deviate from that interpretation now?"

"Because they've failed three times. Lucinda wanted you isolated after I talked about your abilities, to be safe. But these guys probably don't know you are so powerful. I'd assumed you weren't a virgin..."

I risked looking at Marlow and thinking about the night before. "No, I'm not."

"They probably assume that as well. I think you are the perfect vessel. But as long as our killers don't know that...you should be safe."

"Not safe from you all," I said, aware of Marlow watching me close.

"Selene, you have more raw death magic than anyone else in Goat Hill."

"Great, thanks. I can use that on my business cards when this shit settles. Find me something we can use."

"I will keep working on this night and day," I rolled my eyes and walked in a circuit around the apartment. "I must ask you Selene, the vampire that you summoned, who is he? And have you always been able to command the undead? Did Dot know?" I could hear that same note of awe in his voice, like Lucinda. Fucking power-hungry necromancers.

"That's none of your business, Karl. Besides that, you've shown I can't trust you. Also, he's a cop. So, tell your cabal morons that if I even suspect one of them is near me, they will either be exsanguinated by my friend, or hauled into the police station for kidnapping. Or both. We clear?"

"Crystal, my dear. Again, my apologies."

"One more thing, Karl, Lucinda said that if it wouldn't potentially cause the end times or whatever, that she would just give me to *them*. Which implies she may know who they are."

Karl was silent a beat, long enough I was about to repeat his name. "She had some theories."

"You want to start paying me back? You get me those theories."

"I will."

"It's the least you can do. I can only imagine what Dot would say about this. I thought I could trust you." My voice cracked, as much as I hated it. Let him know how hurt I was. Dot would have skinned him alive.

"You're right, Selene. She would have probably killed me herself, then brought me back to kill me again. She was brutal and protective of those she loved. She loved you like a daughter."

"Yeah." I hung up, swiping my damp eyes. Marlow came up and put an arm around me, I stiffened. Were we rushing things? Was this too fast? Regardless, I didn't push him away.

"You okay?" he asked gently. I nodded. "Did you volunteer me to kill those necromancers for you? Not that I mind entirely."

I laughed, "I did. I'm glad you don't mind."

"How about we take it easy the rest of the weekend, avoid kidnappers, murders, and all that unpleasantness?"

Peter was sitting at his desk early Monday morning drumming his fingers, scrolling across police reports and activity when he saw it.

An APB for Selene Shade on Friday night, for a possible abduction.

He doubted there was more than one Selene Shade in the city. His blood had turned to ice in his veins as he stared at her name on the screen. He found her number in his phone and called. It rang and rang, then voicemail. He left a message to call him as soon as she got the message and that he was worried. For good measure he fired off a quick email as well.

Peter was not a crime reporter, he was the local events and music features guy for the *Goat Hill Examiner*. He fantasized about writing something meatier, and his piece about half-lifes could be just that. Their date hadn't been stellar and he knew he'd offended her somehow, but he still liked her enough to worry. There was a killer on the loose. Her line of work was dangerous, and while Goat Hill was known to be pretty liberal about the inhuman elements, still had plenty of folks who'd be happy to bring back witch trials.

Was it an upset client? A jilted lover? A fanatical religious sect who thought she was evil? Or the cult killer on the loose? Crazy times.

What he learned in the time he'd been working on his article was that resurrectionists were feared, even as their services were becoming more popular and mainstream. While the baby boomers did not want to die, even if that meant being undead seniors eating mice, a lot of society didn't love it. It was easy to blame the only people who could bring the dead back.

Enough to kill her over?

He was debating driving over to her office, when his editor stuck his head in the doorway. Chet smiled wide, which could be quite intimidating, as he was a giant wall of a man that filled the doorway.

"So, I finally got around to reading your multi-issue story pitch, Pete," he said, voice low, Barry White low.

"Oh yeah, Chief." He'd been compiling his notes all week, getting everything together, wanting to get the half-life piece greenlit.

"I think a story about half-lifes and resurrectionists, the business of it, and its effect on our community is a great idea. Especially considering your own father is entertaining becoming a half-life himself, it'd bring in a real human-interest element to be so close to the story." Chet entered the small space and lowered onto a creaky old office chair. He crossed his huge arms over his barrel chest. This close, Pete could see the sprinkling of salt and pepper in Chet's close-cropped hair. "I liked what you have given me so far, so let's run with it. Your other assignments will take priority. But yeah, I'll sign off on your pitch. We've done other half-life stories over the years, but nothing this thorough."

Peter grinned wide, feeling elated that one of his ideas, finally, was getting the go-ahead. He'd been taking methodical notes from Harley and the other nurses at the hospice, as well as from his father and Selene. He planned to also go see Dania Barabas with his sister Iris, check her out in comparison to Selene as far as pricing and business went. He planned to interview half-lifes and their families. This could be the real deal. A darker part of him knew that he could even incorporate Selene going missing into the story. It would be a sensational element.

"Fantastic. You will not regret this!" he said smiling ear to ear.

"Let's hope not," Chet said rising, "I want the rough outline on my desk next week to look over, got it? Stick to the facts, I don't want some lurid tabloid piece. I want thoughtful, scientific, pulling heartstrings, real. Ok?"

Peter nodded excitedly, already picturing the Pulitzer he'd win. Probably a little ahead of the game, but strangely very little had been written in depth about the half-life phenomenon and the individuals in the community who could literally raise the dead. It was about time.

The weekend went by in a lazy blur of television, takeout, and elaborate acrobatic sex acts. Mid-Saturday, my cell phone had run out of battery, and I didn't even bother to charge it until I went to bed Sunday night. I just couldn't be bothered. In short, it was probably the best weekend I'd ever had. But, by Monday morning, the world beckoned, and I had a business to run, and Marlow had to get back to stopping the cult and saving the world.

We were halfway to my house when I remembered Germaine Whately, my new hire. I had forgotten so completely about her in the craziness of my abduction and rescue that I almost felt guilty. I filled Marlow in, discussing the pros and cons of an apprentice, but also that she fit the profile eerily well.

"You think she's in danger?" he said, thoughtful as he navigated the thick morning traffic.

"If I were hunting virginal, powerful resurrectionists, she checks a lot of boxes."

"So, while everyone is running around trying to protect you from being the next victim, you think we should be trying to protect someone you forgot to tell us about?" he chided.

I grimaced, "Yes, that does sum it up. If nothing else, I should warn her now, and if I take her on as an apprentice, then at least we'd be together." I groaned into my hands hoping nothing happened to her while I was on my little weekend vacation.

"First things first, let's get you packed up, then I will take you to the office. By then, I should be able to get a detail assigned to you and maybe her. After my shift today, you and I can follow up with Persimmon, okay? She called and left a message that they may have a lead."

He met my eyes, and I felt a confidence there, he had my back, he wanted to be on my team. It would be a lie to say my alarm bells didn't start ringing something fierce as well. Trusting someone to watch my back was very, very against my nature. The few times I had, it burned me in the end. My parents, Persimmon, Greg my college boyfriend. Dot, who up and died on me. I'd often felt it was better to go at it alone, at least you know who you can count on. But Marlow, like a foot jammed in a door, got in. It scared me.

We got to my place and I ran in, packing up a suitcase with work clothes, some pajamas, my entire underwear drawer and some toiletries. I watered my few neglected plants and tossed out anything in the fridge that would rot or stink up the place. After making my bed, cracking a window, and taking the trash out, I looked around the place and wondered when I would feel safe there again. Wondered if I would ever feel safe alone anywhere again. I shut and locked the door.

"Goddamn, do I have a backlog of emails and voicemails." I groaned as I settled in at my desk to work: a few deaths had happened since my abduction and sleepover, eager clients waiting to arrange resurrections. More future clients looking for consultations. Then, a frantic voicemail from Peter Partridge asking me to call him.

There was also a strangely vague message from Amar Patel, the half-life I saw at the restaurant the other night, asking me to call him back and let him know I was all right.

There was a message from Dania Barabas asking to call her when I had a moment, regarding the murders. Also, kismet as she was about to get a lot of referrals from my office until this cult situation could be managed.

Most importantly, the message from Germaine Whately accepting the job

"God, I am the worst." I muttered, "Prime virginal sacrifice victim comes right to my door, and I am too distracted by my own shit to warn her properly."

Marlow sighed and sipped his coffee, "Give yourself a break, you did get *kidnapped*."

"Yeah on *Friday*, it's Monday. Whew, okay you should go. I have to play catch up now." He appeared conflicted, like he didn't want to leave me, and that feeling of something: excitement, arousal, hope... fluttered in my chest. *Please don't hurt me, please let this be something real*, I chanted internally.

"Ok, yes, you stay here behind security doors and cameras and don't go see any clients until your unmarked escort arrives okay?" I rolled my eyes, waving him off as another series of emails flooded my inbox. He took a few steps to the door, froze and came back, circled my desk and leaned down, brushing his lips over mine. I smiled despite myself, pleased when I saw a mirrored expression on his face. "See you later."

Later.

"Germaine, hello this is Selene, so sorry not to get back to you sooner," I said to her voicemail, "I would love to have you come in and start an apprenticeship, do call me back ASAP to talk scheduling. I... also wanted to talk to you a bit more about a police case I am helping with. As I told you the other day, and again I don't want to freak you out, but it does look like the killer is targeting young resurrectionist women around your campus. The killer is pretending to be a student, has gone by the name of James. So, if anyone like that rings a bell, please let me know, or call the cops, and please avoid them. Try to travel around in pairs as well. Okay, thanks, and call me back as soon as you get this." I rattled the number off and hung up. Hoping that I didn't just scare the crap out of her.

I was arranging my appointments and resurrections for the day when my buzzer rang downstairs.

"What now?" I mumbled, checking my calendar and seeing no appointments for another hour. My personal security cop had not arrived yet. At the door was Peter Partridge. He waved his hands frantically at the camera and I buzzed him in.

He must have flown up the stairs because a moment later, he was pushing into my office, out of breath with relief plain on his face.

"Thank God, I was really worried about you! Saw your APB on the police blotters. What the hell happened to your face?!" His arms were outstretched as if he would embrace me but then dropped them, thinking better of it. In all the busyness, I'd forgotten about my banged-up face. "The APB said possible abduction! I really thought you were dead! What happened?"

This was tricky, Peter was a reporter and in the short time I'd known him, naturally curious. While it was flattering that he was worried about me, especially when I thought no one in the world would be, it was also difficult to know what to tell him. On the one hand, feeding him any information could actually help stop the killers; on the other, it could also compromise the investigation causing the killers to move to another city or burrow deep and go into hiding. I touched the fading black eye with delicate fingers.

"It was a weird misunderstanding," I finally said lamely. Deciding better to be vague.

"A misunderstanding! The police were involved. And your face!" He plopped down into one of the chairs facing my desk. Had it only been days since he was there as a client? Had it only been four days since our date? It felt like a lifetime had passed.

"It..." I paused buying time, sipped my rapidly cooling coffee out of a mug with a tombstone on it and met his frantic eyes, "...was a misunderstanding where the police thought I was in danger, but I wasn't. And this," I gestured to my black eye, "was just a weird coincidence where I fell in the parking lot and hit my face on my car." He did not look like he was buying what I was selling. Not surprising as I was a terrible liar. I plodded on, "When they found me, they dropped the bulletin. You must not have seen that part. Besides, why are you looking at police blotters? Aren't you in entertainment?"

"Normally, yes, I write about events. But I am working on something...different, something I wanted to talk to you about. Wait, what do you mean *when* they found you?"

"It's nothing really, just an odd turn of phrase. As you can see I am okay."

"Why didn't you call me back? I've been really worried."

"I took the weekend off, left my charger at home, and now am crawling out of my mountains of emails and voicemails. Really. I'm sorry you were worried. I know it all looks bad but it was really just a series of odd events."

He blew out a breath and raked his hands through his hair, sending it skyward. "Well, good. Though it sounds like some sort of battered wife, 'ran into a door' bullshit to me, but fine, you don't want to tell me the truth, fine. I will drop it. I'm glad you are okay. Now, with that sorted, I had a nice time the other night and I would like to take you out again on another date and tell you more about an article I want to write."

I am sure that I grimaced then, before checking myself. First, I had to lie to him about my adventures with the necromancers and now this? I wasn't sure if he was asking me out or wanting to interview me, or both. I guess it wasn't my imagination that the first date had felt a little like an interview.

"I had a nice time too, Peter, really. But I started seeing someone else—"

"When? Since Friday?" he responded, quick as a viper. Something about the shift, from concerned, to flirtatious, to nasty, raised my hackles. Peter Partridge was charming, but he was also the type an old lady would call a cad, and he probably did not get told no a lot. People like that, who waltz through spaces and always get what they want pretty much always put me off. "Who are you seeing? Or are you just trying to save my feelings?" I put my hand up, trying to stay civil and not just kick him out.

"Not that it's any business of yours, as we just shared one meal, but this other situation progressed this weekend, more exclusive, taking me off the market," I think, I hope.

"Oh wow, okay then. You aren't just saying this to soften the blow, right? In the 'it's not you, it's me' style? Because I do like you. I hope you wouldn't make up some fake guy because you think I'm a creep." *He's fishing.*

I shook my head no, smiling. "No, I would not protect that ego, Peter. I really am seeing someone, a police officer. He is real, I assure you."

"Okay fine, not my business, but would you be willing to get a drink—or coffee—with me, as a friend then, to talk about this article I'm working on? Help demystify your trade? Give your perspective to the suspicious and prejudiced?" He smiled wide, his slightly crooked teeth and mop of hair making him look boyish.

My first instinct was to say no and kick him out, but part of me paused. There may come a time when knowing a reporter, one who wanted to cover resurrectionists in a positive light, could be really handy. He could help scrub our reputation. Hell, he could aid in stopping the killer even. Perhaps I was giving too much credence to Peter's journalistic prowess, but better to keep him at the ready and friendly.

"Yeah, Peter, that could be arranged."

He stood, "Okay! That's great. Getting this article greenlit is a big deal for me, for my career, and I want to do it right." He took a few steps backwards still wearing that boyish grin, "A cop huh? Can't picture you dating a cop. Well that's fine. If this cop thing fizzles, you'll remember me, won't you?" I nodded, rising as well.

He was at the door when he said, "My dad is still on the fence, about it all, so I will be in touch about that too...lots of questions."

"Yes, keep me posted on your father. And, Peter, thanks for checking in. It's good to know people are looking out for me." I blushed a little at my honesty. He winked and let himself out, ever the cool guy.

FIFTEEN

Marlow got to the precinct, the guilt for leaving Selene alone dogging him the whole way. She was a grown woman, and she would be fine he repeated over and over again. Especially now that she knew to keep her eyes open.

Robinson was at her desk, paging through files, she looked up with a smirk when he passed her.

"Well?" she said.

"Well what?"

"I'm curious about your weekend. Last I heard you were running around here screaming like a madman and terrifying young rookies that our resurrectionist may have been abducted. Then we get a quick 'never mind, found her.' Then nothing and model employee Marlow, who never takes a day off, cashes in not one but *two personal days* during an active murder investigation. Now you come in here, looking fresh as a daisy, may even be a blush on those pasty white cheeks..."

"All right, Regine, fair enough. I will give you an update, but it stays between you and me for now. Very need to know. Okay?" He pressed her until she shrugged, glancing around to make sure the coast was clear.

"Okay spill," she said.

He eased into his chair and rolled over to her side of the desk,

"Selene was abducted the other night. Not by our killers, by a random cabal of necromancers."

"You're kidding?! What the hell for?"

"Well this is why I didn't file a report, yet, I don't want a paper trail. In part because we don't know who up the chain would see it. But they felt that Selene is either the next victim or the perfect victim, and they were trying to 'protect' her. So, their hearts were in the right place, theoretically, but their brains..." He dropped his voice to a near whisper. "They knocked her out and tied her up in a basement."

"Holy shit. Is she all right?"

"Banged up, the dickhead who snatched her smacked her around, but otherwise fine. Obviously a little freaked out. She decided against filing a report, to again, keep things quiet. If one group thinks she may be the right type of sacrifice, it wouldn't be hard to get others thinking it too."

"Jesus." Robinson squinted at him, wheels turning. "So, hold up, you went and rescued her, with no backup and no one knowing you were there? And you used police resources to locate her?"

Marlow leaned into his partner, his face gone serious, "I don't know who we can trust about any of this. The department is not set up for...*supernatural* crime, you know that. They try, but one old occultist is not going to do it. I did not bring my weapon, and it was not so much a police mission as a friendly neighborhood rescue. Figured it was better not to bring any attention, especially possible media attention to this situation. We don't know who may be in cahoots with these groups. I made the choice to protect her, over protocol. But I am telling you."

"Where is *Selene* now?" Robinson asked, eyes shrewd. She may not know what her partner was, but she had been on the force fifteen years, and she could smell bullshit from a mile off.

"She's at work, with a detail assigned her in case anyone else decides to 'save' her."

"And all this weekend? Where was she?" His eyes slid away to the stack of paperwork. He started to roll away but her hand shot out and grabbed the arm of his chair. "I tried to call you a bunch of times, all I got was that cagey one-sentence text. 'Found her, see you Monday.'"

He debated how honest he wanted to be. "She was pretty rattled after being kidnapped, so I took her back to my place." Robinson's eyebrows touched the ceiling. He put his hand out to silence her, "She needed a safe place to crash and collect herself. As I said, I wanted to keep it all quiet."

"And because you like her. I knew it, I freaking knew it."

He groaned and wiped a hand over his mouth, "Fine, and maybe because I like her."

"*Did you lose your mind*? She is part of an ongoing investigation. This is all sorts of sloppy."

"That is not entirely true, Regine, she's a consultant on an investigation, there is nothing forbidden about fraternizing with people aiding in a case. She's not a suspect."

"No, not on paper. But she is a potential target and I am not sure if sleepovers are going to keep you unbiased in your investigation."

"I assure you, it's not an issue. This stays between me and you, for now. Partners, right?"

She gave him a withering stare and sniffed, "Fine. Sure. Though between us, *partners*, I have to say I don't get the draw. She's spooky, and uptight, and spends her days with dead bodies. Why don't you go for a nice girl, who wants to settle down, start a family, normal stuff."

He barked out a laugh that drew a few pairs of eyes over computer monitors and cubicle walls. "Wow, Regine, I don't think you know me very well at all. I don't want kids and I like spooky stuff."

A few hours later Persimmon Shaw was on the line.

"Sorry for the delay in returning your call, Ms. Shaw."

"Is our girl, all right? There were some rumblings along the divination trail that she was in danger."

Marlow lowered his voice, "Necromancer cabal, Order of Yama, snatched her because they think, much like you, that she is the perfect vessel. They wanted to stop the apocalypse, by tying her up in some suburban basement."

She swore, "Amateurs. Is Selene all right?" There was a genuine note of concern in her voice.

"Yeah, yeah she is. I don't think she needs to worry about them for a while. The leader, Lucinda..."

"I know of her," Persimmon replied, her feelings about the woman plain by her tone.

"It was her call. She was there. Selene threw some zombie mice at her face, scratched her up pretty good."

"Ha, good. You better keep her close now, until we can find these guys."

Marlow scooted to his computer, opening a sticky note on his desktop to take notes. "Which is why I hope you are calling with some good news."

"Yes, my coven's been weaving a spell that may help identify potential resurrectionists. Come by this evening, I should have something to show you. If it works, that should help identify any future victims. But the real issue, for me now, is how long before our killer's get the same idea about Selene being the vessel. That and I still can't find who is behind this. I am trying to discreetly put feelers out into the various supernatural communities, see what kinds of whispers come back. Normally this kind of death cult, end times, silliness just burns out or is pretty obvious. But my intel is coming back with some genuine anxiety about this ritual, that they may be pretty close to actually doing something."

"The necromancers think they will keep hunting for virgins. For now."

"Let's hope that is true. Word down the pipeline is that some big nasties are behind this. Things from behind the veil, creatures of immense power and inhumanity."

"Well, I like this world as it is, for the most part, I would like to stave off an apocalypse if I can."

"That's why we are a great team, Detective." Her sultry voice was back in place, "Bring Selene tonight. Leave your partner, if you can, I prefer this to stay in the family."

"Bigot," he teased.

"I prefer to think of it as a mercy. Let's not reveal how dangerous we can actually be to them. They are so delicate."

"Goodbye, Ms. Shaw."

Germaine listened to the message a few times, her mouth drying out. She glanced at her roommate Jasmine, who obliviously bobbed her head wearing headphones and staring at her computer screen.

She'd gotten the job.

She was also, potentially, the target of ritual serial killers.

She was trying to find an emotion that could combine both feelings, but came up empty. She wanted to be happy, her money woes would be over, the giant stone that was her loan debt would lighten.

But there was also a killer afoot, one that apparently had a thing for young resurrectionists. Since she had only met one other in her life, and that was just this past week, she had to assume that she was probably one of few on campus

A fleeting thought skittered by, John. He was handsome, he'd come out of the blue, and he liked her against all odds. No one in her small circle knew he existed outside the staff at Java's, and they were probably too busy or oblivious to make a note of who she had been sitting with. Even if she had been going there daily for nearly two semesters trying to be a regular.

It was all too much, she needed a second opinion, "Hey Jasmine, can I talk to you about something?"

Ten minutes later, Jasmine was sitting cross-legged across from Germaine with a serious look on her face. Finally, she blew out a breath and patted at one of the many tight braids that hugged her skull.

"Okay, so you are a resurrectionist and you may have a boyfriend, and you may be the target of a serial killer, and you didn't think I would want to know?!" Jasmine was, similar to John, seemingly too cool for Germaine to have become friends with in the wild. It took nearly a month of sleeping two feet from one another and eating meals together out of desperation to carve out anything past loose acquaintances after all.

Germaine avoided Jasmine's stare, sure her cheeks were bright red like two candy apples. "Are you freaked?"

"Freaked?! No way, it's all pretty cool, if you ask me. Here I thought you were some boring girl from farm country and you have been holding out on me! Even wearing fake contacts all the time!" Jasmine smiled, braces-straight white teeth, a toothbrush commercial's smile. "We're cool, just be honest with me, okay? I can take it."

"Thanks. Wait, you thought I was boring before?" Germaine responded, feigning upset. Jasmine heaved a pillow at her.

"Shut up, I was joking. Now I think the main thing we have to do is make sure that Mr. John is actually on the level. And I can think of an easy way to do that, we schedule a double date."

Germaine chuckled, "I don't know about that, Jasmine, I mean I've only been out to coffee with him and it's not like anything was laid out official-like. Don't want to scare him. I know I'm just being paranoid."

"Better safe than sorry, right?" Jasmine stood and opened her closet. Germaine could not help envying the mile of long dark legs encased in tiny cut-off Daisy Dukes. Jasmine was on the swim team and was nearly six feet of muscled limbs and flawless skin. Germaine was sure she could have been a model instead of an athlete.

"Well, when you do decide to get serious, we will go on a double date. Then, me and Trey can get a look at him and make sure his gentlemanly intentions are purely of the getting in your pants variety." She winked and Germaine buried her face in her hands.

It was weird having an unmarked police car tail me through my day. I had three resurrections lined up back-to-back in the afternoon, mercifully two were at the same hospital morgue, and I had an hour in between to grab a coffee and sandwich at the hospital cafeteria. It was a challenge seeing clients, and trying to convey austere professionalism, all while sporting a shiner on my face. The makeup hid it some, but I felt self-conscious enough to leave my hair down and shift the part to cover that side of my face more.

Midway through my sandwich, sitting in the hospital cafeteria, I was aware of someone watching me. My pulse was racing, mouth tangy with adrenaline when I looked up. He was middle-aged, Asian, male, and was wearing blue scrubs and had a stethoscope around his neck. When our eyes met, he stood and started toward me unbidden. He walked stiffly, with determination, straight toward me. I made note of the exits in case I had to run. Guess being abducted had made me jumpier than I realized.

"I'm sorry to trouble you, my name is Dr. Chen, you are the resurrectionist, yes?" I swallowed the lump of subpar tuna salad in my mouth and nodded.

"Selene Shade." I didn't reach out to shake as the man's nervous energy made me nervous.

"You mind if I sit?" I did. He saw my hesitation, "I just wanted to ask you a professional question, really quick, then you can get back to your lunch." I wanted to say no, but I also didn't want to make a scene. If he was a spell-slinger he could alter perception, so no one noticed me being dragged out, he could knock me out, he could kill me right there. He sat when I did not answer right away and leaned in as I leaned back. "Thanks," he said quietly as if I had invited him after all.

"I've seen you here before, at the hospital, been trying to get up the nerve to talk to you."

"I don't mean to be rude, but my day is pretty packed," I muttered, meeting his brown eyes. Dr. Chen was probably about forty, shorter than me with a thick head of black hair that had a few sprinkles of gray. He wore tortoise-shell glasses and had a smooth unwrinkled face. His aura looked human.

"I understand, I won't take up much of your time, I promise. I have an odd question for you. Please."

I put my sandwich on the cellophane and met his eyes, "That seems to be the only kind anyone has for me these days. Shoot."

"Okay, I met a woman recently, through the hospital. She's a volunteer, very beautiful, and very aloof. Blonde, pretty, out of my league." He chuckled and I resisted the urge to roll my eyes. "After a bit of back-and-forth flirting, she finally agreed to go out for a drink with me. She's quiet, as I said. Mysterious. We've seen each other a few more times and I am falling for this girl."

I stared at Dr. Chen, waiting for the punchline and why he would be asking me any kind of relationship advice. "On the third date we go back to my place, making out and all that, when she stops me and says she has to tell me something."

"She's a half-life." I chimed in, relieved to be moving toward the end of the story.

He nods, "Yes! I couldn't believe it. Blew me right away. She seemed so *alive*, you know. She wasn't this cold dead thing. Sure, she's a little quiet, a little distant. But I had no idea. She said she liked me, but she wouldn't feel right taking things further without being honest. She said she'd give me some time to think about it."

"And what did you decide?" I asked, genuinely curious. In truth, I worried for the creatures I sent back out into the world, worried every day that I was making a mistake giving them another life. That it was cruel, maybe even a form of torture. After all, I knew how hard it was living apart and being feared.

"I haven't talked to her yet. That happened just this weekend, then when I saw you here, recognized you, I figured it wouldn't hurt to talk to a professional. So, what should I do?"

I rested my chin on my hand and regarded Dr. Chen. He wasn't bad-looking and a doctor, so he probably didn't have that hard of a time dating. But he was also kind of annoying. "You seem to like her."

"But she's...a zombie. She eats little animals so she doesn't go crazy or decompose. She's kept alive by magic."

"So? Do you eat meat?"

"I do."

I finished the dregs of my coffee. He waited.

"Well, Dr. Chen, it's not that different. You eat the flesh for the nutrients. She may have died, but her body is alive now and she does have a soul in there. She may not feel things as intensely and she may be a little distant, but those are the qualities that drew you to her in the first place are they not?"

"Can they even have sex? And enjoy it?"

"They can and do. They are different, but they also are still people. I am sure she has hopes and dreams, goals. She returned from the dead after all, that says she is someone who wants to live. She may be looking for love as well. Clearly, she respects you and wants to be honest with you. She could have not told you."

"But does she age? Will she just be the same forever?"

"No, they do age, if she eats her regular critters, just much slower than a regular person, but the body is still flesh. Flesh breaks down."

He seemed to digest all of this, thoughtfully. As much as I wanted to enjoy a quiet lunch in peace, educating the public, especially those in medical fields, about half-lifes was important. Preternatural biology was barely a week-long unit in med school still, in part because it was so unlikely a half-life or vampire would show up in an ER. I felt I was doing a civic duty. "Half-lifes cannot get cancer, or ordinary diseases. Which we can't say for regular human partners."

"Okay, last question and I will let you go. If zombies break down, why don't vampires?"

I stood, gathering my trash and gestured for him to follow me, "I have another client, so let's walk and talk. This, Dr. Chen, is where things get a little weirder and more *magical*. A half-life exists because someone, like myself, puts the soul back in their dead body. My magic binds the two together and restarts the body. The half-life consumes small doses of lifeforce to keep their body from breaking down and to keep the spirit and body together. Half-lifes also wear a magic object, called an animus, which helps keep the body and soul together. Like an anchor. You will notice she probably wears a necklace or ring or something."

"A locket I think."

"Right. So, a vampire is different because they have undergone a cellular change to their body, the magic, or disease, whatever you want to call it, is in their blood, in every cell. A magical infection. This cellular change causes the body to continue living outside of a human life cycle with constant infusions of human lifeforce. They consume much more lifeforce much more frequently and it powers their body. They use magic to continue unchanged and they can spread the magic infection."

Dr. Chen blew out a breath, "In med school, preternatural biology was a really weird section. Since so little can be verified with science. So, who created the magical infection originally? Necromancers?"

I shrugged, "Hard to say, I think it actually may have been witches. Necromancers raise the dead using remains, or their 'salts,' creating a temporary and grotesque facsimile of the deceased that has access to its memories. They are more like a ghost in very temporary flesh. Vampires seem, to me, less unnatural and more part of the world, like big ticks. They are more tied to nature. Like a virus. My guess is that vampires were originally the result of someone way way back trying to raise their own half-lifes. But I really don't know."

Dr. Chen sighed, "Yeah, must have been nice when this was all make-believe and late-night movies."

"We were always here, you just didn't know it. I think if you like her and she likes you, and you can get past what she is, it may be worth giving it a try."

"Yeah."

"I really have to go. Did this help you at all?" I asked.

"It did, I think. I do like her. She doesn't look dead or smell weird." He bit his lip, "I think I am going to call her back. Thanks, for your time and advice."

He turned and walked off, leaving me by the trash cans a little bewildered and begrudgingly wishing them all the best. Maybe Marlow had turned me into a romantic. In my head, I could almost feel Dot gloating.

I had never personally been intimate with a half-life, but from what I have heard, it's not that different than being with a living person. They may not be as responsive and may have some difficulties reaching completion, but that wasn't the end of the world. Plenty of ordinary living people dealt with those challenges every day.

I wanted to believe they were capable of deep love, and real closeness, that they could be with a normal mortal and find happiness. It may not be the happiness of their mortal lives, but I hoped it was better than being dead.

I had my share of clients who came back and wanted to die. A few a year. A lot of them were people who wanted to be resurrected for unfinished-business-type reasons: they were terminally ill, or had some goal they wanted to complete, or it was tied to their families. Once that individual completed the business, or gave up on it, they came back to me, ready to be done.

I wouldn't classify it as suicide, since they had died and come back and were now dying again, though it did always feel a little sad releasing a body I had brought back. Dot and I spent hours discussing the ethics of resurrectionists bringing back, then taking away, lives. And we would always go out for a lot of drinks after freeing someone. The end result of all those discussions? There was something beautiful about taking control of your destiny and picking your moment to leave this coil for the second time. Most people don't get to choose when they live and die.

That inevitably made me think of Marlow. An eternal creature. Had he thought of killing himself over the years?

All immortals must.

Sixteen

Marlow hated to admit how happy and relieved he was to see Selene emerge from her office. She waved and strode over to his car. The bruising faded enough around her eye that makeup hid the bulk of it. Her hair was in a loose ponytail, thick and wavy with a few strands left out to hide her face. It softened her not having it scraped back in her usual severe bun. She smiled and something in his chest tightened, he couldn't remember the last time a woman had affected him so.

"I had some time, so I dropped your bags at my place already," he said when she got in, debating on if he should lean forward and kiss her, deciding against it at the last minute.

"Thanks." She blew out a breath and smiled at him, "I had a very weird day." She told him about Peter rushing in worried about her. After an internal debate he watched play over her face, she mentioned he'd asked her out again.

"Oh?" Marlow hated that he felt jealous. Hoped his tone sounded casual.

"I told him that I was off the market. He told me to keep him in mind if things changed."

"Considerate."

"Unless...you felt I was rushing things."

"Well, I am happy that you are not going out again with this Peter guy." She chuckled at that and took her ponytail down, shaking out her long dark brown hair. It fell well past her shoulders. She scratched at her scalp and sighed, leaning her head back against the car seat, eyes closed. He grinned, enjoying how un-self-conscious she was.

"What?" she asked, cracking one eye open to look at him. "Ponytail was giving me a headache."

"You look nice with your hair down."

"Smoke and mirrors: I painted on a pound of concealer since I had clients all day, wouldn't do to look like I just crawled out of a boxing ring."

"It's looking much better. Hopefully, whatever ritual Persimmon wants us to see is brief and successful."

She groaned, "I don't want to see Persimmon."

"We will go have a nice early dinner, you can tell me more about your weird day. I can tell you how my partner does not approve of our seeing each other. Then, Persimmon will wow us with magic, and we will leave."

"It's been seven years since I've seen her."

Marlow took Selene to an intimate seafood place that was right on the water and not too far from her office. Though she'd never been to Siren, she was excited, as it was always written about. She told him she'd always wanted to go there but never had a date good enough to bring, or a friend she felt close enough with, to sit in a dark room by candlelight and waterfront sunsets, eating gorgeously prepared, expensive fish.

Marlow ordered the trout, Selene the halibut. They sipped wine, she nibbled bread from the basket. He liked watching her eat, she was not a dainty eater, instead she seemed to truly savor and appreciate her food. She talked with a full mouth, and tried to feed him things off her plate.

His fish, what little he ate, was well-seasoned. He even ate a little potato and greens. His stomach was small, as he told her, and his body needed little to no food. If he overdid it, he'd make himself sick, which wouldn't do for their first real date.

He often thought that the only reason vampires could eat at all was to fit in with humans. People were a social food culture after all, so much of human life events were spent breaking bread, drinking, celebrating. A creature who ate nothing, drank nothing, especially in times where food was sparse and generosity of sharing a table prized, it would be awfully suspicious. A person wouldn't trust someone who refused a meal with them.

Selene devoured her food and happily finished his as well. He could almost hear his mother, a woman dead over seventy-five years, say, "For a thin thing, she certainly has an appetite on her. Must have a hole in her leg." It made him smile. He had a hard time summoning his mother's face, but her voice, tutting and playful, he could remember that clear as day.

Selene told him about her odd encounter with Dr. Chen at the hospital, leaving him feeling conflicted about their possible romance. He made the error of telling her that.

"Why conflicted?" She'd asked over dessert, some sort of fruit tart that looked too lovely and sculptural to carve into, though Selene did, with relish.

"This will make me a total hypocrite, but dating a half-life does seem strange," he said.

"Really?"

"Again, it may be my personal bias, those I have met have always come off so...empty."

"They've been through a profound experience and live in a society that doesn't totally embrace them. I don't think empty is fair."

"Yeah, true."

"I think they are people and deserve every happiness and experience they can get their hands on. That's why they transcended death, no?" Her voice was hard. Clearly, he'd hit a nerve.

Marlow backed off, noting the pink in her cheeks and the fire in those strange blue eyes. Of course, she would defend them, they were her children in a way. And she their master. He tried not to think too much on that, since it rode in with memories of Persimmon talking about half-lifes and resurrectionists being unnatural and created for a darker purpose. He also didn't want to skirt too close to the discussion on why he, and those like him, were closer to half-lifes than people. If anything, it was probably more unnatural for him to be dating her, or anyone, because he was basically an undying parasite. It was a lot of territory to avoid.

"Let's change the subject, this may be too heavy for our first official date at a nice place. We already get to spend the rest of it with my nemesis." She ordered a refill on her coffee.

"Tell me something about yourself." She said.

"Like what?"

"Well, I know you are ninety-something, and that you used to be married. I don't know, what else?"

"I love winter, it's my favorite season. And I always live in places with long winters."

"Interesting, why?"

"Nights are longer, it's quieter, I think the snow is pretty. I like burrowing in with a book, a fire, and no place else to be."

"That's nice, me too. Tell me something else."

"I have a little brother. I helped raise him, times being tough growing up. Even after I was changed, I kept up with him, every time I changed identity, all of it."

She was surprised, "What's his name?"

"Henry. He's in a nursing home now, up north in Portland, Maine."

"Are you from Maine?" She asked, reaching her hand across the table and taking his in hers. He squeezed back and nodded, unable to recall when last he'd told anyone about Henry. Or even if he had.

"Yeah, a really small town up near Acadia. My dad was a fisherman, my mom a seamstress. It was a different time then, especially way up north. The wars, the famine, the plague of black pox that traveled through that area, it was hard. There were eight kids in our house, I was the second oldest, Henry the youngest. But by the time I was a young man, only Henry and I were still alive. My father died in a boating accident, my siblings from various things: war, injuries, infections. Then, my mother died from cancer when Henry was only a teen. My wife, Min, she wanted me to have no ties. But I would never leave my brother alone.

So, I got some money together and sent him to boarding school and later college, all behind my wife's back. He made himself into a fine man and a scholar. He became a professor, specialized in vampirism actually. Wrote a few important books, was praised for his inside knowledge." Marlow smiled sadly and raised Selene's hand, kissing it, enjoying the jump of her pulse under his thumb.

"Henry had a wife, and children. Those children have children now. And they always knew me. Uncle Will. It's nice to have family, think it has kept me more connected to the world as I have gotten older. It also made me a savvy investor, setting up little trusts for each of them. I think for vampires, once the world you knew is gone and everyone dead, it's easier to stop...thinking like a human. It's tempting to detach. But my family keeps me in the world. They make the future a less lonely place." Marlow was surprised to see Selene dab at her eyes.

"Thank you for sharing that with me. I'm envious of that. I only had Dot and she's gone now."

He pressed her fingertips to his lips again, tempted to prick one against his sharp teeth. But he pushed down the urge and contented himself being drunk on her attention alone.

"You're very welcome. Let's go see a witch about a spell," he said.

———

I looked up at Persimmon's chic little bungalow and tried to rub off the nervous sweat that sprung from my hands. It was impossible to ignore the memories of being a weird orphan in second-hand clothes, in the shadow of the charming and glamorous Persimmon. Rich witch parents, great style, charm for days. *Who's your friend?* Being asked about me with veiled contempt. I was wiping my hands absently on my thighs when the door opened and there she was in all her glory.

She hadn't changed much, her face had matured and lost some of its roundness. Her eyes were harder. When she saw me she smiled brightly, her arms opened wide, the silk kimono sleeves waving like flags, and she pulled me into a tight embrace.

Her perfume was cloying and musky, probably something that made men into her slaves. I hated the pang of protective jealousy for Marlow, well aware that it was PTSD from having a boyfriend stolen by her in the past.

"Oh my god, Selene! You look amazing! You've really come into your own." She looked me up and down and my skin crawled, I felt like a little kid getting my school uniform inspected. I was glad that I left my hair down and put on a little lipstick in honor of Dot. If I were being petty, it was also to show that harpy Persimmon that she wasn't the only game in town—even if I did have a gnarly black eye.

"Hello, Persimmon, you look amazing, as always," I ground out. She took the compliment like a pro and turned back into the house waving me, and Marlow at my heels, inside.

"Come in, come in, Detective, nice to see you again." They shared a weighty look and something went between them. The jealous feeling surged.

She was talking and walking, I noted the lush decor and the veil of incense clogging up the air. I could hear chanting toward the back. "So, my coven has been working tirelessly all weekend and I think we have found the perfect spell."

We were soon out the back doors standing in a preternatural garden that was easily twenty degrees warmer than it actually was outside. The walls of vines reached high overhead in all four directions, creating a very quiet, very private oasis. The walls also felt, to me, like a prison. A verdant one with beautiful tropical flowers everywhere, but a prison nonetheless.

The coven sat in a circle on the ground. The ground being packed earth that had been drawn upon with hundreds of sigils. A line of salt and herbs kept the coven in the circle. Although I did not practice any magic outside my own brand of death magic, I could sense the power of the circle and those inside. It felt like a static charge, and I wondered if I reached toward it if my hair would stand on edge.

She gave me a sweet look and squeezed my shoulder, I fought the urge to shake her off and claw at her face. "Let me introduce you to everyone."

Everyone, consisted of five other members, with Persimmon I would gather to be the sixth and leader. Covens needed an avatar for each element: earth, air, wind, water, fire, and one for spirit, which I again assumed as coven leader was Persimmon. Also, because I knew she'd never excelled at a certain element in college.

The group ranged in age, weight, and ethnicity, virtually nothing was alike among them save the silver amulet each wore on a leather cord around their necks. It depicted the full moon, with a pentagram drawn over it. I expected Persimmon's coven to be filled with unnaturally beautiful people, a gaggle of models, naked and boldly powerful. It surprised me that everyone looked so...ordinary. This could be a series of people standing behind me at the grocery store, they were that random.

But they were all watching us now, eyes darting between Marlow and myself, and none seemed too pleased by what they saw. An older Black man with a puff of white hair around the back of his head and bald on top gave me an outright baleful glare.

"Everyone," Persimmon called out, voice commanding, "I would like you to welcome Selene Shade, resurrectionist, and Detective William Marlow, vampire." I shot a glance at Marlow, his face was tight, mask on. I doubted he liked being introduced like that. I, on the other hand, was pretty used to it.

"They've come to see the spell we've woven to find possible future victims. If you two would please stand over here to the side." She took my arm and I fought the urge to shake her off, disliking how much she had touched me in a short time. I wasn't overly fond of physical affection with most people, let alone a frenemy blast from the past. But I was also an adult, understanding lives were at stake, and so I went to where she led. Even allowing her to position me, then Marlow beside me, in a corner of green away from the circle. "Great, now I have here a map. As you two may, or may not know, tracking spells are nearly impossible. People are constantly moving and it's just hard to get a bead on them in real time. As opposed to say, an object or a dead body. With a living person, by the time you try to locate someone, they have moved from that place."

The coven knelt in a circle, a middle-aged woman with a shaved head rolled out the map Persimmon handed her, weighing it down at the edges with stones. It showed Goat Hill and a little of the neighboring towns.

"What I've done instead is try to find the homes of the resurrectionists. A place where they rest their heads, and leave a lot of energy. We've been meeting late at night to work the spell, in hopes of catching them all at home, fast asleep. Now I feel pretty confident we know where all the resurrectionists in the city reside." Persimmon turned back to Marlow and I, her eyes triumphant.

"Shall we show you?"

Marlow and I exchanged looks before both nodding.

"Great. Let's begin." Persimmon stepped into the circle and came to the center, which she shared with the rolled-out map.

She remained standing, while the coven around her continued to kneel, their arms outstretched reaching toward the center and Persimmon. She had her eyes closed, her mouth moving in a fast whisper. Sounded like Latin.

Suddenly she threw her head back, eyes and mouth opening, and light like a spotlight shone out from them toward the sky. The air felt thick and electric, each hair on my arm stood on end. I risked pulling my eyes from the spectacle to Marlow. His face was grim, mouth in a tight colorless line. He didn't seem to like this any more than I did. I felt his hand grasp mine, and the dry coolness, the firmness of his grip, forced me to relax a few notches. I had always had a reluctance around magic outside of my own. Many people with magical ability sought out more and more, attracted to the power, and the knowledge. I had never been like that, instead finding myself wary around it. Meddling in things we weren't meant to. Persimmon always found that strange about me. But in magic, like most things, she was fearless. Persimmon cried out now and her body shook as if seized, the rest of the coven trembled and writhed on the ground and the air smelled of ozone and smoke. I noticed the map in the center was burning.

And then, in a blink, it was over. Persimmon dropped to the ground gasping, and the rest of the group sat up, rubbing at knees and elbows, mopping sweaty brows.

Persimmon was flushed, sweat forming tight blonde ringlets around her face. She dabbed at her face with the sleeve of her kimono and then gathered the map. The other members had risen and stepped out as well, a few were heading toward the house.

"Whew! That was intense. But I think this is the best I can do for you." She extended the map to Marlow, who took it and held it up to the light. I could see tiny burn holes, I counted ten, scattered on the map. Curiously, I glanced at my address and saw nothing. Then found my office, saw nothing, then found Persimmon's address and a small pinhole for myself. Huh.

I didn't want to stay longer than we had to, the map helped to a point, but I still wasn't entirely sure how we would find these girls besides knocking on doors in the general area, which took time. The witch coven had all gone inside, leaving Marlow and Persimmon and myself.

"You look disappointed, Selene," Persimmon said, voice concerned, or faux concerned.

"This still would only give a general area to find them. If they stay put. Do you think this was the spell our killer used?"

There was a small metal bistro set beside the back door, and Persimmon eased into one of the chairs, thoughtful, and poured herself some water from the carafe on the table. "I have been thinking about that as well. I think that they must have, though this would be a tough spell to spin alone. But it would just give the vicinity, as you said, they would have to then go and hang around those areas. Perhaps they are able to sense resurrectionists when close to them, they may even have a talisman or something that would signal them being near..." She rested her chin on her fist, mind working. I recognized the pose from years of studying next to each other.

"So, you think they used a spell like this to get to rough areas, and then the killer staked the area out, until he found the target?" Marlow said, thoughtful and pacing. He spun to me, quick.

"Selene, can you sense other resurrectionists?"

"I can if close by, through auras. Can either of you?" I looked between him and Persimmon.

Marlow shook his head, "No, I feel a pull toward you, like the undertow of the ocean, but it's subtle. If I was looking into a crowd, I doubt I'd be able to pick you out."

"And I can only see auras if I use a charm, and yes, yours does look strange. But I would need to be in touching distance, otherwise I can't sense you are anything other than human."

"What do they look like to you? Resurrectionists?" Marlow asked me.

"A void, like the eye of a hurricane. No color. Humans have colors and movement. Vampires and half-lifes do as well, to an extent. But resurrectionists do not have anything besides this void. Like black tentacles."

"So not human at all," Persimmon said as her and Marlow exchanged another look that I didn't like. I felt a stab of guilt. Marlow must have gleaned something because he stepped closer and put his arm around me, making a statement to Persimmon and to me.

"What does it look like to you? With a talisman?" I continued, trying to shrug him off without it looking like a dismissal.

"Strange and yes, something of a sucking/seeking quality." Persimmon said, looking at me with renewed interest. "We really should discuss, when we have more time of course, why that is. It's fascinating."

"Okay, so our killer has to be able to find resurrectionists, young ones, untrained, virgins even. He may be using a location spell, but you are a powerful witch with a coven, and it still took a few days to get a reliable bead on someone. Even still, that would only get you into the vicinity. So, he must be staking out the areas, and he must be able to sense resurrectionists. Either by seeing auras or by using some sort of charm, like Persimmon's. That's the only way it seems."

I snapped my fingers, "He could be a half-life. They would have a natural attraction to resurrectionists as well. They can sense us across rooms." I couldn't believe I hadn't thought of that until then.

"Ok! Okay, and if he were local at all, odds are good that your records or...the other resurrectionist..."

"Dania Barabas," I supplied.

"Yes, between the two of your offices, there is a good chance one of you raised him. Shouldn't be too hard to look up young white twenty-somethings with brown hair."

I thought on it, feeling a distinct discomfort at the prospect that a half-life could be behind it. But I couldn't argue the logic, it felt the closest to a lead. I tried to ignore the faces flipping past, the scores of dead I had personally reanimated. Could one of them really be raping and killing to bring about something so horrible?

But again, why would *anyone* want to? I never understood the suicide bombers, the terrorists, the world-ending cultists. The world was not a perfect place, I understood that, and people suffered all the time. Terrible things happened daily. But so too did wonderful things. I just couldn't understand the compulsion to flick the kill switch and send it all down the tubes.

I had been ignoring Marlow and Persimmon as they talked, trying to figure out how next her coven could help. He was asking if they could make a talisman or something that would allow the wearer to sense resurrectionists in the vicinity.

"—you okay Selene? Seem to have lost you." Marlow's voice was gentle, even worried.

"Oh yeah, it's just been a long...week."

"I think we have all we are going to get from these guys, let's go," he said. The coven was still in the house but avoided us by keeping to the kitchen and living room, and as we popped in to say thanks, they barely could muster a nod of goodbye. Weird.

"Let me know if you need anything else," Persimmon said as she waved us off.

By the time we reached Marlow's loft, I could barely keep my eyes open. I could tell he was wired though, staring at the map, wanting to talk to Regine and his team.

"You should go, work on the case," I said through a fog as I pulled on pajama pants, too tired to care about changing in front of him.

"Are you sure? I don't want to leave you alone, if you are scared."

"Go, go. I am too tired to be scared, and you are positively buzzing. Go be a night creature, and I will get some sleep."

I could see he was torn at the thought of leaving me alone, and it was touching. "Just go, I will be fine. No one knows where I am and the building is secure. I'll call with any trouble," I waved my hands at him while batting away a yawn. The yawn seemed to seal the deal and he nodded, stepping toward me.

"We are burning through days to the new moon, but we have some good leads to start looking into. Thanks for understanding." I nodded and smiled, when he leaned forward, room-temperature hands framing my face, black-brown eyes looking into mine. "I won't be too late." Then his lips were on mine. The kiss delicate, intimate. I smiled into it, not knowing what we were doing, or if it was safe, if anything was safe. But appreciating the small moment, the sweetness, like a drop of water in a desert. Precious. And rare.

Then the vampire was gone, and I crawled into his bed alone.

PART THREE: FULL MOON

SEVENTEEN

The Plains of Anchu were never still, battered down by hot stinking winds from the southern lakes which mixed and tangled with cold snowy winds from the northern mountains. Over the last few decades, the storms had been getting both worse and longer with less quiet in between them. Less quiet meant shorter time to rebuild, or for the scrubs to regrow, or for the hardbacks to forage on those scrubs, or for those that lived in the clay beneath to come out of their underground burrow-cities to hunt the hardbacks. And when the ground dwellers stayed below, the sky creatures could not hunt them, causing whole herds to drop from the clouds, littering the craggy surface with their rapidly deflating and rotting corpses.

Their world was dying. The gaseous air and acid water too harsh even for its heartiest and most toxic of residents.

The underground dwellers were resilient though. When they ran out of things to eat, instead of succumbing and dying, they began to eat their magic, best they could. Creatures of the flesh were not made to live off of energy, though. The years of doing this had made them much stranger. Like the snake eating its own tail over and over. They'd become less alive, less natural and of the world, any world. They'd become predators of their own people. Like an ouroboros, they were recycling energies and remaking reality over and over. Their world was becoming more and more depleted and fragile for it. They knew it wasn't sustainable, they *could only feed off themselves for so long. So, they frantically looked for doors to other worlds, other places that could house them and make them a great civilization again.*

They wanted to go back to the time before, the times of plenty, when the rivers and mountains had provided life and not death. When they were more than cannibals of the soul and the flesh. They knew there was a way out, because when the sky initially fell and the water and air soured, one of their own escaped using Nigrum Porta. He claimed he would bring them all through. But he failed, or abandoned them, and never returned. The Plains of Anchu was dying and the wisest scholars spent all their time searching for how to summon Nigrum Porta back, how to use him as a gateway to salvation.

Time was running out for the hungry and desperate of Anchu.

James looked at the calendar, two weeks to go. He rose from his desk in his small garden-level apartment, furnished mostly by the Salvation Army, the walls whitewashed to bring light into the dank musty space. One corner was devoted to spell crafting, with a map on the wall, *X*'s and pins narrowing the areas where the resurrectionists lived. Scattered on the desk below were dossiers on the girls once he found them. Stacks of folders, photos, and notes.

The other girls had been imperfect, not powerful enough, not good enough, not virginal enough. But he had a feeling about Germaine. She was brighter, both her abilities and personality were more vibrant. She hid it, as she'd trained herself to do, growing up in a Podunk town that treated her like an outcast. Idiots. If he had even a splash of that kind of raw power, well if he had, he wouldn't be working for the Patron now, functioning as a minion for bigger players.

The thing about Germaine though, besides being more inherently powerful, was that he actually kind of liked her. Which surprised him as she wasn't his type at all. But there was something about her. James' mind flashed to the girls' bodies, ripped apart and destroyed by Nigrum Porta, and told himself it was because they were unworthy. It wasn't his fault, they were just bad vessels. But that didn't stop the screams, the sounds of bones breaking, flesh rending, the snap and cracks of cartilage and tissue, from haunting him. Even now, in his over-lit, whitewashed apartment, he could smell the rupturing of organs, the meaty metallic miasma of so much blood misting into the air. His gorge rose and he willed it down. He didn't have a choice.

"Don't be a pussy, James," he muttered, marching toward his coat and shoulder bag hanging on a hook near the door. "To make an omelet, you have to break some eggs. What's a few girls to create a new world order, to live as a god? Keep your head in the game."

He hadn't always been so ruthless, he knew it. He still wouldn't, couldn't, think of himself as a rapist. It was the *ritual* after all, if there was a way to do it without having to fuck the girls, hell, without having to hurt or abduct the girls, obviously he would do it. He didn't want to hurt anyone. But if it worked, if the Patron and his cronies could deliver on the promise, everything would be different. If he and Nigrum Porta could make it happen? He'd get everything. The world would be his oyster. Their deaths would mean something.

If there was a little voice in there, one that sounded a lot like his mother, a quiet whispery voice in the back of his head always asking: "And what if they are wrong? What if nothing happens? What if this was for nothing? What if you killed them for nothing? Or worse, what if they are lying to you?"

Then he would be a murderer, and a rapist, and a traitor to the human race, conspiring with outsiders to destroy the world. An inter-dimensional Benedict Arnold. He laughed at the thought, despite himself. It didn't matter regardless, it was too late. He was in it, he was doing it, and he prayed to god—Gods?—to whoever was listening to see this through, and that Germaine Whately would be the vessel. The last girl he would have to drag into the damned woods.

"Eyes on the prize, James," he said to his reflection, eyes locked to eyes, meaning it.

He marched out of the house, a man with a mission.

Germaine sat stiffly in an office chair, trying to balance her laptop on her actual lap while holding a stack of manila folders between the keyboard and her stomach. She looked at her new boss, Selene, working away at her own desk, headphones in, ignoring Germaine, and then looked at the empty, somewhat dusty desk that was unoccupied.

Obviously, it would be easier for her to be working on a flat surface designed for...work. But Selene hadn't even offered the desk, instead pushing a chair against the wall for her. She had Germaine entering in a huge mountain of files into the computer, case files, raisings, updating addresses.

She'd been working for an hour in this position, her neck had a crick in it, and her legs were cramping. She shifted and a folder slipped to the floor, spilling its contents, and she sighed annoyed, loud enough for Selene to look up.

"All ok?" she asked, voice distracted as she pulled out an earbud.

Germaine fought the urge to glare, since it was only her second full day after all, "It's just a little hard to work like this." She gestured to her lap. "Can I please work at the desk over there, I need to spread out, and it would be much faster."

Selene frowned, her eyes glancing at the empty desk, and a wave of emotions crossed her face. She let out a patently fake chuckle, stood and circled her desk.

"Where is my head at? Of course, you can use Dot's, um...use the *empty* desk. Let me just clean it off for you." Selene passed by her quickly, digging out a roll of paper towels and some cleaning spray from the closet next to a water bubbler.

"I can do that if you want to get back to work," Germaine offered, noting the jerky way her new boss was moving, and the way she chewed her lip. Like she was trying not to cry.

Selene shook her head forcefully, causing a tendril of hair to slip from behind her ear into her face. She blew it out of the way as she scrubbed, more vigorously than necessary. "No, no please. It's long overdue. This was my former partner's desk for so long, practically an extension of her. And she hated when people touched her things. But it's just a desk and you need one to work."

Selene picked up a box next to the printer while she talked, avoiding Germaine's eyes. Selene started to fill the box with items on the desk's top, including the sweater on the back of the chair. When the top was clear she pulled the seat out and forced a smile.

"All clean and ready for you to use. I'll do the drawers later. Sorry about that." She stiffly turned, placed the box beside her desk, returned the cleaner, and disappeared around the corner toward the bathroom. Germaine felt enormously uncomfortable because she knew, just knew, that her new boss was going to the bathroom to cry.

Everything about Selene telegraphed that she was always trying to stay in control. The tidy office, the tidy clothes, her slicked-back hair.

But in the little time Germaine had known her, she could see the cracks.

Germaine set out her computer and files, breathed in the pine cleaner scent, and since she could hear the sink running in the bathroom still, slid open the drawers, curious if there was anything interesting remaining of this mysterious Dot. She found some dog-eared paperbacks, all romances with muscled hunks and languishing ladies. Old tins of mints, many pairs of multicolored reader glasses, some covered in rhinestones. Tubes of bright red lipstick, most down to the nub. A brush, with long gray hair in it. Way down in the bottom drawer, she found a picture, in it a plump older woman with red lips and wild gray hair piled high on her head, had her arm around a much younger Selene. She had a short punkier haircut, dark eyeliner and a guarded smile on her face. They stood out in front of the building they were in now.

She heard the bathroom door open and quickly put the items back, closing drawers and started typing.

Selene settled back at her desk, smiling tightly when Germaine made eye contact. Her hair had been wetted and slicked back, the bun tight and freshly wound up at the back of her head. Her eyes were puffy and skin taut.

"Better?" Selene said tightly.

"Oh, yeah—yes, ma'am, I mean, thank you. I know it was your partner's..."

"It's fine, should have been done ages ago, I have just been busy. My caseload is a mile long, and helping the police has been time-consuming." She paused, obviously thinking something over, or rather debating to tell Germaine something.

"You should know that target is virgin resurrectionists. He's killing them ritually on the new moon. If he sticks to his pattern that is under two weeks from now and they still don't know who it is."

Germaine opened her mouth, then closed it again, unsure what to say. Selene waited a beat and continued. "Now we are trying to find potential victims, to warn them, to keep police on them."

"Yeah, yes. You told me that. I have been careful, I promise." Not to mention that there definitely had been a more prominent police presence.

"So, if there are any new boys coming around..."

Germaine felt the hotness in her cheeks betray her, and an image of

John was there, smiling, handsome, a bit too good to be true. Was he? Her stomach twisted at the thought, the blooming of a familiar shame not far behind. But no, coincidences happened all the time. Just because she started talking to a guy, a guy who didn't know who she was when he talked to her, and happened to like her, and happened to be handsome and smart, and she happened to not be. It didn't mean he was a killer.

A wave of anger drowned out the other feelings, anger at Selene for thinking she couldn't take care of herself or see the difference between a guy grooming her for a sacrifice and one who wanted to go out with her.

"You okay? I know it's pretty scary to think we are being hunted like this," Selene said, watching her with shrewd eyes. "I just want you to be safe, and you are so similar to the other victims."

Germaine bit the inside of her cheek to stop from saying something she'd regret to her boss, "Because you think I'm a virgin?"

Selene put her hands up in defense, "Hey, this is work and not my business. It's because you are a young resurrectionist at the college. I didn't mean to pry or insult you. I'm just passing on what I know, we need to stick together."

Germaine nodded and went back to her folders, embarrassment keeping her eyes on the desk. "Got it, thanks."

It was then that the buzzer downstairs went off, startling them both. Selene's face brightened as she looked at the monitor and buzzed them in. Boyfriend? Germaine wondered, more curious what kind of boyfriend someone like Selene, the Ice Queen, would have.

A moment later, a tall, pale man, with a square jaw and military brush cut strode in, he wore a tan trench coat with a gray suit underneath. He stopped in front of Germaine's desk as if startled to see her there.

"Why hello, you must be the new trainee, my name is Detective Marlow." He smiled tightly and did not extend a hand.

Germaine met eyes with him, but just barely, something about his aura looked weird, "Germaine."

Germaine knew something was off about this guy. Creepy even. His aura was flat and muted, past that, he gave off a vibe. Like a cold gust of wind. She hadn't realized she was staring until he cocked his head, an odd movement, something seen more in birds than people, and his eyes seemed to shift from an ordinary brown to the shiny black of an insect. She gasped and looked down, when she raised her eyes, his looked as ordinary as before.

"Hope everyone is settling in well," he said coolly as Selene came around her desk, happier than Germaine had ever seen her; it was obvious that Selene liked this creepy guy, but for what reason she couldn't tell. Pasty, weird aura, and a *cop?* Though she had to admit his face lost its hardness when he looked back at Selene, the two of them instantly transformed into kinder and gentler versions. His hand went to her waist, leaned in and pecked her on the cheek, and Selene flushed a little. Gag, young love.

"Any new leads?" Selene asked, as he shucked off his jacket and she took it to hang up.

"Well, Persimmon delivered an amulet to the station that can read auras." He sat down in the client chair facing Selene's desk. "We sent a sensitive officer out canvassing in the areas on the map wearing it and he managed to locate another resurrectionist. So, with you and Germaine here, and this officer with an amulet, we're moving along. I'm waiting on Dania to give us a list of how many women she has working for her. But I think only six more to locate."

"How many days till the new moon?" Selene asked pouring herself coffee.

The detective leaned back and covered his eyes, pressing his long white hands to his temples. "Ah, don't remind me. Hey, Germaine, you don't happen to know any cultist end times murderers, do you? Really make my job easier." He grinned at her.

She smirked, "Sadly no, but you'll be the first person I tell." He chuckled and nodded, his smile revealing shockingly long sharp teeth. Her skin crawled.

"Joking aside, you haven't seen anyone suspicious, have you? Been followed? A new guy coming around, twenties, brown hair, white?" He watched her, face gone cop cold. Her heart sped up. Why did they all assume if a boy was talking to her it was because he wanted to kill her? Is that really what they thought of her? She knew they were just grasping at straws and women had been dying, but it still stung. Made her feel like the same old Germaine from Bixby, homely, spooky, unwanted. Like John only liked her for what she was, not who she was.

"No. No, I told Selene already. No weirdos looking for virgin sacrifices." Germaine's voice had been louder and more emotional than she intended. Embarrassed, she stood, "Do you mind if I head out a little early? The bus takes forever and I have a paper to write."

Selene and the detective exchanged a quick glance before she nodded, "Of course. Good work today, you are so much faster at data entry than I am. I appreciate it. See you tomorrow?"

Germaine nodded, gathered her things and headed out, aware they were watching her. Just some fat awkward virgin. Ripe for the pickings of a cult killer. Once in the elevator, she swiped at the sweat gathering on her upper lip, and let out a breath. John liked her, *he liked her*. They connected, she was sure of it. She wasn't some hapless victim. She wasn't a child or a fool either. Germaine had hoped college would be a fresh start where she would be taken seriously. She spent her whole life being bullied and teased, she knew the difference between fake and real friendships. She'd been the butt of so many jokes back home, but John saw her, he really did. She wasn't going to rat him out to the cops for talking to her and buying her coffee.

Eighteen

I watched the door with raised eyebrows as Germaine left. The girl was red as a beet and near tears when she dashed out. I walked to the large windows and spied her practically running across the craggy parking lot toward the street, and ultimately to the bus stop.

"That normal behavior from her?" Marlow said stepping beside me, his cool hand at the small of my back. "I think she knew what I was and it freaked her out."

"She's normally weird, but not that weird, you may be right. She looked guilty to me, too," I leaned into him thoughtfully.

"Guilty like maybe there is a boy...and we implied he may have ulterior motives?"

"Maybe, she was all sort of flustered about the virgin stuff earlier when I asked. But I was also a shy outcast once, hell, I still am, so she may be just super awkward. Either way, someone should be keeping an eye on her."

"I agree, I will call Regine, see what she is up to since she is still on duty."

He stepped away, phone to ear and I noticed how gaunt he looked. It had been a few days since he'd drank my blood, and I wondered if he'd had enough, or even what enough was for a nearly century-old vampire.

I was finishing up on my computer, about to close up when my buzzer sounded. Marlow looked up from his call, no doubt due to my facial reaction. It was the half-life, Amar Patel. He'd left a few messages over the last week, but with the abduction, and the murder investigation, and my sheer caseload, I kept forgetting. Now he was here.

Marlow was at my side in a blink, looking down at the screen. "You know him?"

"I raised him, he's been trying to get ahold of me, I've just been so busy."

"Let him up, I'm in no hurry. It could be important."

A moment later Amar entered my office, and I was again struck by what a lovely man he was, soft eyes, long lashes, and lustrous black hair long enough to curl. He came in eyes a little downcast and clearly nervous.

"Amar, I am so sorry..."

"I have been trying to reach you for days, and I..." He petered off as he took in Detective Marlow standing in the corner near the coffee pot. Recognition followed as he looked from Marlow to me and back again.

"Anything you say to me, you can say in front of my friend here, I promise. Unless you'd prefer privacy?"

"It's not privacy for me, but for you, Ms. Shade."

"Sit down please, call me Selene, you want a drink or anything?"

"No, no. Just to talk to you, just to make sure I am not going crazy, or that there isn't something wrong with me. That I came back wrong somehow."

"Whoa, whoa. Okay I need you to start from the beginning, you need to catch me up."

He rubbed at his eyes, it was a very human gesture. No shambling zombies here, obviously now was not the time, but I was proud of my work.

"After I saw you at the restaurant, you were in my thoughts. I'd wanted to catch up with you, just check in really, since you are kind of my...maker. But that was all really. As I told you before, I have a job, a boyfriend, things are okay. It was more just for coffee and because, if anything, I felt like *you* needed a friend. That night, I could sense a sadness in you, all the way across the room. As if you wanted me to come to you. Not summoned, but just a need."

I swallowed, avoiding his eyes. Tried to cast my memory back to that night, it was the date with Peter Partridge the journalist. Is it possible that distress activated one of my half-lifes? I suppose it was, but it was embarrassing and showed a lack of control. *Or too much control?* A smaller voice whispered. The kind of control a Master of the Dead would have? That any nearby half-lifes could be so in tune with my emotions and ready to act was chilling.

"I thought little of it at the time. But then the next night I was at home, I live in Peak's Corners." My blood chilled, already knowing where this was heading, since Peak's Corner was the Goat Hill neighborhood on the west side, where I was kidnapped in a basement. Marlow moved from behind me and was now standing behind Amar leaning against Dot's desk. "I felt this compulsion, like a signal or a siren in my head, ordering me to get up and find you, to save you, and I was out of my house, on the street, looking for you when the signal just disappeared as if it had never been. I was left standing in the street and then I saw you, and you," he turned back to Marlow, "fleeing a house, running away, bloodied and scared. I hid and you never saw me, but I saw you."

I met Marlow's eyes across the room now, and debated what to tell this man. That he was summoned to the house revealed something about my nature and abilities. It proved that those who feared what resurrectionists can do weren't entirely wrong. I cleared my throat.

"I was taken, by a cabal of necromancers, over a misunderstanding. Detective Marlow over there rescued me."

"Well, aided in the rescue, you had it under control," he said quietly, small smile at the corner of his mouth.

"I panicked when I was trapped there and I sent out a call, or a signal as you put it, to any dead in the area. They had a ton of mice in the walls. I had no idea you were out there, or so near. Or that I could summon you in that way. I promise. I thought my life was in danger."

I could see the anxiety in Amar, could imagine how scary it would be to realize someone could literally control you and puppet you around to do their bidding. Half-lifes did not sign up to be slaves, and the real fear of Zombie Queens was in just that. They could use the dead as their minions. All the dead. That familiar feeling, from all the way back to my parent's funeral returned. The feeling of being a true monster. Something rightfully feared.

"I understand that people like you have an enormous power. But I didn't think you could control me. Make me move, make me think a certain way."

"Most can't, right, Selene? This was an extreme life or death situation," Marlow chimed in. He was curious, probably just as curious as Amar, since theoretically I could control vampires as well under that logic.

My pulse was in my throat, I hated the way Amar looked at me. "Yes, you are right, it is not common, and Amar you shouldn't be afraid," I flinched at the word as it came out, because his face went from nervous to angry.

"You messed with my mind! You controlled me."

"That was a freak situation! I was kidnapped for Christ's sake. My life was in danger."

"So you are saying at any point, if you are in danger, or someone like you is, I may be called into duty, activated like a robot, yes?" Those velvety eyes were hard now.

"I don't want to lie to you, Amar, so I will say I don't know. But I also have never experienced anything like what happened the other day. If you were in the vicinity and someone like myself needed help to fight..." Something in Marlow's expression caused me to pause, like a light bulb had gone off over his head. "What? What is it?" I asked, Amar's head bobbed between us, annoyed at being sidetracked.

"A Master of the Dead is believed to be able to summon armies. The mythology of the Zombie Queen is all about using an army of the dead, hordes of zombies to fight an enemy right?" Marlow said.

"What are you on about? I am talking about my free fucking will!" Amar shouted.

Marlow continued eyes bright. "I think the necromancers and the witches were wrong. About your purpose. What if the resurrectionists are a line of defense for the world? What if a Master of the Dead is actually designed to protect the world using half-lifes like soldiers?"

Amar looked to me, "Is that true?"

"I'm as lost as you are here, buddy," I replied.

"This isn't a joke," he said, furious.

"No one is joking. Seriously, Amar, I have no designs to enslave you, I didn't even know that I had. I was afraid for my life and I went into survival mode. You were nearby and so caught the signal that was meant for a bunch of *dead mice*. Please, don't be offended by that. You own your life and your body. Yes, my magic is what binds you together on this plane, but I never want you to think your life and your choices aren't your own or that I want to control you."

He stared down at his hands, and they shook. "It's funny timing, because finally, I was starting to feel like, well not myself, but someone again. A person. I was feeling more settled. Y'know?" The tears in his eyes filled me with guilt. I nodded afraid my voice would shake. "This experience just reminded me how much I'd lost, how I am not actually a person at all. I'm a thing. A thing that can be manipulated. A tool."

"You aren't a thing." Marlow leaned closer to Amar, his face had what I assumed was "supportive cop" on now.

"See, Detective, that's where you may be wrong. The worst part," he stared up at the ceiling, swiping at his eyes, "was how badly I wanted to save you, how excited I was to fight for you, to kill for you, to be your hero. I haven't felt anything as intensely since being brought back. You calling me unlocked something wild and violent. A hunger. I haven't felt anything so pure since I've risen."

He swallowed, "I wanted to be your slave. It felt good to have purpose. It's what scared me so much, it's why I needed to see you."

I was at a loss for words. What Amar was saying terrified me, what Marlow had said earlier about controlling armies of the dead made it worse. I just wanted to run my little business and eat takeout and be a regular person. I didn't want to control anyone or have hordes of slaves or whatever. I felt raw, sad, and a little angry. I did not ask for any of this. I didn't want to stop murderers or be an important player in the fate of the world or overthink my advanced gifts which had done nothing but alienate me since I was six. Dot knew that, it's why she didn't push or pry, she never had me doing anything out of my comfort zone or that would bring attention to me. She was protecting me from this.

All of this.

Finally, after circling the drain one or two more times, I met Amar's searching stare. "I never meant to hurt you or cause you to question your purpose. I am just trying to live my life as best I can, same as you. But there are things that are bigger than the two of us out there. Bad things. I don't want to scare you, but I also don't know what the future holds. Go, live your life, kiss your boyfriend, cash your paychecks and do not fear me. Please." Then I sent Amar on his way. As soon as he closed the door I had my face on my desk, tempted to bang my head against it when I felt Marlow near me.

"You ok?"

I laughed, a high-pitched hysterical sound, and stared at my hands in my lap.

"No. I just want a regular life."

"What does that even mean? What is a regular life?"

I lifted my head high enough to glare. "You're a clever lad, I'm sure you can figure it out."

He knelt at eye level, "You may not like it, but it is good to know that you can summon half-lifes to you like that. It's an amazing weapon if you need it. He had to be at least a few houses away. That's a great range."

"I don't want to have an impressive range, I don't want the ability to play puppeteer to an unwilling victim. It's horrible."

"Yes. It's just good to know, that is all I am saying. If you are in danger your call extends pretty far, blocks even. Those dead girls, their call was fifty feet, one hundred feet out. But you got a guy down the street in his *house*. And it was by accident. I bet that whole neighborhood is covered with dead things that crawled out to save you. It's pretty amazing. Imagine how far you could reach if you really tried."

I turned my head away from Marlow, forehead against the cool wood of my desk. "I don't feel amazing, and I don't want to talk about this anymore. Please?"

He began rubbing my shoulders, I relaxed despite myself. When I leaned my head back against him with a contented sigh, he blew out a breath and stepped back from me.

"Okay," he said nervously, "I need to talk about something else with you. No big deal, but something we need to work out."

Groan. "What now?"

"Nothing major. It's been a few days since you kindly offered your blood. I don't want to weaken you and am happy to get it elsewhere, I just wanted to let you know. Because even just being this close to you reminded me how starved I am."

"Ah, I thought you looked a little peaked today."

"It's not an easy conversation, so early in our seeing each other for this sort of thing..."

"No, it's fine, really, you can have mine. It's okay."

"Thank you. I normally wouldn't go so long between feedings, but I also felt uncomfortable going elsewhere without talking to you first, I could see how it would look...sneaky." He stared out the window at the water. "I just need to be on my game at work and with the case."

I put a finger to his lips. "It's all right. I promise."

He kissed me then. The kiss turned passionate and toothy, and

before long my pants were discarded, as were his, and we officially chris-
tened my desk. I could only imagine the ghost of Dot bobbing above
with a big pervy thumbs up. Somewhere in there, he drank my blood,
though like the first time I barely felt it, like the pinch of the Novocaine
needle at the dentist.

Afterwards we sat at my desk, he in the chair, me on his lap. He
looked pink and puffy where I am sure I looked pasty and deflated, he
rested his head on the top of mine. I hated to admit how secure I felt,
being held much like a child would.

"So, you think Germaine has a secret boyfriend, and that boyfriend
is the killer?" I finally said, my mind replaying the weird day.

"God, wouldn't that be great? Case closed."

"Yeah."

"Stop!" Germaine said laughing, though there was an undertone of
panic to it. She was standing, balancing, on a banister, looking out
toward the sea. John had his arms around her waist to keep her from
falling, until he'd let go for a moment and she thought she would fall.

"It's beautiful out here," she said looking up, the sky an explosion
of purples and pinks, oranges and pale yellows, reflecting double in the
waves. She breathed in the briny sea air and sighed into John's warm
arms. She was a little self-conscious about her soft midsection, his arms
wrapped tight around it. But he didn't seem to care.

He helped her down and they both sat on the bench looking out,
"I thought you'd like it here. The pier is just awesome at sunset, and
they have this great fish-fry place, and homemade ice cream."

"That all sounds great," she responded, vainly tucking wild orange
hair behind her ear only to have the wind pull it back out again.

"Are you alright? I was just joking about pushing you in, you
know?" She pulled her gaze from the choppy waves to look at him. Her
handsome summer boy with sun-kissed skin and tousled hair. His
strange aura, his hazel eyes; so warm and inviting. If she'd told them
about John, they wouldn't believe he liked her. They would believe he
was using her. For a ritual. That he planned to kill her.

"Germaine, you look like someone just ran over your dog. Are you
upset with me?" Was there a tremble of fear in his voice? Fear that she

was cross? Her chest squeezed, god she hoped so. God, she hoped he actually cared about her, that this wasn't a joke, or worse.

She breathed out, preparing without realizing it. "John, I really like you."

He laughed a bit tensely, "Well that's good, I like you too."

"Do you?" She could hear the fragility, the desperation in her voice and cursed it. "You don't have any ulterior...motives?"

"What kind do you mean?" Was his tone stonier than before? More defensive? The sun chose that moment to dip below the waterline, and it may have been her imagination but the temperature seemed to drop a few degrees.

"There is a killer out there, targeting young resurrectionists, college students...virgins." She risked making eye contact and the expression in his eyes was not what she expected. She anticipated quick denial, even anger, but instead he just watched her, eyebrows frowned into a single line. "You fit the profile."

"How do you know this? *Who told you this?*" he asked, voice barely a whisper.

"The murders are all over the news. But as for the details? My boss did. She's been helping the police. They told me. They teamed up with local witches to find all the resurrectionists in the area using magic. They're rounding them all up now, to protect them from the killer."

He flinched and she just knew. Her heart sunk like a weighted stone, and she felt like a total fool. A gullible pathetic fool: ugly, weird, and unlovable. A joke. She was so overcome with her own inadequacies she didn't even think to be scared.

"I don't know anything about that," he said, but it was too late, the pause too long, and it rang false.

"I am so stupid. No one like you would want someone like me."

"Germaine."

"Please—John, James, whoever you are. Just don't. I won't believe you."

"If you think I'm the killer, shouldn't you be running away and calling the cops?"

"Why are you doing this? What do you hope to do?" she whispered, unsure herself why she wasn't fleeing to safety.

She could see the debate in him to be honest. "Please," she pushed, "I don't actually know enough about you to incriminate you, right?"

He risked eye contact with her and she was shocked to see guilt and shame there.

"I have no choice," he said finally.

She leaned forward, "What do you mean?"

"It's complicated, but I have to do this ritual because I am the only one that can. Or they think so anyway," He glanced at her, again that guilt in his eyes, "The Order of the White Crow. Old guys, heavy hitters. My uncle...he'd been part of their group. They made him and he died. Now they're making me do it. If I don't, I'm dead." Grief flitted across his features and was smoothed away. Germaine could see his pain and felt a little disgusted in herself for it. He was a rapist and a murderer after all.

"So, what makes you so special?" Germaine said, as she squinted at his aura again, it was so strange.

"My mom is a resurrectionist. So is my twin sister."

"I didn't think men could be..." she said but he cut her off.

"Yup." He made an ugly sound, "For all the good it does me, I have no real power. I can sense you, sense your power even. But other than that, it's useless. I can't raise anything."

"Unless—"

"Unless you are the Order of the White Crow and you want to use some freaky shadow monster to open the door to another dimension, and you need a male and female resurrectionist for their 'mating' ritual. Then you are pretty darn valuable. Until they or the ritual kill you."

"Why didn't the ritual work for your uncle, or for you?" Three girls were dead, Germaine thought to herself, three girls he raped and murdered. With her lined up to be four.

"I don't know! I guess they weren't strong enough. They had power, but not enough apparently. They were virgins. Totally green in magic. But they weren't powerful enough. Or I'm not."

"But what if that's the problem?" Germaine said thoughtfully. "Normally, the resurrectionist is in control, right? But you've taken all the power away from them. They are untrained, scared, and they don't want or know what is happening. Raising the dead takes an enormous amount of focus,"

"What are you saying?"

"How are they even using their power? Even in the Bible's virgin birth, she had to *agree* to it."

"You think using magic novices was wrong." James' expression was sour.

"I think the women had no chance. Feels like another situation where the men just assumed the woman would know what to do naturally. But nothing comes that natural, not having babies, not taking care of them, nothing. You wanted them to do a complex spell in the scariest moment of their life while you are killing them? With no warning or training?"

James sighed and turned away, "I don't know! I never asked for this, and I never wanted to hurt anyone."

"Well, you did. Three people are dead." Germaine reminded him, "I don't want to be the fourth."

"If we can do this for them, and succeed, we usher in a new reality and remake the world. They will reward us with real power. Not just the ability to make zombies, but real godlike power. Real immortality. Real magic. More." His eyes gleamed in the dusk light, hungry, perhaps a little mad. "I'm sick of being no one. Aren't you?"

Germaine nodded. Wondering about this new world. Wondering what they could give her.

"I know you have no reason to believe me, Germaine. But I like you, I really do. I think you are beautiful." She rolled her eyes. "I don't want to hurt you."

"I am not that pathetic as to fall for flattery now. Who knows what you said to the other girls."

"I am not trying to flatter you, I am being honest. If I can properly do the ritual, if you were willing to do it with me, be part of it, willingly, you would be the new mother of the world. The new Virgin Mary. You feel powerless and invisible? Feel like a small-town girl who no one even gives the time, right? I am giving you the opportunity to have the world on a platter."

"The world on a platter," she responded flatly, her emotions whirling like a hurricane inside.

"We'd be together, king and queen. You are more than Germaine from the Plains. You are a creature of raw power, power over life and death, you could be the gateway to a new world, with me. Think on it."

"John, how can you think I would willingly..."

"Think on it. Please. I don't want to hurt anyone else, especially not you. I know it sounds lame but: Be my queen. Help me."

"What's to stop me from calling the cops right now?"

He shrugged and gave a half smile. "You don't have much to go on. I use a burner phone to talk to you and a fake name. I wear an obscuring amulet when we've gone out to make me hard to remember."

"And yet you want me to trust you. Tell me your real name, at least," she finally responded.

"My name is actually James. I thought the ritual would work so...it was only after, that I started going by John."

"James, nice to meet you. I don't want you to kill me," she said and met his eyes.

"Then work with me, be my queen. Think it over." Then, before she could stop him, he leaned in, kissed her cheek, and walked away without looking back.

Leaving her alone at the pier.

NINETEEN

"Thank you for coming," Lucinda, head of the Order of Yama, the necromantic cabal and recent victim of zombie mice, said to her guest.

The scratches and bites were healing and should leave no scars, but still looked pretty nasty, marring her otherwise beautiful face.

"I figure now is a time when we all should be comparing notes and being on the same team. It's not a time for tribal infighting," Lucinda continued, walking down the long slick hallway on sky-high heels and opening a door to a conference room. The room was windowless with gray walls and gleaming tile underfoot. The long conference table was a sleek black and could easily seat twenty. The lighting was subdued and the overall impression was austere.

Lucinda pulled out a rolling leather office chair and offered it to her guest, then sat herself in the chair beside it. "Don't you agree?"

Persimmon Shaw, coven leader and one of the most powerful witches in Goat Hill, smiled tightly. "I do, Lucinda, I do. Since we all seem to be getting dragged into this thing whether we want to or not."

"Exactly. Thank you for being so reasonable."

"Do I have a reputation for being otherwise?" Persimmon responded with a tight smile.

Lucinda propped her suited elbow onto the table and leaned toward the witch. "No, not at all. This is purely a fact-finding, or fact-

sharing meetup. I know our tribes have often had issues in the past. I also know we are both reasonable, modern women."

"Don't be so humble, Lucinda, your tribe has had issues with *every* other one in the past, not just us."

Lucinda forced a chuckle, "Be that as it may, we all need to be on the same side now."

"So, just to clarify, when you had Selene Shade abducted, whose side was she on? An us or a them? Just confused on that part. Who is on your side of the gameboard?"

Lucinda sighed, clearly wondering when that ordeal would be behind her, "That was a huge misunderstanding. Our intel indicated that Selene was a Master of the Dead. One that is not tapping into that potential, but has it nonetheless."

Persimmon nodded, green eyes bright, "I would agree."

"We felt that she would be the perfect vessel for the ritual, because of her raw power. Ergo, we felt removing her from the gameboard, to steal your phrase, was the best option."

"And now?"

"Well that is why I wanted to call you here. I know you have been working with the police, helping to locate those that may be possible targets."

"I have."

"We'd also like a copy of that list, I think everyone should be in on this. Our killer so far isn't looking for power as much as—"

"Purity. Virgins. The old classic."

Lucinda smiled, "Exactly."

Persimmon nodded and pursed her lips, thoughtful. "I will give you a list, figure the more people we can have out on the street looking for these girls the better. But no kidnapping, seriously. Since my senses are telling me that this guy won't screw up again."

Lucinda nodded, "Same here, all the spirit world is in a twitter about it, things are rippling along the planes. I would prefer to be on the winning side of that. I have a safe house prepared for the little resurrectionists, so we can keep them with us through the new moon. Willingly, no kidnapping."

Persimmon's eyebrow slid up, "I'm sure the accommodations will be lovely, considering."

Lucinda sighed, "You all need to get over that altercation with Selene, it was a miscommunication by morons. It was handled incorrectly and won't happen again. The safe house is a large townhouse on the waterfront, north of town in Gabe's Bay. I think any resurrectionist with an ounce of survival instinct will come with us and at least stay through the new moon. I don't trust the cops to understand the threat."

"Then what? Do we lock them up every new moon after? Finding the girls is only one part of the puzzle. We need to be working harder to find *him*. Stopping him and whoever he is working for."

"I have an idea about that. I'm going to exhume the last girl, summon her spirit and see if I can't get an image of the guy."

Persimmon grimaced, "You know they already raised her, according to my police contact, Selene and the police that is."

Lucinda continued, "Yes. But I may be able to get more from her than Selene. I had another idea, another avenue to look into. A job for you."

"Oh?"

"They don't like my tribe, won't talk to us at all, but perhaps you could reach out to an elemental? A green guardian of the woods? They could report if our killer shows up."

"That is an interesting idea. Though elementals are...temperamental. On top of that, they don't really understand time the way we do. There also aren't too many green elementals left in the city. But I will look into it. Possibly talk to some weather ones, mix up a bad storm, that'd keep people indoors on the new moon as well."

"Great. I will be in touch with any news, you do the same. Get me that list."

I rolled over and felt the bedsheets, empty and cool. Marlow had been gone longer than I thought. The clock was on my side, and I fumbled for it in the gloom. It being an old wind-up job that did not light up, I had to press it to my nose to see the clock's arms. Marlow had probably been carting the old thing around with him for forty years.

That stray thought reminded me how old he was. I placed the metal clock on the bedside table to continue its ticking. I had woken before the alarm and had plenty of time before work. Plenty of time to think about what dating a vampire really meant. For one, he couldn't have children, not that I had ever really wanted any. He would always be drinking blood from me or someone who wasn't me. He would stay the same and I would get older.

My inner thigh was tender from where he'd bitten me. I knew going forwards that I couldn't be his only donor. I already felt fatigue, that was clearly the early stages of anemia. I would need to be upping my iron and meat quantities if I was going to keep servicing my vampire boyfriend.

Vampire boyfriend. Gods. It was exciting, and scary, and bewildering. And shameful if I was being honest with myself. I was ashamed at how badly I wanted someone to love me. I needed to snap out of this, all of this. There was such a bigger world out there than dating silliness. There were lives at stake. I should be focusing on my business, on training my little protégé. I should be working on the case, finding our killer, saving the world. *Should, should, should.* But my mind only wanted to think about Marlow, think about his arms around me, his lips, his smile, his attention. That was the sexiest thing in the end, his focus on me. No one had ever looked at me the way he had. Since I was orphaned, I'd always felt I was doomed to be alone.

I was sick of my own pitiful mental monologuing and dragged myself from the bed to get my day started. Finishing breakfast, showered and dressed, my phone rang, and it was Peter Partridge. I debated letting it go to voicemail, but curiosity had me answering.

"Hello, Peter."

"Selene, hi, hello, so glad to hear your voice. You still with that cop?" I could hear the smile in his voice.

"Yes, Peter. How's your dad?"

"Old, crazy. It's part of why I called you. He wanted to meet you."

"That can be arranged, I am pretty busy, but luckily just hired an apprentice, so that should help."

"No kidding? Where'd you find her?"

"Craigslist."

"Huh. The mystical and the arcane in the same place I sold my futon. Amazing times."

I glanced at my watch and got my shoes on, heading out the door balancing the phone on my chin, a thought dawned on me. I knew I should go through Marlow first, but we were so close to the new moon.

"I know you want to write an article about me, and am guessing you plan to exploit your father's situation to make it more human interest."

"Selene! How...spot on of a prediction. Wouldn't use the word *exploit* though. What's the point of being a journalist and having an opportunity like this and not taking advantage? Would you do that though, let me interview you?"

"Maybe, when the dust settles. If you do something for me first. It's something for you too, if you can crack this, you may be able to help solve the murders that have been going on."

"I'm listening," he said.

"Get a pen. Okay, I want you to look into using all your reporter skills. There is an old God/entity, named Nigrum Porta or the Black Door. Show me a connection to the recent killings and how resurrectionists come into play, and most importantly how to stop him. As soon as possible."

"Sounds easy." He deadpanned and I laughed as I got into my car, parked in Marlow's guest spot in the basement garage.

"Countdown is ticking, and trust me this could be career-making. You may even save someone's life. Hell, you may save the world."

Peter chuckled, "Well, now you are talking my language. I am guessing you think this is the bad guy that's been killing these girls?"

"Maybe. I look forward to hearing what you find."

"Me too."

Persimmon stood in the forest. She was barefoot although the April evening was cold. She let her feet sink into the earth and forced her breathing and heartbeat to slow. She needed to summon an elemental, and to do that, which wasn't the easiest of feats, she would need to be calm and prepared. The rest of her coven was a comforting presence behind her.

They made the circle and lit the candles. She said the words. Now they waited. She'd tried for two days after talking to Lucinda to get a forest elemental to help with the murders and any information, but the creatures were too abstract to help in that way. Though they did provide her with a list of bodies, none of which seemed recent, which she planned to pass on to the police, most likely Marlow, as she couldn't imagine who else there would understand how she came across such information. For all she knew, they were thousand-year-old Native American remains. But the elementals couldn't pinpoint the ritual or any pertinent details to help.

She'd given up, quietly frustrated that she had nothing tangible to bring back to help as the clock was ticking down the days until the new moon. There was alien energy all around her. Doom portents. She decided the best thing to do would be to try a weather elemental instead. She focused and chanted, and when she was just about to quit, that was when it chose to appear. Appear in the loosest of terms as the elementals were nearly incorporeal. The thing before her was roughly human-shaped made of compressed fog and sparkling dew. It mirrored her appearance in vague approximation, even down to her expressions. Like looking into a fog mirror.

"Great elementals, we beseech you and call for your aid in our time of need."

The fog twin waved her hand in annoyance. "*Speak plain, witch. What is it you seek? There's no drought, the flowers are coming. What is it your mortal heart wants from us?*" Its voice was little more than wind through tall grasses.

"A bad thing comes from another world. A great threat on the night of the new moon. We ask that you make it hard for it to come to pass. That you make it unpleasant for people to leave their homes. We ask you to hide the moon."

The fog creature smiled, "*A storm? You'd like a storm.*"

"Yes, if it's within your power."

"*Oh, this we can do. This will be such fun!*" The fog creature clapped its hands together. "*How wonderful a request. We are so pleased that we shall ask for nothing in return.*"

Persimmon felt a chill up her spine, the elemental was far too pleased with her request, and she feared what she had just set upon her small city. But a hurricane would keep people inside and would make it hard to perform an arcane ritual.

"Till the new moon and no longer."

"*By dawn of that day, the storm will be a memory,*" the elemental said and then vanished, dissipating before her very eyes.

PART FOUR:
WANING CRESCENT

TWENTY

"Two days to the new moon," Robinson said ominously, staring at the calendar pinned to the corkboard beside her desk. She frowned and slowly slid her eyes toward her partner.

"Two days," he parroted back, hoping that they had done enough, at least to buy them another month. The last week had passed in a blur. Police officers, necromancers, and volunteers with magic abilities had managed to track down every burnhole on Persimmon's map. All ten women were accounted for. It was incredible really.

Persimmon and Lucinda had even arranged a safe house for the night of the new moon for all the women who fit the profile. The majority had agreed, which also was something of a miracle. Robinson and a small army of police would be protecting the girls, and going forward, would continue to on the nights of the new moon until the killer was found or scared away from Goat Hill.

Of the women who had refused, only one was giving him pause, Germaine Whately, Selene's new apprentice. He replayed the repeated conversations with her, warning her, reminding her three girls had been killed already.

"I will be fine, I am going to be out of town visiting my family that weekend, so I will be safely out of the state." She'd claimed, which would be great, preferable even, if he believed her. But he'd been around awhile, and he knew a thing or two about liars. He was one after all.

"Penny for your thoughts?" Robinson interrupted, watching him thoughtfully.

"Selene's apprentice."

"The Whately girl?"

"Something is bothering me about her, about the whole situation. I just feel like from the moment I met her she has been lying. That she may know more about this than the others. Still no evidence of a boyfriend?"

"We've had officers keeping tabs, they haven't seen her with anyone but her roommate, but she goes to a coffee shop a lot, and she's gone twice to a huge apartment complex near campus. Could be where he lives?"

Marlow was thoughtful, he replayed every interaction he'd had with the girl, he knew she was uncomfortable around him. But he'd assumed that was because she knew what he was, and unlike the attractively open-minded Selene, most people, especially people from the rural human areas, feared someone like him.

Hell, if Robinson knew, even though they'd been partners for two years, even though he considered her a friend and would protect her with his life, she'd probably request a new partner immediately. The whole station would turn on him. The world was more welcome to magic as it had improved and enlightened human existence, just as they'd embraced technology over time. He's seen a lot of growth these last few years with gay people, different races, and religions. But monsters still had a way to go.

People were only so progressive. Bloodsuckers who preyed on people for food was usually where the line was. If certain lawmakers had their way, he would be up on that pyre burnt up in town square. Or at least on some sort of registry or in a detention camp. There was no place in the new world order for social predators, human-looking parasites, pretenders.

A dark thought skittered by: if we don't save the world, if Nigrum Porta opens the door, would that new world order be kinder to someone like him? Where would he fit in?

He dismissed it, tried instead to think of all the progress they had made on this case. And how much progress he had made with Selene. He was an old man, who'd fallen in love many times, broken hearts, killed lovers even, or lost them because of what he was. But perhaps with someone closer to his side of the divide, a creature of light and dark, of death and rebirth, he could find some sort of companion. He thought of her body beneath his, those icy-strange eyes looking up at him, trusting him. His fangs ached at the gum line, wanting to push down.

Focus on the case, Marlow. You've got two days.

He could barely keep his mind on the case even with days to Doomsday, he knew it was because he was a little starved, a little half-mad. It had been so long since he'd been feeding from one source. It wasn't enough. He knew it.

The case. The case. He wanted to follow Germaine around, grill her a little, dig around and find the truth. Give her a reason to be afraid of him when all he wanted to do was protect her. Bite her. Empty her.

Marlow shot up, startling Robinson who frowned, "What's up?"

"I...I am not feeling myself, think my blood sugar is low. Be back." He was out the door of the precinct, in his car and darting out into the mid-afternoon traffic on a streak of rubber. Hadn't realized he had been so close to the edge, so close to the darker things that controlled him. He glanced at his phone, debated calling Selene, to tell her, to ask for permission, but that caused a twin emotion of shame and anger. He decided against it, he needed blood, a lot, and fast. If he was to stay sharp and human-shaped.

He headed to a brothel he visited occasionally. Catered to all types. As he pulled up he glanced again at his phone, unsure what the modern relationship etiquette was, unsure if it was unfaithful to not want to kill his lover by accident. The world was possibly on the eve of ending and he was fantasizing about killing people, obviously he wasn't at his best.

He headed up the steps, gave the secret knock, and entered, teeth long.

Lila Goodtree regarded Peter suspiciously.

"I don't talk to the press about ongoing investigations," she finally said, her voice surprisingly powerful for such a petite, frail woman. She blinked up at him through thick smudgy glasses, and he smiled, bringing some of the old Partridge charm to the fore.

"I realize that, ma'am. I wouldn't be a good reporter if I hadn't also researched you and all you've accomplished in your career. I assure you, I have no intention of compromising or interfering with the police. I'm here to help." She fluffed up a little at the mention of her accomplishments, but didn't budge otherwise, he pressed on, "I got a tip, did some research on a certain Black Door fella, and what I've found so far, let me say it's disturbing, and if what I have found is true, may be bigger than a case, may be more like end of the world as we know it. In two days' time."

She scowled, reminding him of an old owl, and looked up and down her quiet street as if there'd been anyone listening. "This isn't about a byline, this is bigger than that, got it?"

"Yes, ma'am, off the record, for sure."

The wizened old occultist let him in.

Peter had followed Selene's lead, just two words, Black Door, Nigrum Porta. He plugged them into a search engine and was swiftly sent down the rabbit hole into a world of strange fertility rituals, human sacrifice, interdimensional travel, alternate realities, and a profile of a killer who was trying to open a door to someplace else. There wasn't much on him, this strange entity, save the basics. A few images, most of the murky cave drawing variety, depicted him as a black stick figure, some images were of him just as a black circle. Others had him as a door or passage. Hours and hours were devoured, reams of notes printed out, a few trips to various libraries including the university. Selene had really given him something big. This was why these girls were getting killed. The killer was trying to summon Nigrum Porta. Or use him to bring something else through.

Peter knew that he had something he could take to the Goat Hill Gazette, but something big, front page. Pulitzer.

But he also remembered Selene's warning, about saving lives, about not scaring the killer underground, not messing with the ongoing investigation. He didn't want a dead girl on his conscience. Or the apocalypse. So instead, he kept his head down and continued to do deeper research on Nigrum Porta: who worshipped him, who would even know about obscure rituals like this, and what would their goal be? Somewhere in that research at the college library a name was given to him. Lila Goodtree. Who also worked for the police.

He explained all this and more to the suspiciously elven old woman over a cup of murky tea. He discreetly plucked cat hair from his lips as he eyed the various felines that were moving through the dusty, swaying stacks to get a closer look at him.

"So, my question for you is: why? We know when and we know who the victim type is. We know where, in as much as we can. But what does an order get from worshipping this guy? Why do they want the door opened, and more importantly what is on the other side?"

Lila's eyes flashed, or rather the reflection in her coke bottle glasses did, as she turned her head, "You know I have been wondering that myself. And why now? Why each month? Three in a row. It seems suddenly urgent doesn't it?

"Is it a single guy filling the father/man role, or are there others in the wings? A whole group. Do they want to get out or let something in?

"In my research I found a case, something similar. Down south in Miami, ten years ago. New moon. Guy found dead on top of a young girl in a park, but the strange thing? Her insides were all messed up. Medical examiner said heart attack and uterine hemorrhage. But what are the odds of those happening at the same time?"

Lila raised a gnarled, arthritic finger as she dug with her other hand in the stacks on her desk. She pulled a book from low in a tall pile, and miraculously it didn't topple. Dusting it off she opened it to a page marked with a viciously red ribbon. "In his possessions, he had an old book. I recognized the title because I own a copy. In it a traveler, claiming to be a great leader from the stars, his world dying, sent through a door, trying to find a way to herald his people to safety." She closed the book with a snap, releasing a plume of dust.

"That's the book he had?"

"Yes, it's a compilation of folk stories. The traveler is old, a man claiming to be a god from another world, called himself The White Crow. Apparently, his skin was milk white and he had hair that looked like white feathers. In the stories, he was able to raise the dead, and get this—he married a local and had a strange blue-eyed daughter. This was in ancient Mesopotamia where blue eyes were not common. According to the old campfire tale, White Crow attempted to use a horde of undead to challenge a rival king. The undead horde overwhelmed the human king and the White Crow took the throne. He ruled for a time, keeping a small group of undead soldiers as his personal guard. But all was not happy under his reign and White Crow was assassinated. When he fell, so did his zombie horde. Only his daughter escaped, it is said she started a new life in a far-off land and had a large family, all girls, with blue eyes and power over the dead."

Peter sat up, eyes meeting Lila's, "Blue eyes and raising the dead? Is that a book on the history of resurrectionists?"

She smiled a mouth more gum than teeth. "It's funny, I'd skimmed this odd text maybe thirty years ago. Resurrectionists are so mysterious, after all. But I never thought much about it past that. The only mention of this otherworldly White Crow and his blue-eyed daughter I have ever come across. But a guy dies on a new moon with a girl with very similar injuries and he has a copy with him? Seems relevant, no?"

"You think resurrectionists are descendants of this White Crow guy? From another world? Like aliens?" Peter felt like his head was about to explode at the mere idea of extraterrestrials. He thought about his conflicting attraction to Selene. Lila pulled a face.

"You are focusing on the wrong part. I don't know if any of this is true, it's one mention in one book that is a translation of a translation from over one thousand years ago, but I am looking into it. I have colleagues combing all manners of archives from here to the moon. But what I will say is this: I think there is a good chance that our killer does believe and is trying to open the passageway to the world this White Crow fella came from. I think that is why he needs—"

"A female resurrectionist for the ritual."

She nodded, pleased that her student had put the pieces together. Now the question of what they would do with that knowledge in this time and place was a whole other mystery.

"I still don't understand why here and now? What's the rush?"

Dania Barabas, rival resurrectionist, sat across from me at my desk and adjusted her cat-eye glasses as she sized me up. It was strange we'd never met face to face considering we were the only two resurrectionist firms in town. But then again, she also had bad blood with my mentor and former partner, Dot.

"I figured it was time to meet and discuss what's been going on. And since you haven't returned any of my many calls, well, here I am." Dania was an interesting woman, striking, with an olive complexion and short black hair. She wore a cheetah print faux-fur coat, wound-red lipstick, and loud jangly earrings. It was a lot of look. "Coffee?"

It took a moment to realize she was asking for coffee and not just starting a conversation. Embarrassed, I leaped up and began prepping the pot. Dania assessed the space unabashedly, practically running a fingertip over my desk for dust. I'd sent Germaine to do a resurrection on her own since Dania arrived just as I was walking out with her. It was a bold move, throwing her into the deep end, but she'd been doing solid work.

"I've heard a lot about you. Dot thought you were really something special." Dania had a way of making that sound like an insult. "Then again, the clients you have turned away often comment you're not too friendly." Again, I was tempted to jump in, but was at a loss with what to say to defend myself. I did refer annoying clients to Dania, her being more touchy-feely and new age-y.

She was a big woman, both tall and wide, and the chair creaked as she turned to face me at the coffee station. "Did you know Dot trained me? I was her apprentice. Did she ever mention that?" Dania said, and I splashed coffee onto my hand, muttering an oath as I turned back to her shaking my head no.

"Long time ago now, she was still working with her mentor at that time, Margot, who was ancient even then. We never agreed, Dot and I, she was a really difficult person. Hardheaded. Crude." I was tempted to scold her for speaking ill of the dead, but reigned it in. Dania seemed a woman who liked to talk and bloviate and build up to where she was going. "You don't say much, do you?" She lowered her glasses and speared me with cobalt-blue eyes. They were an odd color, for someone with such Mediterranean coloring. The eyes of a reanimator.

"No, ma'am, I was waiting for you to get to the point. Cream and sugar?" I smiled wide.

"Both, thank you, dear. I will come right out with it, why haven't you involved me in this investigation? I've called and called."

I opened my mouth and closed it, wondering myself. She was too old for a sacrifice, though I was wary to say that. I knew the police had been checking in with her. But I should have called her back. I'd just honestly forgotten. Yet again I was reminded what a terrible team player I was.

"It's an ongoing investigation, and I am merely helping with it. I knew they'd been talking to you," I said lamely, avoiding her eyes.

"You should have called me immediately, Selene. One of the girls that fits the profile is my apprentice, another is my daughter. Did you know that? Two potential victims right there." Angry, penciled frown tight as she watched my reaction. I felt embarrassed, I didn't even know Dania had a daughter.

"Does she have a different last name than yours?" I remembered the lists, and the map, there was definitely no Barabas on that list. Even I was not that oblivious.

Dania nodded. "Donegal. I have twins actually, a boy and the girl, they have their father's last name. My daughter is in training and also in college."

"I didn't realize, otherwise I would have called back sooner. Really."

"We need to stick with our kind, Selene, don't you think? This is a dangerous time, any one of our girls could be snatched up and murdered."

"A lot happened in a short time, Dania. Christ, I was kidnapped by a cabal of necromancers and been working with the witches." I sat back down at my desk, allowing her to process that.

She put a hand to her chest, mouth agape, "You're kidding!"

"No, I am not. And the police had me raise a mutilated murder victim, when you refused to work with them early on, long before we knew anything. I'm sorry I never returned your calls. I wasn't trying to leave you out."

"The police were asking if I'd heard of Nigrum Porta."

"Had you?"

"I had. But I wasn't ready to tell them that. Again, we need to stick with our own kind. You can't trust humans."

"I have been visited by Nigrum Porta in my dreams, have you?" I stopped short, I hadn't intended to share that with her. She sat up.

"No, but my brother was, a long time ago." Dania took a deep breath through her nose, her lips in a tight line, "My twin brother, he'd always had problems. He was always mixed up with bad characters, drugs, just kind of lost. Apparently, he got involved with some group. The magic was very dark, and he killed himself doing something foolish years ago. It's not something that I like to revisit, obviously. The last time I talked to him, he mentioned Nigrum Porta."

"Was it a sex ritual that killed him?" I felt like the biggest fool, had I called Dania back earlier for information; we'd have learned a lot more a lot sooner.

"My brother was troubled. It was inconclusive, but I do think he died doing a ritual."

Speechless, I busied myself fixing my own coffee. I didn't even *know* male resurrectionists existed. "So, you didn't think this information would help the police?"

"You know, Selene, I didn't think it was actually *real*. It all seemed so out there, trying to open doors to let in creatures from another reality through sex? And I couldn't confirm anything, besides some odd conversation with my drugged-out brother before he died. I didn't know much more than that."

"Well it's real. Or at least he is."

"What is Nigrum Porta like?"

The very thought of him and I was coated in a cold sweat, my heart pounding in chest. The first time I saw him, it was in Belinda's death memory and he was crawling over her, tearing her apart from the inside. The second time, he was crouched in my room, hunkered down beside the chair, asking for his door. Was he asking me or telling me? Later, at Marlow's apartment standing over me.

"Scary. And he wants to open a door, that's all I know," I said. "Could your brother see auras, like us?"

"Oh yes, he was very good, better than me. Even in a crowd."

All through the investigation we'd been trying to figure out how the killer was able to locate these girls. It took an entire coven of seasoned witches to even get close using a tracking spell, and that merely provided a map with where they were at that moment. Even if you had the rare ability to see auras, you would still need to be in touching distance to focus on one. It was only after nearly a week of beat cops and psychics within the force searching those areas using charms trying to locate the girls. But what would be the point of male resurrectionists' only ability to be identifying others...

"Is it to breed?" I interrupted Dania, her crisp pencil-lined eyebrows lifted. I rushed to explain my thought process, "I'm trying to figure out what the purpose of male resurrectionists would be. Why would they be able to hone in on females? What if it is to encourage pairing up? To produce more resurrectionists? Or for rituals like this one? Does any of that make sense?" Dania opened her hands, bracelets clanging, similarly baffled. She didn't know.

"How exactly did he die?" Dania had the grace to look uncomfortable, no doubt hitting closer to home than she had wanted. She spun one of the many bracelets around her wrist, eyes downcast.

"The police had found him and a lover dead in a park. As his next of kin, I went down to Miami to identify the body and clear out his possessions from a small apartment. I kept all the arcane materials and books, in part to hide them from the tabloids and sensationalist news, and to understand what my brother had been messing with."

"Do you still have them? The books he left?"

"Some, I'd put them into storage and haven't touched them in years. I can share them with the police, if it could help."

"Yes. I think that would be invaluable. This is the puzzle piece we needed."

I was about to ask her more when my phone rang. Marlow.

"Dania, this is the detective on the case, I am going to put him on speaker phone, he will be so appreciative for everything, trust me."

Dania caught Marlow up to where we were.

"Dania, would you be able to meet an officer at the storage locker today?"

"I think so, let me go home and find the key. It's been a while."

"Okay, let us know as soon as you have it."

After the call, I walked Dania to the elevator. When I pushed the button, she turned to me, "I was thinking...maybe you should go to the safehouse as well. If Nigrum Porta is in your dreams, the necromancers may be right. He hasn't visited me, or my daughter, or my new girl." *Or Germaine*, I filled in silently. "You may be the chosen one after all."

She was a few steps into the elevator, doors sliding closed, "Also, it's not in my nature to gossip, but I think that detective has a thing for you."

TWENTY-ONE

Marlow lay on the dingy mattress, sated.

He'd been walking into the brothel when the guilt overrode his hunger and he decided to call Selene. But instead of a confession, she put him on speakerphone and he was given a huge break in the case. Dania-fucking-Barabas had all the puzzle pieces apparently. He texted the details to Robinson before rushing inside, starved and excited. They needed to get the dead brother's books.

He'd taken much more blood from the donor than he would ever dream of consuming from Selene. Not so much as to leave the girl in the hospital, but if he was being honest, it was close. He knew they were professionals here and she would be given fluids and iron supplements as soon as he left. He floated, content and full, his body rapidly converting her lifeforce into energy. His muscles reknit, his skin renewed, even the enamel on his teeth was stronger. That was the nature of a soul-sucking thief, stealing from others to extend his life forever.

While he knew he needed to stay full to be good at his job, to be able to pass as human, and to not accidentally kill someone, it still smarted and he wished he'd told Selene before. She would understand, she had to. It was just awkward.

His phone buzzed. He'd only been gone an hour; he pulled his phone from his pocket, sliding his human visage back on. He had a job, he was a man. Though this full of blood, he could feel the temptation to regress to the simplest of organisms. A bloated tick. It would be so much easier to hide and sleep.

"Yes, Regine," he said, sitting up as his partner talked, "Great, glad they are sending over the George Barabas files. This is major. Me? Much better thanks, got something to eat. Just been burning the candle at both ends."

He gathered his shirt from the floor and glanced at the girl on the bed. She was wan, skin ashy, eyes half open, but breathing. She would need a lot of juice and cookies, but she'd be all right. He felt a pang of guilt, but this brothel knew what they were getting into. They charged enough. He dressed and headed out, in the hallway he was stopped by Meredith, owner and Madame.

"You leave her alive?" she said, watchful under thick fake eyelashes. She was an older woman, with a build that reminded him of the Venus of Willendorf. She filled the hallway, arms crossed over huge pendulous breasts.

"Yes, ma'am, of course. Thank you for seeing me on such short notice."

"I don't like taking bloodsuckers that are so hungry, not good for my girls."

"I understand, it was something of an emergency. Now if you'll excuse me..."

She raised her hand with long pink talon nails and stopped him short.

"You can take a moment to talk to me. I know you are a busy policeman but you can always give me a minute, right?" The threat was implicit, she knew he was a cop, and Madames always trafficked in the power of knowledge. If he wanted to come back here again, or keep his career, it was best to hear her out.

He acquiesced, folding his arms, "Of course, Meredith, what can I do for you?"

"It's what I can do for you, I got a girl here, a clairvoyant, she gets prophetic dreams, but not regular enough to make a living off it. But enough that she's kind of crazy, which is why she can't have a regular job. Anyways, she had a real doozy of a spell last night, saying some strange stuff. I was actually thinking of calling you about it, on account of it being about that new moon serial killer."

Marlow fished out his phone, texted his partner about this new lead and that he'd be late, "Take me to her."

———————

I watched my new assistant working from across the room. Germaine had her hair up in a high messy bun and was wearing makeup. Her whole attitude when she arrived was peppy, happy, anxious? I narrowed my gaze, noting the way she was singing to herself as she filed. She reported no issues with her first solo raising, I wanted to believe the chipper mood was related to that, but I didn't.

If Dot was here, she would say, *that is a fool in love*, or something akin to it.

With two days to the new moon, we couldn't afford to be pussyfooting around.

"Does your boyfriend live in a big apartment complex?" I asked, smile in my closest approximation of a gal pal, head on fist.

"What?" She replied, startled, her cheeks already turning pink and giving her away. "I keep telling you there is no guy."

"I wasn't born yesterday, and you're being followed by the police. For your safety. Who is in the apartment complex?" I saw the panic in her eyes and pushed. "Why lie, Germaine? This is serious business, people could die."

"I know! But I hated the way you were all looking at me! Like some victim, some little hayseed who wouldn't know the difference between a boy who liked me and a boy who wanted to use me for some ritual. I am not a fool either. You don't know me."

I leaned back in my chair, sizing the girl up. She had more fight than I expected. I sighed, this so wasn't my area of expertise. I was no good with living people, especially someone barely out of her teens.

"You're right, I don't know you. I'm sorry if I hurt your feelings. We just want everyone to be safe and for these guys to be caught. Would you at least stay at the safe house that's been arranged for all the girls for the new moon?"

"For the hundredth time, I am going to visit my parents remember? So, I will be out of the state and far from anyone." She opened her laptop, eyes anywhere but on me.

"Can I arrange a ride to the airport for you then?"

"My roommate is going to take me."

She's lying, I knew it but battled internally on whether it was worth it to call her out on it. My phone was ringing, and I had clients lined up, so I decided to shelf that talk for later in the day. No doubt the stupid girl just wanted to hunker down with her boyfriend instead of a safe house.

"Resurrectionist, how can I help you?" I said distractedly.

Peter sat at the police station in a generic conference room straight out of a cop procedural, tapping his foot. Both Robinson and Marlow were out, and they were the lead officers on the case. A short older woman, with gray hair pulled back into a tight twist, approached him. He rose and they shook hands.

Peter slid the paperwork across the table, "Thanks for meeting with me, Ms. Diomedes. It really couldn't wait."

Ms. Diomedes began paging through the folder. "This is?"

"All of the emails, letters, and phone logs that we've received at the paper regarding the murders and the new moon. If it had been a few I would classify it as cranks. But there are too many, and they are all too specific. I've been working on this story and working with your department occultist. My research on that is all in there, too."

Diomedes nodded, her lips in a tight line, "Yeah, off the record our phone lines have been blowing up as well. Any great aunt who'd ever glanced at a tea leaf is calling. And I'll agree, there is a similarity between the calls and visions and dreams and all that, enough to be worrisome."

"So, should we put out alerts? State of emergency? Some sort of supernatural alarm? There must be something like that right?"

Diomedes regarded him, "I assumed you talked to your editor about all of this?"

Peter nodded. "Something is happening. I think we should alert the public."

"I don't want to cause undue panic, and I don't want people running around in the streets looting, and lynching, and burning witches. But I agree, we can't just ignore this either. I think announcing a curfew and upping police, especially near campus and near any wooded areas. Weather looks to be stormy, that should help us as well. Less people out and about..."

Peter nodded, "Okay, yes, we can do that. I wish there was more I could do."

Diomedes studied him, it was clear she was debating telling him something. After a few seconds, she leaned in, "Off the record, I am not only the PR spokesperson for the Goat Hill Police," she said, weighing her words carefully, "I am also a witch. And I know my coven leader is working closely with some other non-human groups. Lila Goodtree vouched for you, and I know you are friendly with the resurrectionist working the case."

She lowered her voice, "You want to really help? Contact Persimmon Shaw, my coven leader."

Peter was surprised, "Why?"

Diomedes shrugged, "It's not just the folders of crazies or our call-in lines. I've been scrying as well, which is my specialty, and getting the same weird shit. But in one of my last ones, I saw you. It's why I invited you to meet with me when you called."

Peter rubbed his hands over his face, "Saw me? What does that mean?"

"It means you have a part in this. Big or small, I don't know. We need to unify, all of us need to team up. Persimmon can help."

Peter nodded. "Can you get me the best way to reach Ms. Shaw?"

———

The slight girl sat on a twin bed in a room barely bigger than a closet. She had two high-set pigtails and her knees up to her chin, and she watched Marlow cautiously. She was probably early twenties, but the way she sat in the girlish room made him think she was much younger. He had the disturbing realization as he took in the teen hunk posters, stuffed animals perched on bookshelves, and pink everything, that it was intentional, appealing to a certain kind of client.

He frowned but Meredith only shrugged, "Hey Marlow, it takes all kinds to make a world, you should know that better than most."

"This is Suki, Suki this is Detective Marlow." The girl's entire demeanor changed in an instant, her legs dropped, and she sat up. The Asian schoolgirl schtick was tossed to the side, instead the career call girl was ready to ask for her lawyer.

"He's here about your visions, baby, nothing else. He's a client. You can trust him."

Suki sized him up, taking in every detail. When she eventually spoke, her voice was lower and huskier than he expected, "Meredith probably told you I have dreams, sometimes prophetic, oftentimes gobbledygook, and always a bit hard to sort out. I usually figure them out after the event has happened. Which makes me pretty useless as a clairvoyant. Like a weatherman who gives yesterday's forecast." She made a face, Marlow eased into a rolling desk chair. Like everything else in the room, it was pink.

"I have been having this dream, over and over, for months. It's of this weird desert place with a rainbow sky. Storms rage and monsters fly around in the clouds." Marlow raised eyebrows and she waved him off. "I know how that sounds, but the more I go to this place, the more I think it may be real. The people, more like creatures, in the dreams live underground like moles, and they feed off each other, but worse. They suck them dry leaving nothing but a shell, and then they eat the shells. They are all starving."

She was picking nervously at the fluffy pink comforter, "I've visited this place many times, felt the suffering and the hunger, the desperation that forced them to kill their own. In the last vision a door opens, and a man made of shadow emerges and helps them step through. Saving them."

Marlow's throat went instantly dry at the mention of the shadow man and the door. This girl may have just answered the question to what was on the other side. "Do you know where they go? These people." She shook her head, eyes far away, looking past the bubblegum room to some other world entirely.

"I've never seen it in my dream, but I have a suspicion that it is here."

"Why do you think that?"

"Because I had a different dream last night, about these creatures battling a woman with glowing blue eyes, she led an army."

Madame Meredith and Suki were watching him close, no doubt because he had been silent and thoughtful after her fantastic tale. His silence told them it was something more.

"It's real, isn't it? Not just crazy dream visions that need to be deconstructed for allegory and symbols. I thought these felt different, didn't I, Mer?" Suki looked up at the older woman, and she nodded stiffly.

Marlow leaned forward in his chair, hands clasped tight, "Does the blue-eyed woman win the fight? In your dream?" Suki shook her head.

"The dream ends before that, sorry. I told you, my powers kind of suck."

"No, it's helpful, all very helpful." He fished a business card out of his pocket as well as a twenty. He asked her to email him her dreams, just as she told him, in more detail if she could. He asked her to leave nothing out. And to continue to do so if she had any more. Suki agreed, and something in her posture showed relief. Most likely that she wasn't going crazy, though he really wished she was.

TWENTY-TWO

"I wish we didn't have to wait." Germaine said breathlessly, her lips swollen and bee-stung from kissing. James chuckled as he pulled away and stared at the water-stained rosettes on the ceiling. He agreed with her wholeheartedly, but the ritual called for a virgin pure as an unplucked rose.

"There's a lot we could do that would not *pluck* me, no?" She sat up, unself-conscious in only a bra and skirt. Her hair fell long and flame-red along his dingy gray comforter. She felt very adult and womanly, in bed with a man, in her underwear. It was a nice change of pace to her usual self-consciousness.

"Germaine, I don't want to do anything that could jeopardize the ritual." *Or you*, he left unspoken. He gazed at her and she felt powerful: this is what it feels like to inspire lust. He wants me. He's attracted to me.

"In two days' time, if all goes to plan, we will be king and queen of this world, and we can fuck...err...make love all day and night until we pass out from dehydration. But until then, I don't want to take any unnecessary risks."

She hated to admit it, but she agreed. She did not want to get pulverized by some celestial gatekeeper because she could not keep her libido in check. She knew her cheeks must look like two candy apples, the shame burned so hot. It was hard to know where the lust started and her need to prove something, to herself, to Selene, to everyone back in Bixby, ended.

So, they decided to watch a movie and order pizza instead. They settled on olive and green pepper and the movie was a garish action film. But Germaine could barely focus, too absorbed in the feel of James' arm around her shoulder, a satisfying weight. Feet intertwined on the coffee table next to the cooling pie, her eyes roamed around the apartment.

While it was a dark basement with few windows, and damp, even with a de-humidifier humming away in the corner, she found herself liking the place. They sat on a futon in its couch position, and the TV was perched on an overstuffed bookshelf. The shelves sagged with arcane texts, comic books, and pulp sci-fi. The wall over the kitchenette had a city map on it, with various pins and post-its. For the girls. Possible victims.

She knew people, in particular Selene, would think she was positively insane being there with James. Suicidal, even. He was the killer they'd all been looking for. They would think her a fool, a silly Manson girl, a cult-joining type, but it wasn't that. She liked James, liked having the eyes of a handsome man on her, liked the feel of his body beside her. But the more time she spent with him, the more she understood that if they succeeded in the ritual, she would be a god.

The ritual would be the unmaking of Earth as it has been known. In this new order, she could be in charge, important, powerful. Her whole life she'd been a freak and an outcast, and if she just kept on what would she be in the end? A resurrectionist sitting at a desk facing Selene, raising baby boomer zombies until she retired or dropped dead, like Dot. She could see ahead to a lifetime as a lonely outcast in an ill-fitting blazer eating microwave dinners for one. Was it a crime to want to be more than that? To use her god-given powers as they were intended? The world had worn her down enough in the last nineteen years. They owed her.

She also didn't want to die. She had been pouring through the books on the ritual, pressed him for every detail, and they retraced the three previous attempts step-by-step to see what could have gone wrong. She didn't want to be ripped inside out as the door burrowed through them, destroying them. "I want to meet the Patron," she'd finally said to him, midway through the movie. James' face drained of color at that.

"No, we talked about this already, I don't think it's a good idea."

"Please. He needs us, not the other way around, if he wants this ritual as bad as he seems, then we should work together."

"These guys are bad news, Germaine, I don't know what meeting them will do for anyone."

"It will help us understand what the goal is, why they want the gate opened, who is on the other side, how they know there is another side. If the ritual has never worked, what proof do they have it will?" James only shrugged because he didn't know. "What proof do we have that they can actually give you the powers they claim? Or that they can change this world? What if it's all a lie?"

"Because it's very 'do the ritual or we will kill you' with them."

"Maybe he can like give us tips or something on working with Nigrum Porta."

James scrubbed at his eyes, "Tips? Trust me, this guy is terrifying, he is an interdimensional gatekeeper."

"So, he doesn't say anything to you? You don't talk during it?" It. How cavalier to call the rape and murder of a young woman *it*, she mused, but honestly couldn't bring herself to care past saving her own skin. She knew she was doing some pretty elaborate mental acrobatics to both like James and want to be part of the ritual, and also, know that he seduced and murdered three people before her. But she had to.

"I draw the circle, at midnight, beneath the new moon, and I say the words of invocation. He appears. He is like a human-shaped shadow and he communicates telepathically. He, not possesses, but kind of, he goes into me, and we do the deed. And when *we*...cum, it opens the door."

"And you think, if done right, the door opens but the vessel is unharmed? Right? Since the door is spiritual?" Germaine pushed, ashamed that she was a little aroused by the idea of doing this with James. *There must be something terribly wrong with me*, she mused, but pushed the thought aside.

"Right, the portal opens, and the realities merge, similar to the way you bring a spirit back and put it in the body of the dead. It's the same muscles, the same passageway. The resurrectionist *is* the door. I think we're made to do this. Here, look at this quote from one of my uncle's books, it describes a resurrectionist's purpose as 'To ferry the formless into the world of form.'" There was a spark in his eye, this was the excitement that had converted her from victim to participant. It must have been what the first explorers of the sea, or space had felt. There was danger, endless danger, but also such opportunity for discovery. For power. For enlightenment.

"I want you to call on the Patron and the other brothers of the crow or whoever, I want to talk to them, introduce myself, have them test me to see if I am worthy. You know, be prepared for once and not just cross fingers and hope. It's a smart way to do this. Since they plan to kill you if you fail as well. That and I like the idea of these guys knowing who I am and who they are dealing with, the virgin sacrifice fertility stuff, just feels a little sexist, don't you think?"

"Fine, I'll try." James wondered how he'd gotten so lucky. It was a relief to not be alone in this burden.

———

Marlow was quiet and distant when he got to Selene's office. He wanted to tell her about Suki, about the vision, about the huge folder of calls and emails at the station that corroborated Suki's visions. But he wasn't sure how to tell her that without telling her about the brothel.

They wended through rush hour traffic, sticking to small labyrinthine backstreets to avoid the worst of it. His mind was anything but quiet, the world becoming bigger and stranger the more he learned about it. He'd been walking around for nearly a century; in that time, he saw the constant battle between magic and science. Magic was less predictable than sciences though, and often even more inscrutable. Sure, you could cure someone of cancer by making them a vampire, but now you've created a whole new set of problems. You could try to use magic to manipulate the weather, or elements, but magic had a way of coming back thricefold. You make rain for a drought? You may create a flood somewhere else. Marlow wondered if the real problem was the ego of humanity thinking it could control anything.

Witches and scientists both manipulated nature, striving to combat global warming, pollution, and create a more harmonious balance between man and the jungle. Spirits floated around them, fires could be lit with the mind, and creatures could transform from one thing to another, all of this he knew and saw in his time.

But even Marlow wasn't ready for creatures from another dimension. Or that the world could be cut into and passed through like a theater curtain.

"All okay? You've been very quiet." Selene was watching him with those otherworldly blue eyes. Could Selene really be the Master of The Dead tasked to protect the world? He was no student of the supernatural, outside of being a member. In fact, his ex-wife, Min, had accused him of being prejudiced against the inhuman and magical. That he was incurious. That he was ashamed to be *part of their community*, as she used to put it. Perhaps if he was more involved in magic and monsters he would have gotten further in the case earlier.

Stop. You're thinking in circles, there is a woman you care about waiting for a reply. Take advantage of not being alone for once.

"Marlow?" Her warm fingertips brushed gently along the top of his hand. "You're not mad at me about Dania, right?"

He stirred, smiling at her, "No. Of course not. We just didn't know enough to really ask the right questions. I was just a million miles away, deep in thought, sorry."

"You were creeping me out, sitting so still, barely breathing."

"Just thinking about my day, the case, reality."

"Wow, that covers a lot of territory."

He was conflicted. On one side, Selene was helping with the case, and they were in a relationship, so he owed her to share and be honest. But on the other side, how much honesty was he ready to give her? He could tell her about Suki but omit the brothel? Where was the line between the case and what he was? He debated not telling her about the dreams at all, but that also felt wrong. "You tell me about your feelings regarding Dania and your day first, get me out of my head."

"Honestly? I am embarrassed. Embarrassed that I have never reached out to her, that there are two of us in Goat Hill and I'd never met her. I didn't even know there were male resurrectionists! If you can call them that since they can't resurrect anything. Somehow Dot hadn't even bothered to mention that to me. Or that Dania was her freaking protege before me! Or the fact her brother died doing some similar ritual!"

"Yeah, that's the kicker. Robinson is on it though, she requested the old case files from Miami and we're sending an officer by Dania's to get the books left by the brother from the storage locker. Maybe there will be clues to the group he ran with. If nothing else, the books could help us find more on the particulars of the ritual."

"I know what you mean, the clues are all dangling in front of us. I agree that it's most likely a male resurrectionist, and he is able to sense and locate females. He and Nigrum Porta are pairing up for the ritual, if it works, the virgin opens the door, and then something comes in. Now that we have corralled all the available resurrectionists, one hopes, then at least we will buy ourselves another month."

It started to rain, a few pats along the windshield quickly turned into a deluge. "April showers," Selene said quietly. The rain blurred the city into lights and shadows. Bodies ran with briefcases over heads. Umbrellas hung limp and abused by the heavy onslaught and harsh winds. *Could all this end?* He knew climate change and melting glaciers were a ticking time bomb, he knew a possible virus or a celestial event like some hurtling meteor could start another ice age. All these were things that could happen, and as an immortal, things he would possibly live to see. But an invasion from another world? It was so sci-fi. "You've gone creepy undead quiet again, Marlow, please talk to me."

"Creepy undead?" He smirked. "I'm sorry, I am just debating how much to share with you. How to share with you. I haven't been in a real relationship for quite some time and I am a little out of practice."

"Believe me, I know how you feel. You are my longest relationship since a college boyfriend who left me for Persimmon if you recall. I don't have a wealth of experience myself. Out with it, please."

He was having a hard time remembering when he had been so nervous. The rain continued to batter the roof of the car, and he grimaced as he inadvertently splashed a cluster of pedestrians on the corner. "I'm just thinking about the end of the world. Of beings coming here from another dimension and what that would look like. Of a war between worlds. A prophetic dream has come to my attention, today, in it the ritual works and things do come through. They are cannibalistic-energy-parasite-type creatures. And in the dream, someone raises an army of the undead to fight them. The state of the world depends on that army winning. Or something like that." It was Selene's turn to breathe out.

"Well. Shit," she finally said. "Prophetic dreams are far from exact sciences. Or it's merely a possible scenario and not a guaranteed one? There is so much bullshit surrounding soothsaying and clairvoyance after all."

"I totally agree. But the prophecy, I can't get it out of my head. I am looking around at the world, at these random people, at all these old books and rituals, at everything we take for granted wondering if this is the end of it all? If it is, shouldn't we be doing something amazing with that time?"

They reached the rougher South Side, the buildings becoming bigger and more industrial, the streets emptying out. The rain hammered down, flooding the gutters and sending garbage racing down the streets. "What would you do if this was your last night on earth?" Selene said, her voice frightened.

"I would probably open a very good bottle of something I'd been saving for such an occasion, and I would get in the tub with a beautiful woman."

"Then let's do that."

"I was supposed to go poke around the apartment building that your mentee keeps going to with Regine, but I'll just have her bring another uniform with her."

"If you're sure."

"Yeah, yeah, let's go hunker down someplace dry." Marlow said, wanting to push away the traitorous thoughts of feeding on another, of betraying Selene's trust, he didn't want to spend another second on the prophecies, on his ex-wife, on anything but Selene.

Iris Partridge was wailing. She careened down the hallway, face red and tear-streaked, hair mussed, in an oversized Grandpa sweater and pajamas beneath. In short, she both looked crazy and like shit.

She practically bowled over her brother, Peter, her arms wrapping tight around him. They were not particularly close and rarely if ever embraced. Peter tried to hide the shock and discomfort, more so when he caught the nurse he'd gotten together with a few weeks passed. Hollis? Haley? Hazel. *Harley*. It didn't matter, she had already spun on her rubber-clogged heel and walked away, no doubt pissed at him for never calling back.

He had other concerns. "He's dead?" Peter asked, regretting it instantly, wishing he'd said passed on or some other euphemism. His sister pulled away, her fiery bloodshot eyes meeting his.

"*Not yet*, but very soon. Anytime now."

"Then why are we in the hallway? He could be dying as we speak." She realized the wisdom in her brother's words and quickly snatched up his arm, dragging him along the hospital hallway. They were soon back in the room, where his withered old father lay, with skin the same color as the sheets, his breath loud and labored. Peter could see the outline of his skull, and the frantic throb of his father's pulse in a squiggly vein at his temple.

His father was about to die.

Peter instantly saw his entire life with the man in a blink, as cliché as that was. His memories started with the impossibly tall and imposing patriarch who ruled his house like some sort of feudal lord. Then later, the kinder moments like teaching him how to catch a ball, how to drive, or the long summer they painted the house together. They'd spent hours talking that summer. Peter rarely saw eye to eye with the man dying in the bed, they were both too alike and too different to ever really get along. But he knew his father was proud of him, and he knew his father had adored his mother. Her death had hollowed him out, scooped him empty of any warmth, for she had been the thing that softened him.

"Hey, Dad," Peter said, trying to sound normal, not sure how to sound. Iris swayed, shuffling foot to foot, a tissue balled up in her fist, pressed to her red nose. The old man squinted, tried to focus on his son, and for a moment, there was a flicker of recognition before his face smoothed back out.

"He needs to sign the papers, Peter, so he can come back. Dad? Dad? The papers..." Iris was practically shouting at the prone man. She pointed at a folder balanced on the side table, beside a kidney bowl and water pitcher, both items pink plastic.

The old man shifted his rheumy eyes to Iris, she knelt inches from his face. "Remember Daddy? You wanted to be a half-life?"

Peter whispered his sister's name, when she waved him off he dragged her away from the bed. "What the hell are you doing?" he hissed, his anger choking him as he glanced at his father, little more than skin and bones.

"Peter, he's dying. *Dying*. And you won't do anything about it."

"He's dying because he is old and sick. It's part of life. You are an emotional basket case right now, get over yourself, it's his time."

"Oh, please," she responded, her anger rising to meet his. "Excuse me for wanting my father to be in my life, in my children's life."

"He has been! It is not about you. If he comes back, as a reani-mated corpse, into that frail old body, eating fucking hamsters with his dentures...he will be a monster. Besides, you think he will be nicer to your kids as a zombie? Creepy grouchy undead Grampa? Not to mention it's sacrilegious according to *your* religion. He would be giving up heaven and possibly reuniting with Mom. Would you take that from him, really?"

"Don't you dare bring Mom into this. If I could have her back here, I would in a second."

"Thank god she thought the practice was evil and unnatural," he spit back at her.

At the mention of Mom, Peter's father perked up, "Gayle?" he said, looking around for her. Iris sobbed loudly, quickly running to her father and dropping onto her knees.

"Oh, Gayle, there you are, I've missed you so much."

"No, Dad it's—" but Peter put his hand on her shoulder and squeezed, not hard enough to hurt, but hard enough to quiet her.

"You ready to go see Mom in heaven, Dad?" he said, voice cracking. His father's eyes lit up, and he smiled a gummy grin.

"Oh, yes, my Gayle. Pretty as a picture," he said, voice little more than a whisper. "I've missed her so much."

"Don't you want to stay here? With me, Daddy?"

"Of course, I do, Gayle, I always want to be with you and the children, our children." Iris closed her eyes, fat tears sliding down.

"Let him go, sis."

"But what if there is nothing out there? What if she isn't anywhere? That he becomes nothing? Then he is just gone."

"Then he will sleep and rest. He's been sick a long time. It's cruel to keep someone for yourself. This is about you, not him." He could sense the fight in her, the Partridge clan was not one to give up or back down. They watched their father, his eyes out of focus, his breathing rattled, the way his papery eyelids were slowly closing. He'd been whittled down to a frail old skeleton covered in skin, and he was so tired.

The elder Partridge closed his eyes for the last time, and with a great exhalation, died.

Iris wept, her whole body shaking as she lay over him. Peter found himself a little uncomfortable with the physicality of her grief. He allowed himself a tear or two and then stepped into the hall to flag a nurse.

Ten minutes later he stood under the awning in the hospital parking lot, smoking a cigarette he'd bummed off an orderly, thinking about Selene. The rain was so heavy it was like a wall of water around him. Raining like it was the end of the world.

Selene needed to feel what she did was a part of nature, that she wasn't a freak, but he knew that letting his father die and stay dead was absolutely the right thing to do. There was no argument that could sell him on creating a shambling monster out of his father's corpse. He knew she liked to think of herself as normal and her creations as normal, but he knew in his very marrow that she and her offspring were monsters. After his research, especially with Lila Goodtree, he was starting to think that the whole point of resurrectionists wasn't even to bring back zombies originally. That it was to shuttle creatures into different worlds.

If she was the descendant of that original blue-eyed girl, then she wasn't even human or from this world at all. She was an alien.

Nothing made sense to him and he doubted that it ever would again. There were things he knew to be fact, like that the soul was real and that resurrectionists could somehow catch souls and bring them back. His new theory was that the genetic components that made resurrectionists able to find a soul and pluck it from the ether and shove it back in a body were just a bonus and the real ability was to bring other things into the world. They themselves were the doorway, but without the communication from the other side instructing them, they instead used their inherent necromantic ability to restart the dead body by fusing the soul and form together.

But that still didn't make sense to him entirely since being a passageway and finding souls were totally different abilities. On top of that, the fertility ritual was sexual, and the failed attempts had mutilated their bodies. And none of this explained what Nigrum Porta's role was. Fucking magic nonsense. Peter would keep searching and he would keep working with Lila. She'd also recommended he talk to the head of necromancy at the college, Karl Wraith, and wasn't he shocked to learn he had been married to none other but Dorothea Wraith, Selene's mother figure and mentor. A small world where all roads seemingly led back to Selene.

He had planned to meet with Karl that evening but canceled to come to the hospital instead. He knew he should be thinking about his dad, and caring for his sister, and being in mourning, but the nearness of the new moon, the strangeness of this world where death was only for some people, and creatures with immense power pulled puppet strings unseen, kept calling for his attention. His phone was in his hand before he'd even fully thought it out, it rang and went to voicemail.

"Hi, Selene, it's Peter Partridge, I was just calling to say my father passed away and we decided to let him stay dead, or um...not undead. I think it is the right choice, and do hope that there is an afterlife out there and that my parents are together again. Sorry for the ramble. The other news is that I have been running with your tips about the murder and have found out some interesting things regarding the case. I will keep you abreast of and will keep sharing anything pertinent with the cops. Stay safe."

That done, he stomped out the cigarette and headed back into the hospital, avoiding the nurses he'd flirted with and specifically the one he'd slept with, to find his twin and start the unpleasant process of dealing with his father's natural, ordinary death.

TWENTY-THREE

The dead thing laughed, or as close as it could, considering how desiccated all the parts of the body that were in charge of laughing were. A closer approximation would be to say its dusty shoulders lifted and fell while its wobbly jaw swayed and a god-awful wind-through-a-drafty-house sound emitted from its gaping maw.

"You will all suffer and scream, you will be unmade, their hunger is unquenchable!" the dead thing repeated, third time to be exact. It pointed a bony finger at her.

"You will—"

"—Yes, I get it, suffer and scream, endless torment. You have anything else pertinent to tell us?" Lucinda interjected, her patience all but gone.

She was normally a woman who exuded calm, poise, power. But the cracks were starting to show and she had a growing discomfort amidst all the negative predictions. In her periphery, she could see Karl Wraith, looking like the devil himself with his black hair going gray at his temples, the Van Dyke beard, and black turtleneck.

Karl was a few years older than Lucinda, and they'd belonged to the same cabal for twenty years. She knew he resented her for superseding him as leader. She knew he felt he should be running this summoning. The fuck up with Selene Shade had not helped that opinion.

"DOOM!" The thing that was once named Wallace hollered, no doubt offended that attention had drifted from it. Lucinda rolled her eyes at the angry husk and turned back to Karl and the rest of the core members of the cabal. Chairs creaked as weight shifted.

"Everyone get that?" Lucinda stood on a platform, Wallace the Prophet upon the plastic-covered table next to her. The cabal members sat in a circle below, on folded chairs around her. The house lights were off, save a spotlight pointed at her and the dead thing hollering on the table.

"Why did you choose Wallace?" someone called out, she turned to the voice, squinting into the shadows. But she knew who it was, Karl wasn't the only one of the cabal to challenge her authority these days unfortunately. It was Brent, a relative novice and a right prick. She held in a sigh.

"Although Wallace is quite physically destroyed, due to his salts being improperly preserved, no doubt, and while he has quite an attitude problem in general," she paused for effect and also because the dead thing often liked to interrupt. Strangely he stayed quiet, his burrowed-out eyeholes watching her, or at least sensing her, with something like amusement. "He is seldom *wrong*. He was an extremely accurate soothsayer in his time, and he is still quite accurate in his ability to see beyond."

But that was exactly the problem, she thought to herself. Her most reliable dead clairvoyant was predicting doom and destruction. With no alternative. Someone said something similar out loud to the room.

"I don't think we are doomed. I think Wallace here likes to add a little drama to his predictions to make them more interesting," Karl chimed in, tone fatherly to the younger members. Lucinda seethed at his flippant attempt to gain control of the room.

"I have to disagree with you, Karl. Members of The Order of Yama, I am of the opinion that we need to be preparing our affairs and our community for something very serious. Something apocalyptic. Wallace is odious and..."

"YOU WILL BE SCREAMING AS THEY DEVOUR!" Wallace chimed in, interrupting her as if on cue. Lucinda went on to elaborate that all the soothsayers had been foretelling stormy weather ahead. She'd been in contact with the local witches, and they had been experiencing the same. As she was no believer in coincidence, this meant that the future had been decided. She knew that all of this had something to do with sacrificed resurrectionists. She knew they needed to do every-thing in their power to stop it from going down.

Necromancers were powerful. They used death magic to further their knowledge of the past and future, to extend their lifespan and health. To properly invest for the future and to discover treasures long lost. They used the knowledge trapped in the bodies of the dead, summoning their souls through the remaining genetic material of their bodies. It was a similar ritual to that of resurrectionists though their way involved a lot more ritual, and they were unable to create an intact body and intact soul or to keep them together indefinitely. Necro-mancers had to work fast, raise the dead, ask a few specific questions, then let what remained of the body go. One thing they could do, that was different, was raise the same dead over and over. They were also able to raise a fresh corpse with no soul and use it as a puppet or golem. These true zombies explained why some thought necromancers had created vampires in their attempt to create half-lifes. Lucinda had a working theory that vampires were actually a witch creation, using a magical virus.

Whoever did it, the theory went, that vampires were the most successful attempt at such a merging of body and soul after death. Vampires must consume a massive supply of blood, and within it life-force, to keep their bodies intact. They were then able to create more of their own kind, on their own, without any ritual besides the exchanging of blood and a death.

Wallace, on the other hand, was basically a skeleton covered in a layer of greasy old skin with the occasional tuft of hair on it. This was the best body she could conjure from his damaged salts. Salts were the preserved bodies stored in glass tubes for future use. Once she banished him back to death, this skeleton would dissolve back into its salts, they would be swept back into their glass tube, and stored for future needs, breaking further down with every summoning.

The vaults below the Order of Yama were filled with thousands of these glass tubes, arranged by category and year. A wealth of knowledge could be accessed from that vault, accurate history, secrets, and from Wallace and others of his ilk, glimpses into the future. The bodies of clairvoyants, psychics, and the like were precious. Society often sneered at necromancers, but the portions of their souls given to traffic with the dead also gave them keys to the future. In this particular case, it gave them a heads up to try and change the future. A future that could be coming to an end. It was worth raising and dealing with the surly dead to stave off an apocalypse.

"What are these devourers, Wallace? Describe them for me please."

The corpse sighed, annoyance in what was left of eyes, "Hunger incarnate. Generations of wizards, living in a world with no food, eating magic, eating each other's magic, creating a circle of craven endless hunger."

"Where are they now?"

Wallace, shrugged his shoulders as best a skeleton could, "Somewhere else. Both near and far."

"Do they have weaknesses?"

The skeleton cocked his head, vertebrae cracking as he did so, and thought. "They are burrowers, subterranean."

"So, perhaps our sun?" Wallace shrugged again and Lucinda made a note of that with a shaking hand. Her head was throbbing, the magic was draining her, and she knew it was time to let him go. She wanted to ask more questions, but it would have to wait for another time, as he was starting to break apart. A necromancer's control must be absolute. She didn't want the cabal seeing her weak. Since the kidnapping debacle, she was already on thinner ice than she'd like. On top of that, fatigue led to sloppiness. The dead can overtake them, physically, or even spiritually in some cases. The former Order of Yama leader was once such a person, he overextended himself and ended up possessed by a half-mad warlock from the middle ages. Had to be put out of his misery. Both of their salts preserved for posterity. It wasn't pleasant and Lucinda knew better.

"Thank you for your assistance, Wallace, sleep now." She released the body by smudging a sigil on the table. It instantly fell into a pile of brownish dust. An assistant would clean it up and return it to the vault. She sipped some water, aware of the eyes on her.

"So now what?" someone said, breaking the silence.

"Should we go kidnap someone?" someone else said, and a few others snickered. Lucinda scowled. Selene's abduction was a horrible misunderstanding. She'd nearly been voted out of her seat as cabal leader over it. Yes, she probably had overreacted. But in her defense, another dead clairvoyant, one who was universally respected as being accurate, had predicted Selene was a major player, and that Nigrum Porta wanted her. Lucinda still believed that Selene Shade was the Zombie Queen.

Figured it only made sense to take her out of the running as next victim. To save the world. But those fools chucked her in a basement like a bunch of criminals. So much for civil affairs between supernatural tribes. Had they done that to a witch, hell would have rained down on them, an all-out tribal war.

Luckily, resurrectionists were rare, had very little defensive ability, and were often solitary. They also lacked much power beyond the ability to resurrect. Unless, they could control vampires like Selene could. But Lucinda needed to be smarter than all that. Necromancers were seen as a legitimate religion now, and The Order of Yama was a tax-exempt religious organization. This was not the old cloak-and-dagger days when humans didn't know about them.

That was why a botched kidnapping was so embarrassing. She took her job rehabbing the unsavory reputation of necromancers very seriously. Lucinda had spent her ten-year tenure as the cabal leader spinning them as more than weirdos messing with dead bodies. Their cabal was fantastically wealthy, in part due to the secrets of the dead of the past and the future. The largesse went publicly toward charities, non-profits, PR firms, scholarships, plus owning their own galleries, laboratories, and publishing houses. They even offered funerary services to the best and brightest to allow them into the vaults so their knowledge would live long after their deaths. No, she worked too hard, to give all that up.

Not that any of that mattered if the world was going to *end*.

"New moon is *tomorrow night* people. Make jokes if you want, but I suggest all those with the clearance pull up any salts with future seeing abilities or past experience with these rituals. Lessers and noviciates should be hitting the books, researching everything we need to know about these 'devourers from another world,' Nigrum Porta, Zombie Queens, all of it. All known resurrectionists that fit the ritual profile will be held in my safe house for the night of the ritual, buying us some time. Stockpile weapons and supplies and settle your affairs. You don't like Wallace's predictions? Prove him wrong. Dismissed."

Regine Robinson cursed the rain, the murder case, and her partner. All while lifting her soaking foot, which had just sunk a foot into a misleadingly deep puddle. The rain continued to hammer down. She squinted around the dingy apartment courtyard, which consisted of cracked concrete and overflowing drains, lawn chairs were knocked on their sides, and the few decorative trees, battered and drooping, losing to the rain.

Marlow was supposed to be with her, but he'd gone off looking into prophecies. There weren't any officers free to tag along with her, so she decided to do it on her own. Gave her time to wonder about prophecies reported from a notorious brothel to him directly, that he'd gone solo to check out. She didn't like to doubt her partner, it could be dangerous or even fatal to lose trust after all, but sometimes it felt like he was keeping things from her. And this was one of those times. Granted, she would rather knock on doors than hang out with psychic prostitutes at a well-known whorehouse.

Germaine Whately had been coming to an apartment in this large building. Robinson was annoyed to discover how many apartments could be accessed from the courtyard, and resigned herself to going one by one and hammering on doors. She discovered after a look around that the basement-level apartments opened to the outside, where the rest of the apartments had an exterior door and a buzzer system. Regine decided to start with the basements then. The first was an old lady, practically deaf, who didn't know her neighbors. The second was a Korean family who spoke little English. Third wasn't home. Regine could feel water squelching on the inside of her shoe. It soured her mood.

She hoped Marlow's hunch that this Germaine girl was hiding something led somewhere. She hated the idea of having another mutilated girl on her shoulders. She just wanted to catch this guy, even better if she got to shoot him a bunch in his head, guaranteeing that he was totally dead and unable to come back or get into any trouble. Magic criminals convicted and sentenced to death often did have their heads removed and bodies cremated, to prevent any type of reanimation. She wasn't a violent person per se, but there had to be a line. And this creepy fuck crossed it ripping apart these girls the way he had. Monstrous.

Regine was deep in thought when she hammered on the fourth apartment door. Noting the address on mailbox read, J. Donegal. The stairwell did little to relieve the sideways rain, in fact, it was functioning as a small waterfall, and she hunched into the doorframe, the water pooling around her ankles, pounding one last time.

"Yes?" a male voice called, peering between the chain and the door, squinting at the detective.

Young, brown hair, male Caucasian, first name J, really fit the profile, her pulse sped up. "Police. You got a moment?"

"What's this about?" Did he look nervous? Yes. Regine had been a police officer for nearly twelve years, and she could say with surety he did. Now was that because he had a bong sitting on the coffee table, or recently written some bad checks, or was it because he was a serial rapist, she couldn't say. Not yet.

"My name is Detective Robinson, I am investigating a murder and hoped I could ask you a few questions."

"A murder?!"

"Sir, please can I come inside? It's raining cats and dogs out here. The sooner we can talk the sooner we can all move on with our lives." He was clearly reluctant as he opened the door to let her in. Robinson felt her own reluctance, those internal bells clanging inside, at being alone without backup. A voice said she should radio in and at least let someone know where she was.

Tomorrow was the new moon. No time.

She stepped inside and he closed the door.

TWENTY-FOUR

I wasn't positive I was dreaming. But I wasn't positive I wasn't either. I knew I was in Marlow's tub, the water so bubbly my body was hidden save my toes peeping up in the corner. Marlow had gone out to fetch another bottle of wine and put on some music. It was steamy and I was relaxed. Maybe the rain would stop the ritual and buy us another month.

In the tub I could almost trick myself into believing that in twenty-four hours nothing would happen, and I would go back to work and my life.

I was staring at my unpainted toes and through the closed door I could hear jazz, with Marlow whistling along.

Then Nigrum Porta was in the room with me, as if he'd been there all along. He was standing just out of arm's reach, above me, looking all the more horrible and otherworldly in the bright lights of the bathroom. His skin, if you could call it skin, was alive. Sliding and rippling, like a starfish underwater. I moaned, but no sound came out, and although I was frantically commanding my body to get up, to scream, to move, *nothing* happened. Just muffled jazz and the cloying smell of lavender bubble bath. Nigrum Porta lowered, kneeling close to me, his hollow eyes boring into mine, seeing into me, through me. I could almost feel him in my mind, it was a fluttering sensation like the delicate bat of moths' wings against skin.

Then, a mouth formed, one moment it was just a smooth space where the lips would normally be, and then a small slit, prying open, becoming a terrible black hole, the interior spinning round and round. Ink going down a drain. It reminded me, improbably, of the villain Penguin. *Stand still a moment and watch my spinning umbrella, won't you?*

And round and round, round and round, until he was nearly close enough to touch, close enough to kiss. The terror was choking me, I was paralyzed, unable to even blink in panic. Slowly his hand came up —if you could call it a hand—since he didn't have bones, or muscles, or anything but the viscous mass he was made out of. While my body was still as stone outside, inside, my heart was threatening to burst through my chest, and my frantic lungs were not getting me enough air. Small starbursts erupted behind my eyes, a mini-fireworks show just for me. And then that hand touched my face, his fingertips gentle and strangely warm.

With the touch, I was instantly teleported, out of my body, out of the bathroom, out of my world entirely. Instead, I was still immobile but now encased in something moving. Like what I imagined wearing a space suit would be like. Something with limbs and a head. With dawning horror, I realized I was inside Nigrum Porta's body. I could feel his mind brushing against mine, and it was an alien thing. I couldn't dwell on the fact I was out of my body because I could see out his eyes. And we were looking at a landscape like nothing I'd ever seen. Sharp rocky desert extended in all directions, the rock formations iridescent, striped in purples and greens, golds, and grays. In the distance, a jagged cluster of mountains, nearly hidden in a haze of a rainbow-colored shimmering mist.

I, he, *we*, looked down at our feet and could see a large crater, perfectly round, and worn smooth on its sides like the top to a glass bottle. The winds howled and tore along the rough terrain, but a different howling came from the black hole at our feet. These were screams, almost human, sounding utterly terrified. I didn't want to go into the hole, but the body moved, dropping us into the black nothingness without any reservation, fearless. The screaming grew louder as we were submerged into absolute darkness, moving closer to the source. Nigrum Porta could see, its vision shifting to something between a grayscale and what I imagined a bat's sonar would look like. It walked